W9-AGZ-426

MORE PRAISE FOR DEBORAH LEBLANC!

"A spooky-as-you-can-get ghost story. LeBlanc has created a tight horror tale filled with memorable characters...and creepy scenes. Fans of spooky ghost tales will love the author's smooth prose."

—*The Horror Fiction Review*

"[A] hair-raising tour de force...that is as darkly disturbing as it is utterly readable....An irresistible blend of horror, mystery and dark fantasy."

—Barnes & Noble.com

FAMILY INHERITANCE

"The sticky Louisiana bayou comes alive in first-time author LeBlanc's imaginative chiller about family curses and witch doctors....LeBlanc's dialogue is spot-on...riveting."

—*Publishers Weekly*

"Storytelling brilliance...a tour de force."

—*L'Observateur*

"A super-tight suspense tale that features elements that reminded me of several horror film classics....*Family Inheritance* is a sure-fire bet for fans of character-driven horror novels."

—*The Horror Fiction Review*

"What unfolds before the reader is an engrossing—at times terrifying—and altogether enjoyable story that is richly woven and told with passion. Deborah LeBlanc holds the readers' attention and never once drops it."

—*Dread Central*

THE REACHING FINGERS

Olm walked over to the kitchen sink and turned on the faucet. He leaned over and with shaking hands cupped water into his palms, meaning to rinse out his mouth. That's when he caught movement out of the corner of his eye. He froze, turned his head ever so slightly and saw a black, translucent figure peeling itself from the wall opposite him, like wallpaper that had lost its adhesive backing. It had no distinct features, only the obscure form of a human—a man. Another figure quickly followed the first, this one oozing from the wall like gray smoke.

Olm took a step sideways—and the utility drawer beside him suddenly slid open—the drawer to the cabinet that once held the cereal slammed shut. On the floor, Fruit Loops crunched beneath unseen feet. *They* were heading toward him now, wavering forms that reeked of malice—and gasoline. The temperature in the room abruptly plummeted to freezing.

"No!" Olm shouted. "Go away! What do you want from me?"

A burbling sound—a *glub*, like a pocket of air breaking through the surface of heavy oil—and the apparitions moved closer. The burbling seemed to be the sound of their movement, as purposeful as footfalls on dry leaves, as the flap of a jacket as one walked through a brisk wind. It meant movement, movement toward him.

"Who *are* you?" Olm yelled, backing away slowly, slowly. "What do you want?"

Burbling gray, glubbing black—now with fingers, long reaching fingers…

DEBORAH LEBLANC

WATER WITCH

LEISURE BOOKS NEW YORK CITY

For the Magic Man

A LEISURE BOOK®

October 2008

Published by

Dorchester Publishing Co., Inc.
200 Madison Avenue
New York, NY 10016

ISBN 10: 0-8439-6039-6
ISBN 13: 978-0-8439-6039-6

The name "Leisure Books" and the stylized "L" with design are trademarks of Dorchester Publishing Co., Inc.

Printed in the United States of America.

10 9 8 7 6 5 4 3 2 1

Visit us on the web at www.dorchesterpub.com.

WATER WITCH

PROLOGUE

After soaking his father with three gallons of gasoline, Olm lit a match and tossed it onto the old man's body. With a loud *whoosh*, blinding orange heat towered toward the night sky. Olm took a few steps back, watching in fascination as clothes and hair disintegrated instantly. Soon the pop and sizzle of burning flesh outsang the chorus of nocturnal swamp life that had deafened him for the last two hours—clicks, whines, buzzes from insects too vast in species and number to count, the croaks and *whomps* from frogs and alligators, snakes with bodies wider than the circumference of a man's arm. All of them raising their voices to Brother Moon, to one another.

Skin and thin layers of fat slipped away from bone, the flames licking across the scaffolding that held his father's body, and Olm hoped the wooden beams would hold until the ritual was completed. So much work had gone into making this happen. He'd cut thick cypress branches to just the right length, soaked them in water, hoisted the weighted logs by himself into a wobbly skiff, then transported them through the dead of too many nights, through sloughs and flats clotted with water lilies that eventually led to a

1

U-shaped, ten-acre knoll in the farthest corner of the Atchafalaya Swamp, far away from prying eyes. Although it had been difficult to lift, hammer, and construct the burial shelf without any help, Olm's greatest challenge had been to steal his father's body from Sasaint's Funeral Home before it was embalmed, and to do it without getting caught. The struggle and hard work had been worth it, though, for now that everything was in place, Olm's life could truly begin.

Although this wasn't the traditional Pawnee burial his father had requested before he died, it was the fastest way for Olm to be rid of the body, which he needed to do if he was to follow through with a crucial, albeit extinct, Pawnee custom. One his father never embraced.

As legend had it, in order for a son to acquire the knowledge of all the leaders in his ancestral line, he had to offer his father's body to the elements at the time of his passing. When only bleached bones remained, the father's spirit would then be released, and all a son had to do was call upon what was rightfully his. To Olm, acquiring that knowledge meant ultimate power. For surely in the roll call of his ancestors, there had to have been medicine men, chiefs, warriors, and mighty hunters, those whose dance offerings and sacrifices, human and animal, changed weather patterns, and produced bountiful harvests. Olm had no intention of planting anything. He figured the same wisdom that created abundance in fields and swamps throughout past generations would adapt and supply the needs of a leader in the twenty-first century. Waiting for his father's bones to bleach might take weeks, though, even in the ruthless Louisiana heat.

He'd already spent thirty-seven years waiting for this moment, and Olm didn't want to wait a second longer than was necessary. Since his father was only one-third Pawnee, and from the Skidi tribe, Olm didn't think the alterations he'd made in the burial custom would make a difference. As far as he was concerned, he'd followed more than half the custom by bringing his father's body to the swamp and building the burial shelf. How the bones were exposed shouldn't matter.

As the fire roared, and flesh and muscle slipped away, Olm walked toward the ritual circle that lay two hundred feet away. Even from ground level, it looked like a monstrous, unblinking black eye staring up toward heaven. He'd made it after building the burial shelf, using only a hoe, a shovel, and a few ragged memories. The hoe had worked well for marking out the three-hundred-foot circumference and for clearing the swamp grass, vines, and bramble from its surface. Once the black earth lay naked, save for a few earthworms, he'd used the shovel to dig the inside of the circle to a three-inch depth. The memories were the only tools that gave him problems.

When he was a boy, Olm's grandfather had told him stories about how the Pawnee, especially the Skidi, used annual sacrifices to ensure bountiful harvests on land and water. He told how they'd danced the Ghost Dance, pleading with Tirawa, the god of the spirit world, for the return of their dead ancestors so the tribe would be strengthened by their collective wisdom and, of course, how a son offered up the bones of his dead father. So many stories, but all of them told so long ago, the details of the rituals were hazy and overlapped. Once again, Olm took the route of improvisation, trusting that he'd be granted dispensation since his father hadn't bothered to teach him much more than how to chug twelve-ounce bottles of Budweiser without belching.

At the northern perimeter of the circle sat a small wire-mesh cage Olm had brought along with his father's body. Inside the cage lay a fat nutria, which he'd captured a week ago and had been caring for since. The rodent appeared mesmerized, small black eyes locked on to the fire. It didn't even twitch as Olm approached. Once beside the cage, Olm pulled a Buck knife out of the back pocket of his jeans, opened it, and flicked his thumb over the six-inch blade. Confident it was sharp enough, he leaned over, stuck the blade into the ground, then righted himself and began to undress. He couldn't remember a time when he felt more excited. Just thinking about the new life that lay ahead made him giddy, almost light-headed. No more being laughed at or the brunt of anyone's joke. After tonight, he'd harvest money, women, knowledge, and strength in abundance. He'd finally be the one to have the last laugh.

Wearing nothing but gooseflesh and a smile, Olm squatted, opened the back of the cage, and quickly pulled the nutria out by its tail. He held the squealing, writhing rodent at arm's length, pulled the knife out of the ground with his free hand, then stood and

4

stepped into the circle. After he reached the center of the circle, he glanced over at the burial shelf. The fire was receding—his father's bones were exposed.

It was time.

Olm faced west, lifted his arms high above his head, and shouted, "*Tirawa!*" The nutria clawed and bit at his forearm, but he ignored the pain, concentrating instead on the few Pawnee words he'd learned from his grandfather. The ones that called upon Father Sun, Brother Moon, Mother Earth, Sister Water. He'd practiced for weeks, stringing the words together into a chant, reciting them over and over until they rolled off his tongue with little effort. The words might not have been the same as the ones used by his forefathers during their rituals, but surely these held enough power to gain an ear from the netherworld.

With the nutria's teeth buried in his arm, its body twisting and slapping against him, Olm closed his eyes, pictured himself at the head of a tribe of thousands, and began to chant.

"Kiitsu—Sakuru—Poh—Piita. Kiitsu—Sakuru—Poh—Piita . . ." Olm repeated the words again and again, louder each time, until his mind held nothing but the rhythm of the chant. His feet followed that rhythm, stomping the ground, first with his right foot, then with his left. A breeze kept time with him, as did the trees, their leaves rustling a soft percussion.

Right—*stomp*. Left—*stomp*. "Kiitsu—Sakuru—Poh . . ."

Right, left. "Piita—Kiitsu . . ."

Right-left, right-left, right-left—circling, circling.

"Sakuru—Poh—Piita!" The vibration of the words ran through Olm's body, and his vision as leader grew sharper, clearer.

It was then Olm opened his eyes, stilled his feet, lowered his arms, and rammed the knife into the belly of the nutria, ripping it open from groin to neck. As the animal screeched and writhed in its death throes, Olm held fast to its tail and covered his body with its blood, letting it splash over his shoulders, down his chest, his back, his groin, his legs. When the nutria finally fell limp, Olm tossed it aside, dropped the knife, lifted his arms above his head once again.

"Great Warrior Spirit, I call upon you to give to me what is rightfully mine. You have promised, through the voice and heritage of our people, that a son only has to ask and you will provide. I not only ask you for the fullness of all that made the leaders before me powerful—I command it! Morning Star and Evening Star will testify to my worthiness, as will Brother Moon, Mother Earth, and Sister Water. Listen to their cry. Hear their testimony of all the years I have suffered, waiting patiently for this moment, enduring hardship after hardship. Do not turn your face from me, oh Great One. I call upon you and all your minions, those from the north, south, east, and west, and command that the promise be fulfilled quickly. You must obey . . . Kiitsu, now! Sakuru, now! Poh, now! Piiti—"

Before he finished the command, a gust of wind slammed into Olm's back, nearly knocking him off his feet. With it came the maddening chitter of insects, the croaks and *whomps* from frogs and alligators, only their calls sounded louder than before. Shivering, he glanced about. The fire had died from the burial shelf, making the night darker; the stars above him appeared brighter, bigger. He heard the loud lapping of water against the shore of the knoll. The fecund scent that had surrounded him earlier seemed more concentrated now. Everything appeared the same, only magnified, amplified. The air was charged with something *different*.

He peered from left to right, turning in small, slow circles, looking, searching for what he felt, but couldn't see. Then, just off to his right, through an eastbound slough, he spotted something odd. At first it looked like a million fireflies heading toward him from a great distance. Olm watched, curious, fearful, feeling very naked.

As the pinpoints of light drew closer, the air grew thicker, charged with an electric current that filled him with dread. The specks of yellow light no longer looked like fireflies, but like eyes. Thousands—no, a million eyes coming toward him—for him.

And in that moment, Olm instinctively knew that he had somehow managed to summon a hell of a lot more than he'd bargained for.

CHAPTER ONE

I don't know which gave me indigestion first, writing a check for twenty-three hundred dollars made payable to the Internal Revenue Service, or the sound of Fritter scratching on the back door. Not that it really mattered. Both were bad news.

Wanting to delay the inevitable as long as possible, I hesitated signing my name. Hell, the IRS got its due whether or not I waited until the last minute, barely making the April fifteenth deadline, something I did every year. There was a point to my procrastination.

For some reason, working as a freelance writer and being an heir to a few interest-bearing accounts made me not only a target for regular audits, but also a test subject for new and useless tax forms. I always imagined some governmental toad eagerly counting off five cents from every ten cents I earned, with a Post-it note stuck to the side of his or her computer that read *Reminder: Fuck with Dunny Pollock, the freak who lives in Cyler, Texas.* As far as I was concerned, the bastards didn't deserve my money any sooner than was mandated. Reluctantly, I scribbled my name on the appropriate line, then stuffed the check into the envelope.

As much as I despised the IRS, at least I knew what to expect from them. Fritter's scratching was a different story. Experience had proven more times than not that the small, wiry-haired mutt had an internal *oh, shit* meter worth noting.

Fritter had shown up about six months ago, pawing at my door and staring through the screen with large, watery brown eyes. Judging by the prominent show of ribs and the lack of a collar, I figured he had no home and wanted food, so I'd tossed out the only leftovers I had at the time. Half an apple fritter. He'd sniffed it and looked at me as if to say, *What, no kibble? No beef?* Then, after batting the stale pastry around a couple of times with a paw, he'd wolfed it down. No sooner had my offering disappeared than he resumed scratching at the door until I went outside to shoo him away. That's when I noticed a reddish sheen rising over the eastern horizon. It had taken a few seconds for me to realize it was far too early in the day to be a sunset, and I was facing in the wrong direction to boot. I blinked, took another look. The azimuthal glow shifted and wavered, as if west Texas had suddenly been awarded its own version of the Northern Lights. It turned out to be a brushfire so large it took three county fire departments to put it out.

About a month later, while I was getting ready for bed, Fritter showed up at my door again, pawing as if he meant to rip through wood and screen. It was late, and I was already grumpy from a looming deadline and an article that refused to gel, so I just grabbed the first thing I happened upon in the fridge and threw it out to shut him up. It was sliced deli turkey, which evidently didn't require sniffing because he simply swallowed the meat whole. I didn't even have time to close the kitchen door before he was at it again, scratching, pawing, whining for all he was worth. Twenty minutes later an F-2 tornado plowed through Cyler, missing my house and the twenty-acre spread that surrounded it by mere feet.

The final incident that forced me to put two and two together about the dog came a couple of weeks later. I'd just climbed into my truck to head for the grocery store when the mutt came tearing around the corner of the house and threw himself at the driver's door. I hollered at him to beat it, but he only hurled himself at the door again. I honked the horn, and he ran off a few feet, then came to a stop and gave me a look that seemed to say, *Listen to me—see me—don't go!* That look was so humanlike, so *readable*, I almost got out of the truck. Instead, I gave myself a reprimanding *tsk* and sped off. Fritter chased the truck down the long gravel drive, and it was about a mile down Highway 142 before I finally lost him.

On my return trip from the store, bench seat loaded down with eggs, milk, bread, more sliced turkey, cans of beef stew, and orange juice, I was T-boned by a teenager speeding across an intersection in his father's red Camaro. Luckily there'd been no serious injuries. I managed to walk away with only a bump on the head, a scratch on my right knee, and the inside of the truck covered in egg slime. When I got home, Fritter had been waiting. He yapped and raced about my feet, evidently glad to see me, then trotted off with his tail and head held high. There'd been no mistaking the haughty attitude . . . *See what you get for not listening to me, Ms. Thing?* Ever since then, the dog and I had a clear understanding. He scratched, I paid attention.

With my stomach twisting up in knots, I pushed away from the table and went over to the door to see what Fritter wanted. As soon as I turned on the back porch light, I spotted him running in circles, chasing his tail as if something had latched on to it and refused to let go. I pushed open the screen door and quickly scanned the sky. There was no whistle in the wind, no reddish glow. It looked like any other small-town Texas night in April. Cool, dark, and filled with more stars than was possible to count.

I turned to the dog. "What now?"

As soon as Fritter heard my voice, his frantic circling ceased. He looked up at me, and the intensity of his stare sent my heart hammering against my chest.

"What?" I asked again, frustrated he didn't speak English and I couldn't speak dog. All I had to go on were those *looks* he gave me. "Well?"

In response, Fritter suddenly bolted, squeezed himself between the open door and me, and ran into the house.

"Hey!"

The mutt ignored me, toenails ticking, scritching on the kitchen linoleum as he ran across the room. I watched dumbfounded as he finally slid to a stop, right beneath the old telephone mounted on the far back wall. There he sat and chuffed, looking up at the phone, then over at me, then up at the phone again.

I stood in the doorway, unsure of what to make of

the situation. Fritter had never come into the house before. In fact, he'd never stayed in the yard longer than a day at a time. When he wasn't warning me of something, he came and went as he pleased, usually taking advantage of the bowl of water and occasional leftovers I placed near the toolshed out back. Although he didn't belong to me, I'd named him. I had to call him something other than Dog, and Fritter just seemed appropriate. A sort of commemoration of the first time we met.

I closed the door and walked over to him, settling my right hand on my hip. Fritter chuffed again, swiped his tongue over his snout, then flopped onto his belly. He glanced up at the phone, then over to me, and the inside of my chest suddenly felt weighted with a thousand fluttering bats. Was he trying to warn me that something was going to happen in this house? Or that bad news was coming by way of the phone? My stomach churned again, and I tried convincing myself, despite the other warnings, that I was being paranoid. That Fritter was nothing but an old dog that happened to be in the wrong place at the right time. Nothing but coincidence. But I couldn't let it go.

I pointed a finger at him. "Look, if you're trying to tell me something, you're going to have to do better than that."

Fritter glanced from me to the phone again, yawned, then rested his muzzle between his front paws. His yawn caused a few of the bats nesting in my chest to scatter. Maybe his scratching wasn't a warning this time. Maybe he just wanted a warmer place to sleep tonight or a late snack. And even if he meant to warn me about something, it couldn't have been that urgent, he looked too relaxed.

I blew out a loud breath and headed for the pantry to get a can of beef stew. "You make me crazy, you know that?" Fritter rolled his eyes in my direction, as if I were the nuisance.

Shaking my head, I opened the pantry and stepped inside. It was the size of a small walk-in closet and always smelled of fresh-dug potatoes and onions, even though I stored neither on its shelves. That scent had a way of bringing me comfort, a sense of peace, home, and family. I closed my eyes for a moment and inhaled deeply, remembering. There was a lot to remember.

My paternal grandmother had stored potatoes and onions, which had been harvested from my grandfather's garden, in this pantry for as long as I could recall . . . which was quite a number of years. I'd lived here since I was five, along with my younger sister, Angelle, after our mother and father died in a car accident in El Paso. Mom and Pop Pollock had taken us in immediately after the accident, and for years they made sure we never wanted for the basics in life or questioned whether or not we were loved. When it came to food and shelter, love and protection, especially protection from outsiders who wanted to know more about my secret, Mom and Pop Pollock had given all they had. And they continued to give even after they died, which had been about two years ago. Mom passed on after a heart attack on Valentine's Day, and Pop followed a month later from a massive stroke. Their will had been short and simple; everything was to go to Angelle and me. The house, the land, a 1987 Ford pickup with only forty-one thousand miles on the odometer, and a surprising amount of money they'd managed to squirrel away in money market certificates.

The money came from a pool of oil that had been discovered on the south end of their property nearly sixteen years ago. It had been large enough to plop them into the lap of luxury for the rest of their lives. Instead, having always been frugal, Mom and Pop had only bought necessities, preferring to save a good portion of their new income for "a rainy day," which, of course, never came.

With no mortgage on the house, and interest checks coming in monthly, Angelle and I could easily have sat on our butts and grown fat and bitchy over the last couple of years. Fortunately, our grandparents had also left behind a work ethic that kept that from happening. The money did, however, provide us with the freedom to work at whatever we chose. For me, that meant freelancing as a columnist for three large Texas newspapers, one as far away as Dallas. The pay wasn't all that great, but with money not being an issue, I reveled in the opportunity to work independently from home. For Angelle, it had meant earning a degree in education. Now she worked as a second grade teacher in south Louisiana, where she lived with her relatively new husband, Trevor. Angelle loved working with kids as much as I loved working with words.

Standing in the pantry, thinking about my sister, sent a wave of loneliness crashing over me, and I quickly grabbed a can of beef stew and got the hell out of there. There was a significant difference between living alone and being lonely. I'd always managed the former without a problem and fought my entire life to ignore the latter.

To brush away the last of that forlorn web, I shook the can of stew at Fritter. "You better damn sure appreciate this. Ten o'clock at night, and I'm feeding a ragtag dog."

Fritter jumped up, and at first I thought he was excited about the upcoming snack, but then he let out a sharp bark and stared at the telephone, ears peaking. In that instant, the phone rang.

I shot a look at the old beige box mounted on the wall. It had no caller ID, no answering machine, and its ring was shrill and always set my teeth on edge. Even worse, it summoned all the bats back to roost in my chest. I set the can of stew on the counter and took a step toward the phone, which sent the bats colliding into each other. Fritter began to paw the linoleum and howl, his snout raised to the ceiling. Between the scratching and howling, jangling and fluttering, I felt a sudden urge to run out of the house and never look back.

I wish I had.

CHAPTER TWO

Gritting my teeth, I marched over to the phone. "Quit being ridiculous," I muttered to myself, then yelled at Fritter to shut up. He howled louder. I grabbed the receiver from the cradle and yelled into it, "Hold on!" then dropped the phone, scooped Fritter into my arms, and carried him outside. The mutt barked and wiggled, squirmed and howled, as if I were leading him to a torture chamber. By the time I got back to the phone, I was out of breath.

"What the hell is all that noise?" My sister, younger by two years and prettier by multiples of ten in my opinion, never missed an opportunity to get right to the point. We usually talked at least once a week, catching up on what was going on in each other's lives. But the last time we'd spoken had been a couple of weeks ago, and even then the conversation had been short. The school year was rolling to an end, which usually meant Angelle's workload doubled, leaving her little time for leisurely chats.

"Just Fritter losing his shit. I had to put him outside."

"Since when do you let him in the house?"

"I didn't. He just kind of let himself in." Fritter was

still howling, and he began to paddle the door with his paws. Right then I had a sneaky suspicion that whatever he'd been trying to warn me about involved this call. The hair on my arms stood on end. If there was bad news coming, there was no use dancing around it. Just as soon cut to the chase. "What's wrong?"

"How . . . how did you know something was wrong?"

Since I'd never told my sister about the special connection between Fritter and me, I figured it best to tell a little white lie. Better that than have her think I had a few brain bulbs burning out. "I could just tell from your voice." She let out a little sob, and my knees weakened. Jesus, something *was* wrong. I leaned against the wall. "Talk to me."

Angelle sniffled and let out a shaky breath that I could hear even over Fritter's howling. "I don't even know where to start."

"Try the beginning."

"That would take too long." Another sniffle. "Dun, I need . . . I need your help. I need you to come out to Bayou Crow."

My palms grew slick with sweat. "What's the matter? Are you sick? Hurt?"

"No, not that. I really don't want to get into everything over the phone. It would take too long and sound too . . . too weird. I'll tell you all about it when you get here . . . if you'll come."

"Wait, I don't understand. You need my help but can't tell me why?"

"No . . . well, yeah, I can tell you the most important part—a couple of kids from my class are missing.

An eight-year-old boy named Nicky Trahan, and a seven-year-old girl, Sarah Woodard. They've been gone for over twenty-four hours now, and people here are starting to think they've either drowned or got lost in the swamps."

I frowned. "I can understand drowning with all the water out there and everything, but how do a seven- and eight-year-old get lost in a swamp? It's not like wandering off in the woods. You can't just walk through a swamp, right?"

"Not really. There is a good bit of land out there, though."

"Okay, but don't you have to get to that land by boat?"

"Yeah."

"Did either of those kids know how to drive one?"

"I don't think so. I mean, they're only seven and eight."

"That's my point, how would they have gotten out there?"

"Someone could've easily taken them."

What came immediately to mind was, *Why?* But I didn't ask. The question was stupid. There were no real answers when it came to child abduction. Just sick assholes with personal agendas. "Gelle, I don't—"

"B-fifteen!" a woman shouted in the background from Angelle's end of the line.

"Who's that?" I asked.

"Poochie, Trevor's grandma. She does that every once in a while, call bingo numbers I mean. Not sure why." Angelle lowered her voice. "She's a sweetheart,

18

but has always been a little off. Started getting worse over the last two, three weeks. You know, forgetting things, like taking her meds, leaving the stove on, stuff like that. Trevor thought it best to move her out here for a while."

"You mean she's living with you?"

"Yeah. She lived all the way out in St. Martinville, over an hour and a half away. It was hard keeping tabs on her from that distance. She doesn't have any other immediate family but us, and Trevor isn't ready to put her in a nursing home yet."

"Man, that's got to be tough, having her around all the time, huh? I mean, you've only been married a little over a year. Isn't that sort of still in the newly-wed phase?"

"Yeah, well . . . you've gotta do what you've gotta do for family, right?"

I tsked. "No fair. That's a setup if I've ever heard one."

"Dunny, those kids . . ."

I knew what was coming and didn't want to hear it. I wanted to go back to earlier, when opening a can of beef stew for a mangy mutt was my only concern. Right then I almost wished for a tornado or to be driving around and have some pimply-face kid broadside my truck. Anything but what Angelle was about to ask.

"You have to come out here and help find them."

I shook my head. "I can't, and you know why. What about the police? Haven't they been called in? Haven't they sent out search parties?"

"Everyone's been looking, neighbors, teachers, other

students. Bayou Crow only has one cop, so they sent a couple of deputies from Iberville Parish Sheriff's Department yesterday. Problem is they already had to pull them out this morning. Dunny, this town's so small; if those kids were around here, we'd have found them by now."

"Not if someone grabbed them and hauled ass to another town."

"Yeah, I thought of that, but there's only one main road that runs in and out of Bayou Crow. People around here are too nosy to not have noticed a strange car trolling the street. Someone would have seen something—said something. The only logical place those kids could be is in the swamp. And if someone took them in there, and they manage to escape some-how, there's no way they're going to be able to find their way out by themselves. They'll die out there, if they're not dead already. It's as simple as that, Dunny. You have to come. If anyone can find those babies, I know you can."

"Shit," I muttered, then trapped the phone be-tween my right ear and shoulder and wiped the sweat from my palms on my jeans. Fritter was still pawing frantically, but at least his howling had stopped. I fi-nally asked, "Did you tell anyone about me, about what I can do? Does anyone there know?"

"I haven't said a word to anybody. Trevor doesn't even know, and no one has to know. You can wear your gloves like always. I'll just tell them you're here visiting; then when we go out to look for the kids, I'll make sure we're alone. No one will find out, I swear. Dunny, you have to come."

I sighed, suddenly feeling like the most exhausted thirty-three-year-old on the planet. No more fresh-dug potato and onion scents to comfort me. All I smelled now was trouble. "Gelle, I've never done it around a lot of water before. Even if I went out there, there's no guarantee it's going to work."

"But that's just it; at least you'd have tried. Remember all you did even without trying? The water at the Hughes' place—the oil on Mom and Pop's property? And Pirate . . . don't forget about Pirate."

"I don't—"

"Look there's a plane that leaves out of Midland at seven thirty tomorrow morning. It connects in Houston, gets into Baton Rouge a little after eleven. I sent the link with all the flight information to your e-mail address. You won't have to worry about renting a car or getting directions here, I'll pick you up. All you have to do is say you'll come."

Fritter gave a high-pitched yelp, and when I looked over at him, he slammed his body against the door, just as he'd done to my truck. The expression on his face, if a dog could have an expression, and this one certainly seemed capable, read, *Don't even think about it!*

I didn't want to think about it. But what choice did I have? In truth, it wasn't so much a repeat of the past that I feared as it was not finding those kids. Suppose I went out there and nothing happened? Eventually I'd have to leave Bayou Crow knowing I'd failed. I'd have to carry the weight, the guilt, the burden of those lost kids all the way back to Texas. I didn't know if I could live with that. And truth be told, I did worry about people knowing my secret, as selfish as that felt under the circumstances. It had taken a long time to get my life on an even keel, to get people to forget about me and move on to some other freak. Going out there could bring everything back, everything I'd worked so hard to leave behind—everything that shoved loneliness front and center.

"Dunny?"

"Yeah, I'm here."

"So . . . will you?"

"I'll be there," I said quietly, then hung up the phone, realizing only after I turned away from it that I hadn't told my sister good-bye.

Feeling as if the soles of my feet had been painted with superglue, I made my way from the kitchen into the living room and over to the large picture window that took up most of the east wall. Beyond the window, in the center of the front yard, stood a twenty-foot mesquite tree. Its thorny branches didn't flow up and out like an oak's or a pine's. They were twisted and bent at awkward angles, refusing to conform to any standard horticultural symmetry. Pop had worked for years pruning, trimming, literally training the mesquite to be a tree. Left on its own, it would have grown to be little more than a scraggly border shrub, but under his care, it stood tall and birthed beautiful lavender flowers. If only I'd have fared as well under Pop's care as that mesquite.

I placed my left palm against the windowpane and spread out my fingers—all six of them. The extra digit had been there since birth. It had its own bone and was as flexible, if not more so, as my normal little finger. I never asked why my mother and father didn't have the appendage removed at birth. I just assumed it was because they didn't have the money. By the time Mom and Pop could afford the surgery, which wasn't long after the oil well began to produce, I was in my early teens and had become so accustomed to the thing by then, I feared losing it more than I did the ridicule and curious looks it brought from other people.

I was only eight when I learned to fold the extra digit into my palm or to wear gloves while out in public. Gloves were a bit of a hassle because I always had to get two pairs, one a size larger than what I normally wore. That way I could mix the left larger with the right smaller so the extra finger would fit into the finger sleeve along with its sister. As closely as I tried matching them, however, the gloves still managed to draw attention. They were just too out of place in Cyler. It was rarely cold enough here, even in winter, to wear a heavy coat, much less gloves. And as if it wasn't bad enough I had to hide the deformity, by the time I turned ten, I discovered the damned thing could do *stuff*.

The first time I found that out was on a Sunday afternoon, when Angelle and I had gone with Mom Pollock to visit Frieda Hughes, a neighbor. The entire time we were over there, Frieda whined about the number of drillers she'd brought out to her property in the last month and how not one of them had been able to find a freshwater well—and oh, Lord, what was she to do? While Frieda was in the throes of one of her famous pity parties, I grabbed

Angelle, and we escaped to the backyard for a game of hide-and-seek. One minute I was giggling with the anticipation of finding the perfect hiding place, and the next I was standing near an old tractor shed behind the Hughes' house, grimacing in pain.

The extra finger had folded into my palm on its own. And it hurt as if someone had trapped it in the jaws of a clothespin. Angelle, who'd been the designated seeker at the time, found me with little effort. At first she'd laughed in triumph, then realized I wasn't so stupid as to hide out in the open. When she asked why I was just standing there instead of playing the game, I meant to tell her it was because my finger was hurting so bad. Instead, I wound up saying, "Go get Mom Pollock. There's a lot of water under here." Then I pointed to the ground beneath my feet.

Two days later the same drillers who'd been out the previous week found a wide freshwater spring, sixty feet below the ground on the very spot I'd predicted. Dowsing wasn't an unusual occurrence in Cyler, only the known dowsers normally used forked willow branches or thin metal rods. No one had ever heard of a kid dowsing, much less a kid dowsing with a finger.

Word spread quickly after the Hughes' find, and Mom and Pop Pollock did their best to protect me from the clinging people, many coming from as far away as New Mexico, all of them hounding me for help. No one could protect me, though, from the teasing at school. While other misfits were tagged with names like Four-Eyes, Fattie, Banana-nose, or Dumbo, I got stuck with Freak and Water Witch.

The worst of it came soon after I discovered oil on Mom and Pop's property. Although no one in the family had breathed a word about how the oil had been found, people immediately assumed I was responsible. Folks appeared in droves, begging me to search their land for black gold. It got so bad, we had to get an unlisted phone number, and Pop had to put a gate at the end of the driveway to keep people away.

Unfortunately, instead of growing tall and fruitful under Pop's care, like the mesquite, I shrank away from people. Their greed overwhelmed me. It still did. I was a freak that people tried to manipulate with lies and promises they never meant to keep. And that didn't change once I became an adult. I was still a target for manipulation, especially from men. I'd been wined and dined by some of the best, only to find out later that they meant to use my abilities for their own gain.

To make matters worse, I found out about five years ago that my finger's talent extended beyond finding oil and water, lost lockets, and misplaced keys. Back then, Angelle's yellow and black calico, Pirate, who'd been part of the family for years, went missing. I'd searched for that stupid cat, consciously focusing on it and trusting that my extra finger would find it. And, of course, it did. Instead of pulling into my palm and pinching as it had when I'd found the water, though, or stretching outward and aching like when I'd discovered the oil, it had grown limp and cold. By the time I located Pirate's headless, mauled body under a thicket a mile away from the house, my finger had felt encased in ice.

It was then I'd sworn Angelle to secrecy. If people went nuts over water and oil, what would they do if they knew I could locate other things, like dead bodies? Since my sister was the only one to witness my finding Pirate, I made her swear a solemn oath never to tell anyone about it, and she hadn't. I'd also made her promise to never bring the matter up again, and she hadn't. Until now.

The thought of searching through a swamp for two missing children made me queasy and sent a litany of doubts tumbling through my mind. It wasn't about searching through so much water. That had only been an excuse. What I feared most was failure. What if those kids *were* in the swamp and I couldn't find them? Then again, what if they were in there and I *did* find them, only dead? And there was no telling what else my finger might dredge up from hiding in those dark, murky waters.

From somewhere deep inside, instinct warned me to stay home. But judging by the heaviness in my chest, my heart had already succumbed to the missing kids. I had to go.

Drawing in a long breath, then releasing it slowly to calm myself, I dropped my hand from the window and watched the imprint of all those fingers fade away. If only disappearing were that easy. . . .

With my head clogged with worry, I headed out of the living room and to the computer that held the information on the Baton Rouge flight. As I passed through the kitchen, I heard Fritter whimper from behind the screen door. I looked over at him.

"Don't even start," I warned. "I don't want to hear it."

He flicked his tongue over his snout, stared at me.

"They're just little kids. I have to go . . . so quit staring at me like that, goddamnit."

Fritter chuffed once, and in that sound, I could've sworn by all that was sacred I heard the words *You'll be sorry.*

CHAPTER THREE

The Baton Rouge Airport was smaller than I expected. It didn't take long for me to get from the gate to a set of wide glass doors that whooshed open, welcoming me to a warm and humid Louisiana day. Angelle had told me about the heat and humidity that baked the state in the summer, but she hadn't told me that summer began in April. It was obvious other travelers hadn't been warned, either, for a few had arrived in heavy coats and sweaters, most of which were stripped off immediately.

I squinted against the sun and marveled at how green everything looked—grass, trees, shrubbery, so lush and beautiful. In Cyler, spring took its sweet old time coming about. And even then its landscape remained predominately brown because of drought. Back home, the air always smelled of dust and desert, but here it was scented with pine, jasmine, and a hint of something that smelled a little like bananas.

A horn honked, and a gray Camry pulled up to the curb in front of me. No sooner did it stop than the trunk popped open. An elderly woman peered out at me from the back passenger window. She pressed her face against the glass and smiled, lips curling in over toothless gums, heavy jowls jiggling. She had brilliant green eyes that held the expression of a child who'd just seen her first department store Santa—a little fear and a whole lot of wonder.

Someone tugged on the strap of the carry-on bag I had slung over my right shoulder, and I glanced over to see my sister standing beside me.

"Hey, you," she said, and offered a faltering smile. "Sorry if you had to wait long."

I stared at her, unable to respond. I'd last seen Angelle about five months ago, when she and Trevor had flown to Cyler to spend the Thanksgiving holidays with me. At that time, her beautiful heart-shaped face still held the glow of a newlywed. Now her cheeks were sunken, her complexion sallow. Dark circles rimmed her light brown eyes. She wore a blue T-shirt and a pair of jeans, both of which looked as if they'd come from the discard bin at the Salvation Army.

Before I managed to say anything, Angelle's eyes welled up with tears, and she threw her arms around me. "I'm so glad you're here," she whispered against my ear.

I returned her hug, holding her tight. She was trembling, and she squeezed me back even tighter. Having a soft spot for kids was one thing, but Angelle seemed traumatized, as if those missing kids belonged to her. Something bigger had to be going on. I was about to ask her if she was okay to drive, when someone called out.

"Hey!"

Angelle and I turned toward the old woman sitting

29

in the Camry. She had lowered the back window to half-mast and was waving a hand through the opening. "Dat damn door she's stuck, come get me out!"

"You don't need to get out, Poochie," Angelle said. "We're coming right now."

"Mais, den you bes' hurry 'cause I'm gonna pass out in dis heat. Poo-yi, it's hot!"

"You're not going to suffocate, Poochie. The car's still running, and the air conditioner's on." Angelle grabbed me by the arm and led me to the back of the car. She signaled for me to put my bag in the trunk.

As soon as she closed the trunk, the old woman harrumphed loudly. "If dat air condition is on, den de summabitch is broke, 'cause I don't feel me no air."

Angelle gave me an apologetic look. "Poochie's the reason I'm a little late. Normally she's at the B and B right now, but she kept insisting she had to come with me to pick you up." Before I could ask what a B and B was, Angelle tapped a finger against her left temple, looking even more exhausted than she did five minutes ago. "Poochie goes a little off from time to time, and she *never* shuts up. So take that as a heads-up, we may not get any talk time until I drop her off."

I gave her another quick hug and kissed her cheek. "No need to apologize. We'll talk when we can. I'm just glad to see you."

"Me, too." Angelle squeezed my arm, then gave me a real smile, albeit small. "Come on, let's get going before Poochie decides to pitch a hissy fit."

"I heard dat," Poochie yelled out the window as we headed for opposite sides of the car. "What's dat, a hissy fit?"

"Nothing, Pooch," Angelle said, opening her door. "We're leaving, so put your seat belt back on."

As soon as I settled into the passenger's seat, Poochie scooted to the edge of the backseat and put a hand on my shoulder.

"What your name is?" she asked, giving me another toothless grin, her green eyes flashing questions yet to be asked. She looked to be in her mid-eighties, and although her manner appeared brusque, it held the confidence of a woman who felt living eighty-some-odd years had earned her the right to say whatever she pleased to whomever she pleased.

"I already told you her name twice this morning, Pooch," Angelle said as she put the car in drive and threaded her way into traffic.

Poochie frowned as if ready to say, *No, you didn't.* I figured it was as good a time as any to jump in. If I was going to be here for a couple of days, and Trevor's grandmother was going to be part of this, even if only by osmosis, then it was probably better to get some of the basics locked down up front. "My name's Dunny. And yours is . . . Poochie?"

She nodded vigorously, and her cap of white, over-permed hair bobbled.

"Is that your real name?"

The old woman tsked. "What kinda mama you think would give her baby girl a name like Poochie? No, dat name came from my old husband, Maurice, may de good Lord rest him. My for-real name is Patricia. Maurice, him, he just cut dat short to Poochie. So dat's me, Poochie Blackledge. Before I had me a husband, though, it was Poochie Babineaux. I come from

St. Martinville. My grandbaby, Trevor, he's de one dat moved me over here. You know how dat is when you get old, de young people think dey got to take over everything. So, I figure I come live over here for a little while, maybe save on some grocery money, you know. It's not too bad. And you, what your name is?"

I blinked at the onslaught of words.

"She just told you her name, Pooch," Angelle said, and gripped the steering wheel tighter.

I wanted to look out at the landscape, take in the green, green, and more green, but Poochie would have none of it. She tapped me on the shoulder again.

"Oh yeah, dat's true, you tol' me you name. Well, den, who's you daddy? What his name is?"

I grinned in spite of her persistent chatter. I loved the woman's accent, her brassy, outspoken style. "My dad's name was Robert Pollock. But he and our mother passed away when Angelle and I were little girls."

"Oh, *pauvre 'tite fille*." Poochie shook her head. "Dat's so sad you don't got no daddy and no mama. What you mama's name was?"

"Victoria Pollock."

"Aw, dat's a pretty name. I had me a sister. Her name was Valenteen, but she died long time ago, prob'bly thirty-five, forty years now. Valenteen . . . dat's almost de same like Victoria, huh?"

I smiled. "Pretty close, I think."

"Pooch, you already know all about our parents." Angelle slapped the blinker handle down a bit harder than was necessary. "I've told you about them a bunch of times. Don't you remember?"

Poochie huffed. "What, de gubberment pass a law dat says you can only talk about something one or two times, den you can't talk about it no more?"

Angelle threw me a look, rolled her eyes, then faced the windshield again with an exasperated sigh.

Poochie tapped my shoulder again. "Hey, how come you wearin' dem gloves like dat? You a little cuckoo in de head? It's too hot for gloves."

"I just like wearing them," I said.

"You know, dey think I'm crazy in de head." Poochie tsked and tapped her forehead with a finger. "But it's not true, no. Every once in a little while, a few things slip in and out my head, but dat's not too bad, huh? I believe everybody got something dat slips out der head sometime. What you think?"

Struggling to keep up with the constant shift in topics, I only nodded.

"You see?" Poochie tapped Angelle's right shoulder. "You sister thinks de same as me. I tol' you I'm not crazy."

"I never said you were, Pooch."

"Yeah, but I know what y'all been thinking. That I'm needin' to go to de cuckoo house or to de ol' people's house. Dey both de same if you ask me, but it don't matter 'cause I'm not goin' to neither one no how."

Angelle had already turned onto Interstate 10, and I could tell by the way she was white-knuckling the steering wheel and pushing the speedometer past eighty, she was anxious to get wherever we were going.

"N-thirty-two!" Poochie suddenly yelled.

Angelle and I started at the outburst, and although

I figured it could prompt a barrage of words, not one of them answering the question, I had to ask, "Why do you call out bingo letters and numbers?"

"'Cause I like how dey sound. You know how when you go to de bingo hall, and all de little balls is flyin' around in de machine? Den dat machine sucks out one of dem balls, and a man grabs dat ball, and he yells, 'B-two!—N-thirty-eight!—O-fifty-two!' I love when dat happens! It passes me de frissons all over. It makes me feel good, like I'm dat much closer to win."

"What's a frisson?"

Poochie shook her body, demonstrating a sudden shudder. "Like dat—like all de excitement inside you want to come out all at de same time. I can't go to de bingo hall in St. Martinville no more, and dey don't got one where I live now, so I got to make my own frisson. Let me tell you, when you my age, you got to get all de frissons you can where you can get dem."

I chuckled.

"So—how come you got dem gloves on?"

Angelle and I exchanged another glance; then I turned back to Poochie. "Just giving my hands time to warm up." I hoped that would appease her, but I had a feeling not much appeased her curiosity, that it was a constant state of being—hungry, fed, hungry, fed, the cycle never ending. "My hands always seem to get cold, no matter where I go."

"Hmmm," Poochie said, elongating the sound until it reached a pitch of disbelief.

Before she could broach the subject again, I quickly asked, "So, what's this B and B place Angelle says you go to? Is it like a bed-and-breakfast?"

Angelle snorted. "*Far* from a bed–and–breakfast."

"No, dey don't got no bed over dere, but breakfast, yeah, sometimes. When Vern feels like to cook." Poochie settled back in her seat and folded her arms over her ample bosom, which caused her pink house-dress to hike up over her knees. "Vern Nezat, dat's Sook's husband, and Sook, her, she's a cousin on my poor husband's side. Dey own de Bloody Bucket, and I go help over dere most times during de week."

"The Bloody Bucket?"

"Yeah, dat's what I said."

"It's kind of like a combo grocery store and bar and grill," Angelle said, not taking her eyes off the road.

"They name a place where people buy food the Bloody Bucket?" Sudden images of a slaughter-house, cow innards and blood strewn across the floor, came to mind, and I shuddered. "Doesn't sound very appetizing."

"Sound's worse than it is," Angelle said. "There's a pier attached to the back of the building. That way if a fisherman wants to come in for a beer and a burger, he doesn't have to worry about retrailering his boat. He just ties his skiff up to the pier and goes into the bar from the back door. Most of them come in straight out of the marsh, shrimp boots and clothes all muddy and bloody from the bait they've been cutting all morning for trout lines. They used to keep their bait buckets on the back porch, too, until Sook made them stop be-cause it was drawing too many flies. Anyway, that's how it got its name, and—"

"Yeah, most de men over dere's a bunch of slobs," Poochie interjected. "Vern don't care how dey come in de bar, long as dey buy beers, you know? Sook, her, she de one who gets mad. She usually works de grocery side, but at de end of de day, she's de one's gotta mop de mess left on de floor in de bar. Poo-yi, dat makes her mad."

"What do you do over there?" I asked.

"Me, I stay to de grocery side, pass down de aisles and clean de can goods. Corn, Beenie Weenies, okra, stuff like dat. Dem can goods don't sell too fas', so dey get all dusty. And I make sure nobody takes stuff in de store when Sook goes help Vern in de bar." Poochie must have seen me eyeing the folded metal walker that leaned against the seat beside her because she promptly added, "Oh, I jus' use dat walker at de house. I got me some very-close veins on my legs, you know, and sometimes it's hard for me to walk. At de Bucket, though, I use me a scooter. Vern and Sook got me one so I could ride around de store fas' if I need to."

At last Poochie took a breath, unfolded her arms, and smoothed out her housedress so it covered her knees again. "Now, you sister tol' me you come out here to pass a little visit." She cocked her head and looked me dead in the eyes. "But me, I think you here to help find dem li'l chil'ren. Dat's true, huh?"

Oh God, she knew!

CHAPTER FOUR

My heart did a triple beat, and I glanced at Angelle, who went wide-eyed and mouthed, "I didn't tell her anything."

"N-thirty-seven!"

Angelle jumped, which caused her to jerk on the steering wheel and the car to veer slightly to the right toward an eighteen-wheeler. She quickly brought the car back on track, then blew out a breath.

"You know how come I know dat?" Poochie said. "Dat you come to help find dem chil'ren?"

"How?" I asked, the word coming out strained. I wasn't sure I wanted to know how she knew.

"Well, it's like dis. I had me a feeling de good Lord was gonna send somebody de last time I was out to my prayer tree."

"What's a prayer tree?" I asked, and Angelle shot me a *quit asking questions or she'll never shut up!* look.

"Dat's something, yeah . . . when I move over here, Angelle, she don't know what a prayer tree is, neither. Dat's a shame y'all don't have none where you come from. A prayer tree, dat's important. Back to my house in St. Martinville, I used me a chicken tree, kept all de shoes for de souls in purgatory on de

37

right side of dat tree, and shoes for de people dat's still alive on de left side. Over to Angelle and Trevor's I gotta use me a china ball tree 'cause dat's all dey got. It's not big like my chicken tree . . ." She shrugged. "But sometimes all you can do is work wit' what you got, right?"

"Shoes?" I glanced at Angelle, but she stared straight ahead, her thoughts obviously spiraling elsewhere. I turned back to Poochie, who continued to talk . . . and talk . . .

"Mais, yeah, shoes. Dat's what I use to keep close to de people I pray for. Sometimes when a person pass away, de family's worried dey didn't pass right to heaven. Maybe dey did too much bad, you know? So dey bring me a pair of der shoes so I can pray for de soul, ask de good Lord to let dem in heaven."

"Why shoes?"

Poochie shrugged. "Just 'cause. What I do is tie de shoelaces together and throw de shoes up in de branches on de purgatory side of de tree. Now, if somebody wants me to pray for somebody dat's sick or hurt, like dey got a broke leg, den I throw dem shoes up in de alive side of de tree." Poochie grinned, obviously confident that the explanation clarified everything fully.

As colorful as she was I was beginning to believe my sister might be right. The old woman's mind did slip off the track occasionally. Shoes in trees that had designated purgatory branches? Okay, maybe it slipped off a bit more than occasionally. . . .

"Anyways," Poochie continued, "I usually go out

to my prayer tree every day, but las' week when I went out dere, you never guess what I saw."

It took a long pause before I realized she was actually waiting for a response. "Oh . . . uh, I don't have any idea. What did you see?"

"Some of de shoes on de purgatory side was missin'!" She nodded, wide-eyed. "It's de trut'! Now, how bad you think dat is when somebody's gonna steal a dead man's shoes out a tree? Den, don't you know I went back out de very next day, and *boom?*" She slapped her hands together. "Another pair of shoes missin'. So far now, dat's prob'bly three-four pairs gone, and I don't know where dey went. All I know is since dey been gone, dere's been nothin' but trouble. De chil'ren went missin', and de feux fo lais is out in de swamp 'most every night now. I know, I seen dem out by de bayou. Dat makes it all kind of dangerous for de fishermen 'cause it's de feux fo lais's job to make people get los' in de swamps, you know what I'm sayin'?"

I nodded, not having a clue about feux fo lais or their job descriptions.

"And dat's not all I seen, no. Dere's stuff goin' on at de house and even at de Bucket. It's everywhere, I'm tellin' you. Just de other day, I got me a glass of water at de house and put it over here. . . . Poochie mimed placing a glass on a table in front of her. "De next thing I know, de glass of water's over dere." She motioned all the way to her right. "And it's not me dat moved de glass, no. It's like it move all by itself. Den sometimes I catch something out de corner of my eye, like somebody movin' out de room real fas', but I can't look fas' enough to see who it is."

"Poochie, let's give it a rest, okay?" Angelle said, her face growing much paler.

"What you mean rest? If you tired, you can take a nap when we get to de house."

"I mean let's talk about something else."

"Oh . . ." Poochie shrugged. "Okay, but first I'm gonna finish tellin' you sister what I was tellin' her."

There was something about the hard set of Angelle's lips, and the fear that flitted across her face, that made me wonder if she knew more about the story than even Poochie was telling.

"Mais, like I was sayin' . . ." Poochie waved a hand as if to collect all the words she'd spoken so far into one big pile. "Wit' all dat crazy stuff going on, I had to wonder me a couple things. I been wonderin' if some of de people I been prayin' for in purgatory didn't come back for der shoes. Maybe some got mad 'cause I put dem up de tree in de first place. So I go ask God yesterday, I said, 'God, what's going on? I don't understand all dis crazy stuff. You need to tell me something.' Then God spoke in my head, clear, like I hear me talkin' right now. He said, 'Poochie, all de answers not supposed to come right now, but don't worry, I'm gonna send somebody to help find de chil'ren.' So you see, dat's how I know why you here. God said so."

I thought the old woman had not only clicked off the track, but she'd jumped onto a different mode of transportation altogether. One that could possibly lead to a mental health unit. "I don't think I—"

"I know when de good Lord talks wit' me like dat, it always comes true. All I got to tell you is be careful. Dis is nothin' to play wit'. Dey don't got no water where you come from. Dey don't got no swamps, and you never been in de bayou before. I think you cuckoo to even go try to find dem babies like you gonna do, but still, what you doin' is a good thing." She glanced over at Angelle, then back at me. "But y'all gonna need some serious prayer. So I'm tellin' you, first thing when we get to de house, you need to give me a pair of you shoes. I'll put dem in de tree and pray, so de good Lord's gonna keep y'all safe and—"

"Wait, I—"

"I don't know if dem babies is still alive out dere. Me, I can't tell, don't have dat in me to see. I don't got me no ESPN, you know, like de people dat can put dey hand on something and tell where you been or where you goin'. All I can do me is pray. And, Boo . . ." Poochie paused, cocked her head as if trying to discern a strange, distant sound, then tsked loudly. "Poo-yi . . . de good Lord just made Him a little pass in my head right now. He tol' me, 'Pooch, you bes' pray and pray hard 'cause dat woman's sure gonna need it."

Her last few words seemed to drill a hole into the center of my chest. As crazy as they sounded, they held a ring of truth that scared the shit out of me. What the hell was I getting myself into? I looked over at Angelle, saw a tear slide down her right cheek. *God, not a good sign.* Thinking it best not to draw attention to her crying in front of Poochie, I turned toward the passenger window and watched

41

as we topped a bridge that crossed the Mississippi River. I was in sensory overload. So much green—too much water—so much talk—too little known. What the hell was I supposed to do with all this?

Poochie tapped my shoulder again, and when I looked back at her, she winked, then bellowed, "I-eighteen!"

Oh yeah, I was definitely in for one hell of a ride.

CHAPTER FIVE

It took only one bite of dry cereal for Olm to realize they'd fucked with the Froot Loops. When he'd grabbed a handful out of the box, they'd looked and smelled fine. But now, biting into the colored loops, he tasted the bitter burn of gasoline instead of sugary fake fruit. Olm quickly spat out the swill and swatted the box of cereal off the kitchen counter. Froot Loops scattered across the floor like confetti.

Over the last two days, *they* had been slowly and methodically contaminating everything he attempted to eat. It started with the chicken salad sandwich on Wednesday. He'd managed to get half of it down before it curved down gasoline alley and made him puke. Then there'd been the burger and fries he'd craved on Thursday. He'd barely gobbled down two bites of each before they turned bitter. Same with the honey bun and milk he tried eating last night. Now the goddamn Froot Loops. *They* meant to starve him to death, one food group at a time. Either that or drive him mad enough so he'd eat a bullet.

Olm walked over to the kitchen sink, loops crunching underfoot, and turned on the faucet. He leaned over, and with shaky hands, cupped water into his palms, meaning to rinse out his mouth. That's when he caught movement out of the corner of his eye. He froze, turned his head ever so slightly, and saw a black, translucent figure peeling itself from the wall opposite him, like wallpaper that had lost its adhesive backing. It had no distinct features, only the obscure form of a human—a man. Another figure quickly followed the first, this one oozing from the wall like gray smoke.

Forgetting his hands were filled with water, Olm threw them up protectively and wound up dousing himself in the process. He swiped at his eyes, whimpering. Until now, the apparitions had only come at night—whispering nonsensical words in his ears, touching him everywhere, constant probing, jabbing fingers he could never see, robbing him of sleep. Of sanity. He didn't know what *they* were, *who* they were. Not one of *them* ever spoke, no matter how many times he begged for answers. All he knew was they couldn't possibly be his people, not the Pawnee warriors and priests from his Skidi lineage. They wouldn't harm their own. Not like this.

Olm took a step sideways—and the utility drawer beside him suddenly slid open—the drawer to the cabinet that once held the cereal slammed shut. On the floor, Froot Loops crunched beneath unseen feet. *They* were heading toward him now, wavering forms that reeked of malice—and gasoline. The temperature in the room abruptly plummeted to freezing.

"No! Not in the daylight—not in the light!" Olm shouted. "Go away—go! What do you want from me? What the fuck do you want?"

44

A burbling sound—a *glub*, like a pocket of air breaking through the surface of heavy oil—and the apparitions moved closer, their forms growing denser though features no more distinguishable than a moment ago. Thick gray smoke now thicker—black wallpaper darker—nothing translucent now, edges curling in as though charred from a long-ago fire. The glubbing, burbling seemed to be the sound of their movement, as purposeful as footfalls on dry leaves, as the whisper of polyester rubbing between a runner's thighs, as the flap of a jacket as one walked through a brisk wind. It meant movement, movement toward him.

"Who the fuck *are* you?" Olm yelled, backing away slowly, slowly. "What do you want?"

Burbling gray, glubbing black—now with fingers, long reaching fingers. Olm shuddered. Not the touching—he couldn't bare the touching. Especially not in the light . . . not in the daylight.

As if preparing for a dunk underwater, Olm sucked in a deep breath, then grabbed his car keys off the counter and ran out of the house through the back door. He didn't look back—couldn't look back. If *they* were no longer held to the night, then anything was possible now, anything. What else awaited him? What else would they do? What more *could* they do?

By the time Olm reached the blue Impala sitting in the driveway, he was sure he'd pissed himself because his pant legs felt warm and wet. He didn't bother checking, just jumped in the car, locked the doors, and within seconds had the engine roaring and the tires peeling through gravel.

Only after he'd swung a hard left onto Highway 290 did Olm glance down at his pants. He was surprised to find them as dry and wrinkled as when he'd put them on a couple of hours ago. He peered up into the rearview mirror, raked trembling fingers through his sparse brown hair, relieved to see his house fading quickly in the distance. There was little doubt he was losing his shit. Tomorrow night was his only hope. If what he had planned didn't work, *they'd* win. He'd be dead. Olm was sure of it. He would *make* sure of it. No starving to death. No more jabbing, probing fingers. If he was responsible for bringing this shit here and couldn't make it leave, then he'd take himself out of the picture, permanently.

Three weeks ago, when he'd performed his father's burial ceremony and called upon Tirawa, demanding what was rightfully his, Olm's life had immediately taken on a new order of business. One of chaos and terror. Somehow everything had gone terribly wrong. Instead of receiving wisdom and strength from his Pawnee ancestors, he'd grown mentally and physically weaker by the day and so fearful he often jumped at his own shadow. He'd obviously done something wrong during the ceremony, but wasn't sure what. And even if he did know, there was no way for him to go back in time and correct it. All he knew to do was try and appease whatever he'd pissed off and keep calling to Tirawa.

Tirawa . . . seemingly insatiable, demanding more, always more. Was there truly any way to get the ear of this great spirit? To get it to manifest itself? Or had his grandfather just been full of bourbon and bullshit when he'd told him the stories? Olm remembered the tales sounding so real, remembered seeing the conviction and passion on the old man's face as he told them. It was so raw, so real, it literally transformed his appearance, brightened it somehow. Olm had to believe they were true—had to. There was no turning back now, anyway. None. He'd already crossed over a threshold that most men would never even have approached. . . .

Thinking the nutria he'd first sacrificed hadn't been sufficient, Olm had returned to the knoll night after night, offering reparation with larger, more intense sacrifices. He'd trapped a fox, beheaded it while it was still alive, then doused himself in its blood. When the fox didn't work, he'd brought in a calf; ripped its belly open from stem to stern, sliced off its head, then burned its entrails on a small burial shelf. It, too, produced no results.

In total, Olm had made six offerings over the last three weeks, the last one being a horse, one big enough, strong enough to kill a man with one kick. But nothing happened after he'd sacrificed it. Not one change. All of his efforts, all of that blood, and everything only seemed to be getting worse.

The apparitions showing up in his kitchen squashed any hope that things might be on the mend. *They* were revealing themselves in the light now, which could only mean they were getting stronger. He only wished he knew what *they* were. What *they* wanted. Other than to destroy his life. Not being able to sleep, to eat, to walk down a hallway without constantly glancing over his shoulder. How much more could a man take? Even the people in town, those he'd once considered friends, were turning their backs on him, skittering off in another direction as soon as they saw him approaching. What was he supposed to do? Just allow himself to fade away as though he'd never existed in the first place? Let *them* win? Not a chance— not when there was a chance. . . .

Desperate times called for desperate measures, and Olm was ready to measure desperate any way he had to, to force things in a different direction. When the horse offering didn't work, he'd spent hours peeling through childhood memories, desperate to recall everything his grandfather had told him about Pawnee and Skidi customs and the ways of their people. Searching for something, anything that might turn things around. That's when he remembered the ceremony dedicated to the invocation of Tirawa. As far as he knew, the ceremony had no name . . . only a purpose.

As legend had it, the two most prominent star powers in the universe were the Evening Star in the western sky, also known as the goddess of darkness and fertility, and the Morning Star in the eastern sky, known as the god of fire and light. The supernatural controlling authority at the zenith of the sky where these forces met was known as Tirawa. And, according to Olm's grandfather, there was only one way to capture Tirawa's complete attention, to call upon his absolute power so that it might be infused into the tribe. And that was through a human sacrifice. Not just any human sacrifice. It had to be a young girl.

According to the story, in the days of old, Skidi men would raid an enemy village and capture a girl, preferably one between the ages of seven and thirteen. At the moment of her capture, the child was dedicated to the Morning and Evening stars, then brought to the camp and ritually cleansed in preparation for a three-day ceremony. During those three days, the girl was fed, bathed, the entire village celebrating through song and dance, everyone focused on the girl's needs. But all that changed in the last hours on the final ceremonial day.

On that last day, the child was stripped naked and tied to a scaffold that held her upright and spread-eagled. Once she was secured, two tribal leaders would walk toward her from the east, each carrying a flaming brand. When they'd reached the girl, one would burn her armpits with his brand, while the other used his to sear her groin in honor of the Evening Star, the goddess of fertility. While the child screamed and writhed upon the scaffolding, four warriors from the tribe were called upon, and each had to approach the girl and lightly touch her on the head with his war club. Touch her—prepare her for the coup de grace—which normally followed immediately.

Amidst the girl's screams and the zealous chanting from the tribal members, the man responsible for the child's actual capture ran toward her from the west— ran toward her with a bow and sacred arrow—ran toward her and shot her through the heart. The moment the arrow impaled her, the four warriors began beating her on the head with their clubs, and they continued beating her until the officiating priest approached the scaffold.

With much pomp and circumstance, the priest

would make his way to the girl, then circle the scaffold four times, all the while calling upon Tirawa. After his last round, when he faced the girl for the last time, the priest would slice open her breasts with a flint knife and smear his face with her blood. The man who'd captured the child and shot her in the heart was made to collect some of her blood on dried meat, and that meat had to be shared with the rest of the tribe. Once this meal of dried meat and fresh blood was consumed, each male member of the tribe, no matter his age, had to shoot an arrow into the girl's body. Then the entire tribe circled the scaffold four times before walking away, leaving the girl's corpse to the elements. Only then was the ritual complete.

As far as Olm knew, this was the most powerful sacrificial ceremony ever performed by the Skidi. If this didn't get Tirawa's attention, nothing would. It was his last hope—his only hope.

CHAPTER SIX

Olm knew from the beginning that recreating the ceremony wouldn't be easy. Not only would he have to perform it alone, but he had no sacred arrows or war clubs. That meant he'd have to improvise, again. This time, though, instead of jumping ahead like a zealous idiot, Olm had made certain to think things through carefully. He considered the possible reasons a young girl was chosen back then instead of a boy. Why she was branded and clubbed on the head? If blood was the only sacrifice needed for Tirawa, why not just slaughter her immediately? Why the torture?

The only answer that made sense to Olm was fear. The whole ceremony, even the part where they fed her, cared for her, was a buildup toward the inevitable. Surely the victim had to have known that. Certainly her fear over those three days, particularly during the last, had to be near mania. It had to be more than just about the blood. It had to be—blood *and* fear. That had to be the answer to it all.

And if blood and fear were indeed the keys that unlocked the powers of Tirawa, then Olm wanted to do everything possible to amplify their affect. No more pansy-ass nutrias and foxes. This time there'd be no slipups. He not only wanted to make sure the ceremony worked, but he wanted to force it to greater heights, beyond what his ancestors had accomplished. Surely that would please Tirawa, make him banish the shadow people that tormented him, cause the great spirit god to shower him with gifts for years to come.

All this made sense to Olm, the reasoning behind the fear and blood, the ceremony, why he should push it to greater heights, why that would please Tirawa. . . . The problem was figuring out *how*. *How* was he supposed to take a ceremony of that magnitude and make it greater?

The solution came to him a couple of days later, while sitting in his truck, waiting behind an off-loading school bus. As he watched a half dozen or more kids scamper from the bus to their respective homes, it dawned on him; if one child's fear and blood had worked for his ancestors, then the blood and fear of two children should work twice as well—right? And—what if he changed the way they were sacrificed? Maybe slow it down instead of the quick kill to the heart. Wouldn't that heighten the fear factor significantly? Quadruple it possibly?

Keeping all those things in mind, Olm had set up his plan. He carefully calculated the time, date, and work that needed to be done so the climax of the sacrifice would occur at the very moment the moon waxed toward its apex. It was crucial to have all things culminate at this time, for Brother Moon sitting full-faced in the heavens was a major power in and of itself. It would be his failsafe against failure. Olm was convinced of that, and he worked meticulously through every detail, making sure everything was measured down to the minute of that crucial juncture.

When it was time to gather the children, Olm envisioned himself entering an enemy's camp, just like his ancestors, and seeking the perfect offerings. He found them easily enough. A boy and a girl about the same age, height, and weight. Both had light brown hair and brown eyes. From behind, they could easily have passed for brother and sister, only their facial features told different stories. The girl's face was round, rosy cheeked, and had a wide forehead. The boy had a narrow face, a pointed chin, and a pug nose that tipped up at the end. Both were beautiful in their own right, and Olm had had little trouble luring them away. He'd simply lied to get them into the truck, then kept lying when he transferred them from the truck to the boat. The performance he gave as he drove them out to the knoll and the sacrificial circle deserved an Oscar, in his opinion. Considering the circumstances, all had gone amazingly well. Quiet and orderly—well, until he'd bound their hands and feet, anyway. Then the screaming began.

The children's shrieks didn't worry him, for the knoll was so far back in the swamps, God Himself couldn't hear them. If anything, their cries for help encouraged Olm. It meant their fear had already started. To encourage and feed that fear even more, he'd tied them back to back against a cypress tree and made them watch while he dug two holes, both three feet wide by three feet deep—a hole for each of them.

As soon as he reached the appropriate depth for

each hole, the rich black earth beneath his shovel grew spongy, just as he'd suspected it would. That had given Olm hope, for it was just another step in the plan that had gone without a hitch.

The only real hiccup had come when he'd grabbed the boy to put him in the first hole. The brat bucked and wiggled and refused to keep his legs outstretched. It was only when Olm threatened to bash the girl's face in with a shovel that the boy quieted down. The girl gave him no problem at all. In fact, she seemed almost paralyzed with fear.

Once the children were settled in their individual holes, Olm had moved on to the next part of the plan. He collected silt in a metal bucket from the edge of the knoll, then dumped that silt over their legs. It had taken several trips to bury both children waist deep, but once that was done, all he had to do was stay mindful of the schedule he'd set, the one that ran in conjunction with the waxing moon. From there, it was only a matter of waiting.

Waiting—simple—simple pimple.

But it wasn't simple. The waiting drove Olm mad. He wanted to move on with his new life *now*, wanted whatever he'd fucked up to be fixed *now*. But only so much silt could be added *now*. Too much too soon, and the whole schedule would be thrown off. He had thirty-one hours and twenty-two minutes left before he could bring the ceremony to its climax. That was a lot of time—for fear.

Olm imagined the horror raging in the children's minds as they felt bucket after bucket of silt dumped on their bodies, the level of muck rising higher and higher, pressing against their chest and back. He wondered what their reactions would be once the mud reached their shoulders and inched up to their chin—covered their mouths. Then what terror, what glorious terror might fill them as the ceremony rolled to its conclusion. The last bucket poured—pushing the silt past their noses—finally suffocating them in mud. What could possibly generate more fear than that? Then to join that apex of fear to the fullness of Brother Moon—the entire plan was pure genius.

After the fear element was offered to Tirawa, all he'd have to worry about was the blood, something so easily remedied. He'd make certain the children were dead, then dig them up one at a time and wash their bodies with swamp water. Once they were cleaned, he'd cut out their hearts and place them on a burial shelf, where they'd be burned in honor of Tirawa. Then it would be done.

Olm felt no guilt or regret for anything he'd done or would do to the children. It was the way of his people, something he accepted wholeheartedly. Besides, it was either them or him, and which offered more by way of societal contribution? The children were simply two brats on an already overpopulated planet. Kids understood little more than take, take, and always wanted more. He, on the other hand, not only had the wisdom of additional years; he had a bloodline that had led an entire nation of people. Yes, who contributed more, indeed.

All he had to do was survive the next thirty-one hours and a handful of minutes. And he would, no matter what it took. He'd hide out if he had to, do without food or water until this was over. It didn't matter. Nothing mattered but this ceremony and getting his new life started. He was willing to do whatever needed doing to turn the universe in his favor.

Having calmed considerably, Olm pulled his truck over to the side of the road and stared out at the bayou that ran parallel to the road. Down those murky waters, through the sloughs and channels, across the flats, down into the darkest parts of the Atchafalaya, where the cypress tress grew so thick their branches seemed conjoined, sat his two aces—in the hole. He considered the wild game, snakes, and alligators that populated the swamp. There was always the chance the children might wind up as a meal before ceremony time. That thought sent a slight flutter of concern through Olm, but he quickly squelched it. In truth, collectively or independently, mud, alligators, spiders, and snakes bred fear. Wasn't that what really mattered, the fear? If nature got to the kids before he did during the full face of the moon, there was nothing he could do but accept it as fate. Surely Tirawa would take everything into consideration. The children's fear would still be a part of the ceremony, even if he didn't get to witness it.

Olm smiled. It felt good to have a plan come together, especially one this intricate and of his own making. He wished his grandfather was around to witness the ceremony, maybe take part in it. He imagined the elderly man standing tall, chest stuck out with pride over the work of his grandson.

With a contented sigh, Olm turned, ready to tap the accelerator and pull back onto the highway, when he heard someone call his name. A deep, raspy sound that sent dread rumbling through him.

Not wanting to look but unable to help himself, Olm glanced in the rearview mirror. The sound had come from behind him—the backseat—the back—behind. He saw it immediately. A black, translucent *thing*, wavering, bobbling as though having difficulty maintaining its shape. It looked similar to the ones he'd seen in the kitchen—the ones that haunted him night after night, the ones that touched him, kept him from sleep—the ones that contaminated his food.

Only this time . . . this one had teeth.

CHAPTER SEVEN

Bayou Crow gave me a new appreciation for the term *small town*. Although it held the standard one red light, one main road attraction of most rural blips on the U.S. map, it was the first one I'd seen with a levee wall flanking its entire east side. Beyond that wall was nothing but swamp, which wasn't surprising. Most of southern Louisiana appeared to be swamp, a giant fertile womb always giving birth. It kept its offspring close, nurturing it with an exotic amniotic fluid that created beauty out of dark and foreboding. The population of Bayou Crow might have numbered only six hundred, but what lived and thrived in and on these waters was countless. I felt it, saw it as we traveled near its banks. So many birds—reptiles—animals—insects . . . To someone whose total wildlife adventures consisted of running into an occasional jackrabbit or groundhog, maybe even a scorpion or rattler, and, of course, kept company with a mangy mutt, it was all a bit intimidating.

Aside from its swamp, Bayou Crow didn't offer a hell of a lot. A few beat-up mobile homes and weathered clapboards lined its west bank, along with a beige metal building that held a large red and white sign that read DALE'S TRADING POST. Just below that sign were notices that DALE'S now carried live bait, served frozen daiquiris, and had a thirty percent sale on Blue Bell ice cream. One block past Dale's was a squat, pale brick building that, judging by its sign and the crooked cross on the roof, was the Unified Kingdom of Christ Church. It looked more like a post office with a broken weathervane.

Angelle took a left on a side street that ran alongside the church, her foot still heavy on the gas. I couldn't blame her. For the past half hour, Poochie had been talking nonstop about ghosts, the feux fo lais, and shoes that disappeared from china ball trees. The only time she came up for air was when she asked a question, and even then you had to answer quickly or she'd fill in the blanks for you.

"You see dat?" Poochie said, tapping a finger against her window.

"The church?" I asked.

She nodded. "Dat's where de little girl lives."

I glanced at Angelle. "The girl who's missing?"

"Yeah," Angelle said. "The preacher there is Sarah's uncle, Rusty Woodard. They live in that old house, just behind the church."

"Dat man's cuckoo in de head, yeah," Poochie said. "He can't hardly keep track of his own self. No wonder dat baby got los'."

"Where are her parents?" I asked.

Angelle shrugged. "Sarah's lived with Woodard as long as I've been here. I've never met her parents."

"I don't know about de daddy, but I know about her mama," Poochie said matter-of-factly.

"How can you know?" Angelle said. "You've only lived here a couple of weeks."

"Sook tol' me, dat's how I know. She said when dat little girl was three, four years old, her mama just drop her off in de church like a sack of dirty clothes and tol' her cuckoo brother she didn't want her baby no more. Sook said de mama was trash, all de time jumpin' from boyfriend to boyfriend. I guess she didn't want no baby around when she did her jumpin' so she brung her here."

"Why do you keep talking about Woodard that way?" Angelle asked. "I've met him a few times, and he didn't seem crazy to me. A little enthusiastic maybe. . . ." She turned left into a parking lot that fronted a run-down metal building with glowing Budweiser and Miller Lite signs in the windows.

"Meetin' dat man on de street ain't de same. I'm tellin' you, he don't got all his marbles in de same sack, no. When he's in dat church, he gets all crazy, jumpin' up and down, wavin' his arms in de air, and talkin' stuff dat don't make no sense."

"Maybe he's a fundamentalist?" I offered. "You know, speaking in tongues and all that."

Poochie tsked. "De good Lord gave you a tongue, me a tongue, him a tongue. Just 'cause we got one don't mean we s'pose to run around and talk stupid."

I turned away, hiding a grin. The woman had a point.

"Enough about him," Angelle said, killing the engine and opening her door. "Let's get you inside, Pooch."

"Where are we?" I asked, following her out of the car.

"This"—Angelle spread her arms out wide in mock presentation of grandeur—"is the Bloody Bucket." She rolled her eyes, then opened the back car door. After pulling out the collapsible walker, she opened it, then helped Poochie slide out of the backseat.

Obviously happy to be mobile again, Poochie clomped off with the walker like someone eager to lead a Mexican standoff—pretty impressive for someone supposedly unsteady on her feet. Angelle followed with less enthusiasm, and I trailed behind, worried about what had my sister looking so bad, so exhausted. I had to admit spending that much time in a car with Poochie Blackledge prattling on nonstop *was* tiring. Although far from boring, being confined in a small space with her was like playing tennis in a closet—in the dark. You couldn't tell where the ball was coming from next or at what speed. Living with the woman twenty-four-seven had to require the patience of a saint, and even then it wasn't hard for me to imagine Mother Teresa doing a few eye rolls.

The sound of arguing reached us before we made it to the front door. A man and a woman from the sound of their voices, and if volume had anything to do with surmising the winner, the woman was way ahead.

". . . and you know that doesn't make a lick of sense, Vernon Francis—"

"—*said* put it on."

"It's too deep, doggone it!"

"Just listen to dat," Poochie said with a snort. "Dem two is at it again." Having reached the glass door first, she turned her walker sideways and hipped her way into the building.

Once we were inside, it was easy to see why Angelle had laughed when I'd asked if the place was a bed-and-breakfast. Judging by the four aisles filled with assorted foodstuffs, we'd entered the grocery store end of the Bloody Bucket. The small place looked clean but old, and it smelled of grilled onions and fresh fish. The short, narrow counter near the right wall was crammed with various displays—chewing gum, cigarette lighters, artificial fishing bait, rhinestone bracelets, beef jerky, and Eveready batteries. There was hardly room for the cash register, which was a punch-key model circa 1953. Butted up against the back end of the counter were two tables, both with faded red bench seats made out of hard plastic. Each table held an ashtray, salt and pepper shakers, a bottle of ketchup, and an even taller bottle of Tabasco sauce. On the other side of the room was a set of old saloon-type swinging doors, which I assumed led to the bar. And to the right of the doors stood an elderly couple who appeared to be in the middle of a hand-wrestling match. The woman was nearly half a foot taller than the man and probably outweighed him by a hundred pounds.

"What's all de noise about?" Poochie demanded. "We could hear y'all big mout's all de way 'cross de bayou."

The wrestling stopped immediately, and the couple turned toward her at the same time. Angelle let out a little gasp, and my heart did a *kerthunk* when we caught sight of the generous amount of blood smeared on the front of the man's white T-shirt.

CHAPTER EIGHT

"Merciful Jesus and all de saints!" Poochie said, her face growing pale. "What you did, Sook? Stab him?"

The woman tsked loudly. "No, the darn fool did it hisself." Grabbing the man's left hand by the wrist, she pulled it into view. A blood-soaked paper towel covered his palm. She yanked it off, revealing a deep gash that promptly sprouted fresh blood.

The man grimaced. "Damn it, woman! Look it, you got it bleedin' again. Now I gotta start over with the paper towels."

"Don't you 'woman' me, Vernon Francis Nezat, and don't you be cussin' like that in front of comp'ny. That thing needs stitches and you know it."

Poochie nodded vigorously. "Dat's for sure. Sook said it right on de nose."

"And quite a few stitches from the looks of it," Angelle said, grimacing. "How on earth did you manage to do that?"

He pulled his hand out of Sook's grip and hissed in pain through his teeth. "First off, ain't nobody takin' after me with no needle and thread. I can fix it my own self. Nothin' a little rubbin' alcohol, paper towel, and freezer tape won't cure." He marched over to the counter, grabbed a roll of paper towels, and tore off a few sheets.

Sook stuck a fist on her hip and huffed. "Freezer tape ain't gonna hold that, you old hardhead."

"Then I'll use duct tape, goddam—" He threw me a quick, sheepish look. "I mean doggone it. Sorry."

I grinned. "No problem."

"Now, ain't that a fine howdy-do?" Sook said, and headed toward me. "We standin' round here like fool idiots that ain't got a lick of sense for introducin'. You've gotta be Gelle's sister. How you doin', sugah?" She held out a hand, which I quickly scanned for blood before shaking. "I'm Sook, and that skinny piece of man over there with blood all over 'im 'cept for that darn camouflage cap on his head is my husband, Vern."

"Dunny," I said, still holding my grin.

She gave my gloved hand a curious look, and I saw the question flash in her eyes. She didn't ask it, though, only released my hand and grinned back up at me. Her smile appeared easy and genuine, but it did little to soften her face. Sook's head and neck looked as if they belonged on a linebacker, her nose to a boxer who'd been in too many fights. She wore a red smock, baggie denim, knee-length shorts, and green flip-flops that revealed bright red toenails. Her dark gray hair sat near the base of her neck in a haphazard bun.

"Angelle says this here's your first visit to Louisiana," Vern said, his hand now gloved in paper towels and duct tape. "That true?" He cocked his head, sizing me up, taking in my boots, jeans, long-sleeved button-down shirt, black gloves. His eyes settled on my left hand, and I crossed my arms reflexively over my stomach, meaning to hide both hands from view.

"Yes, sir, first ti—"

"Hey, where's my scoot?" Poochie asked. She took off for the back of the store, her walker thumping the floor with each step.

"Back in the storage room," Sook said. "Vern fixed some kinda spring thingee on it this morning. Saw it pokin' out one side of the seat; didn't want you hurtin' yourself on it."

"It's good to go now," Vern said.

"'Preciate it," Poochie said, then disappeared down one of the grocery aisles.

"You really should have that cut looked at," Angelle said to Vern.

"Nah, it's all good." He held up his hand. "See? Hardly bleedin' anymore."

As deep as his wound was, I was surprised to see that he was right. There was only the smallest dot of blood in the center of the paper towel.

"How'd it happen?" Angelle asked.

"You know that big jar of pickled eggs I got behind the bar?"

"Yeah."

"Fool thing up and broke. I was pickin' up the glass from the floor when one of the pieces up and stuck me."

"Whadda ya mean it up and stuck you?" Sook said. "You wasn't payin' attention and grabbed that piece of glass wrong, that's what happened."

He scowled. "I already told you I wasn't even

reachin' for one when it happened. I was sayin' somethin' to Pork Chop and next thing I know, I'm bleedin'.'"

Sook snorted. "That's what I said. You wasn't payin' attention."

Batting away her words, Vern stormed off toward the swinging doors, mumbling to himself.

When he disappeared into the next room, Sook shook her head. "I swear that man's gettin' more senile by the day." She sighed, then went over to one of the tables and dropped onto its bench seat with a grunt. She patted the space beside her. "Y'all come sit, take a load off. Y'all hungry? Thirsty? I can get Vern to cook up a couple burgers real fast."

"Thanks, Sook, but we have to get going," Angelle said.

Sook's thick eyebrows peaked. "Already? Y'all just got here."

"I know, but Dunny hasn't even had a chance to unpack yet. We came straight here from the airport. I'm sure she'd like to freshen up." Angelle looked at me, her eyes holding a clear command. *Just tell the woman you'd like to go freshen up so we can get the hell out of here.*

I was about to comply when I heard the whir of a small motor behind me. It was Poochie, driving up on her scooter. The thing looked like a revved-up wheelchair with handlebars.

"Hey, y'all come see!" Poochie said to no one in particular, then zipped past us and headed for the swinging doors. She bumped the doors open with the nose of her scooter.

"We're leaving," Angelle called after her.

"No, no, come see first!"

"What's wrong, Pooch?" Sook asked. "You look like somebody stuck a bee in your butt."

"Just come on!" Poochie insisted, then disappeared behind the doors.

Angelle sighed. "All right, all right, we'd better go. If we don't, she'll just wind up chasing us down the highway in that scooter until we do."

For some odd reason an image of Fritter came immediately to mind. Him chasing me down the highway, barking and snapping. Instead of seeming funny, it worried me.

Sook chuckled. "You know her too good, Gelle. She'd for sure do just that." She shook her head in an appreciative gesture. "You've gotta admit, for her age, that old woman's still got a lot of piss and vinegar left in her."

I heard Angelle mumble a concession that Poochie was indeed full of something before she pushed her way into the next room.

As I'd suspected, a bar lay behind the swinging doors. It was dark, the room much smaller than the grocery store. A man with a handlebar mustache and a surly expression sat at one end of an L-shaped counter. His potbelly and barrel chest had a camouflage T-shirt stretched to capacity, and the pant legs of his jeans were tucked into rubber boots.

" 'Bout time," he said, and tapped the bottom of the beer can he was holding on the counter. "Was gonna send out a search party. Fixin' to hit dry hole here."

"Where's Vern?" Sook asked.

He shrugged. "Either chockin' his chicken or stirrin'

the chili in the back. Fetch me another beer, will ya, Sook?"

Poochie pulled her scooter up beside him. "Pork Chop, you all de time got a dry hole. Whatchu doin' here dis early anyhow? It's not even one and look at dat, you already guzzlin' like an old Ford."

"Just leave him be, Pooch," Sook said, detouring behind the bar. She grabbed a Bud Light and handed it to the man.

"Yeah, leave me be," Pork Chop agreed. "Ain't none of your bidness, anyway, Poochie. You ain't my mama and you ain't my wife." He popped the top on the can, pulled long and hard on the contents, then let out a belch that sent beer and garlic fumes wafting our way.

Even in the gloom of the bar, I saw Poochie's face darken. "No, thank de good Lord dat I'm not you mama."

Pork Chop snorted and took another hefty swig from the can.

When he came up for air, Poochie held out a hand. "Lemme see dat."

"I thought you were all fired set to show us somethin'," Sook said.

Poochie ignored her and waggled the fingers of her extended hand impatiently. "I said lemme see."

"What?" Pork Chop asked.

"Dat can."

"How come?"

"Something's on it."

Frowning, Pork Chop examined the beer can. "No, there ain't."

"Yeah, dere is. I'm gonna show you."

"Where?" He leaned toward her, holding out the can of beer.

"See?"

"I don't see nothin'."

"It's right . . . dere!" At the word there, Poochie backhanded the can out of his hand, and it went sailing across the room, beer splattering across the wooden floor in an arc. The can hit the floor with a loud *thunk*, then rolled out of sight.

"Hey! What the hell'd you do that for?" Pork Chop shouted.

"Talk sass to me again and see what else you gonna get," Poochie yelled back.

Just then Vern appeared in a doorway behind the bar. "What's goin' on out here?"

Poochie harrumphed. "Just Pork Chop actin' de donkey. Go get de mop so he can clean up dis mess." With that, she revved up her scooter and headed for the back of the room and a door that stood open about fifty feet way.

Pork Chop sat openmouthed, watching her, the fingers of his right hand still curled as if holding a beer can.

A deep laugh suddenly erupted from a dark corner of the room, startling me. Evidently, I wasn't the only one surprised, because Angelle grabbed hold of my left arm, and Sook gasped and slapped a hand to her chest.

"Lord, Cherokee!" Sook said. "You dang near scared the earwax out of me. You got to start wearin' somethin' other than black, sugah. I didn't even see you sittin' over there."

I heard chair legs screech against the floor and squinted to get a better look at the man getting to his feet from behind a small table. He looked to be in his early forties, and his body unfurled to at least six foot two. He sported a Vandyke, wore a black Stetson low over his brow, and a long black leather coat over black clothes. "Sorry, about that, Sook." His voice reminded me of fine leather, rugged yet soft.

"I thought you was goin' out with Leon and Mark to hunt for them kids," Sook said.

"Already been and come back." He stuck a hand in the right front pocket of his pants, pulled out a few dollars, and dropped them on the table.

"Any luck?" Angelle asked, releasing my arm.

Cherokee shook his head; then the Stetson slowly turned in my direction. In that moment, Poochie saved me from further scrutiny.

"G-fifty-three!"

We all turned in time to see Poochie's scooter bop over the back-door threshold as if it were a speed bump.

"Where the hell you goin', Pooch?" Vern called after her.

"To de pier!" she yelled back.

"Whoa, hold up!" Sook took off after the old woman, the bun on her head bobbling as she went, her shorts flapping around spider-veined legs. "That old pier's on its last leg. You're gonna wind up in the water if you're not careful!"

Everyone hurried after Sook, Pork Chop taking the lead.

"Jesus," Angelle said, darting past me. "Does that woman *ever* stop?"

By the time we all made it outside, Sook was standing near the edge of a dilapidated porch, hanging on to the rear wheel lip of the scooter, trying to keep Poochie from going down the rickety-looking pier that butted up against the porch. "Would you stop already?"

Poochie waved a hand, motioning toward the end of the pier. "Go, then! Go look. I seen it from out de window in de storeroom."

Without a word, Vern headed down the pier. Pork Chop followed him, as did Mr. Stetson, whose angular face, black eyes, and high cheekbones were finally revealed in the sunlight. The rest of us took up the rear.

When Vern and Pork Chop reached the end of the pier, Pork Chop let out a low whistle. "Holy shit-eatin' crackers."

"What is it?" Angelle asked.

"Looks like Woodard's cow," Vern said. He glanced back at us. "Stuck 'tween them pilin's. The head's cut clean off, and it's gutted like a fish."

"How do you know it's his?" Sook asked.

"The W brand on the rump."

At the end of the onlooker train was Poochie, and she slapped her hands together. "You see, I tol' y'all dat man was cuckoo."

I was about to ask Angelle what a preacher was doing with a cow, when a sharp pain shot through my extra finger. I bit my bottom lip to hold back a gasp and clutched my left hand with my right. The finger pushed against my palm as if it meant to force its way out of the glove and fold over backward. I'd never felt such pain from it before. It made me sick to my stomach. It had pinched when I hunted for water, but this was way beyond pinching. Not even close. The pain was so excruciating I could barely draw a breath. I felt sweat trickle down the sides of my face. Then Angelle's face entered my line of sight, her eyes filled with concern. I wanted to say, *Get me out of here, get me somewhere else, now. Now!* But I was afraid if I opened my mouth, a scream would fall out.

"Hey, where's everybody at?" someone called from inside the bar.

"Out here, Beeno," Sook shouted over her shoulder.

A short stocky man dressed in a police uniform appeared in the doorway. "What's going on?"

"Dat tock-uh-lock preacher done cut off his own cow's head, dat's what," Poochie said.

Sook admonished her with a tsk. "We don't know that Preacher Woodard did this, Pooch." She looked over at the cop. "Just a dead cow, Beeno. Vern says it's carryin' the Woodard brand."

Pursing his lips, the cop stepped onto the pier. He acknowledged me with a nod, and I returned it, working hard to keep a grimace and whimper in check. It felt as if someone were trying to saw my extra finger off with a dull knife. As he drew closer, the cop asked, "Who're you?"

Before I could answer, Sook said, "Look at me bein' rude again and not introducin' a one of y'all." She waved a hand in front of her face as though fanning

away a fart, then pointed to me. "That there's An-
gelle's sister, Dunny. She came all the way from west
Texas. Dunny, this here's Beeno Leger, the deputy in
Bayou Crow. And that one there in the shrimp boots,
that's Pork Chop, and the big one over there, that's
Cherokee."

Afraid my teeth would chatter with pain if I spoke,
I nodded a greeting to each. I had to get out of here,
had to get away from the water and whatever was
in it. Had to get out—the pain—stomach starting
to churn, knot up. It took every ounce of willpower
I had to keep myself calm, my expression cordial. I
didn't want to attract any more attention than necessary.

"Don't talk much, huh?" Beeno said, his eyes hard
brown marbles rimmed with suspicion.

Angelle grabbed my right arm and gave it a tug, signaling it was time to leave. "She's just tired from trav-
eling and has a bad headache. We came straight here
from the airport, so the poor thing hasn't had a moment to catch her breath. I'm going to take her home
now so she can rest." She gave him a quick smile, then
tugged on my arm again. "We'll be back to pick you
up at four-thirty, okay, Poochie?"

"Yeah." Poochie's eyes darted from my face to my
clutched hands back to my face. The sparkle in her
green eyes told me she knew the headache excuse was
a crock, and she fully intended to uncover the truth.

Uncover the truth . . .
The truth shall set you free . . .
Not always—not for everyone . . .

As those unbidden thoughts tumbled through my mind, a horrible sense crept over me, making me shudder. Uncovering truths in this place might very well mean the death of us all.

CHAPTER NINE

Angelle's house was only three blocks away from the Bloody Bucket, but even that short distance seemed to do wonders for my finger. The pain had eased to a dull throb, and it had finally stopped feeling as if someone meant to saw it free from my hand. Now that we were alone, I took off my gloves, tossed them on the kitchen table, and let out a huge sigh of relief. My hands were wrinkled from having been stuck in their own personal sauna for too long. It really *was* too hot for gloves here.

"Want a Coke?" Angelle asked.

"Nah, I'm good."

Angelle headed for the fridge. "Don't see how you're not thirsty. Heat's different here than back home, don't you find? Out there dehydration sneaks up on you because the humidity's so low. Here it just smacks you in the face. I'm thirsty all the time. Gotta drink more water, though. You know what they say about too many Cokes. . . ."

It was the first time she'd spoken since we'd left the bar. I knew my sister, knew she was holding back an avalanche and was using small talk as a way to gather her thoughts. I also knew from experience that it was best to wait and let her drop the first rock. I pulled out a chair, sat at the table, and began massaging my extra finger. Starting at the knuckle that met my hand, I pressed and kneaded, working my way up to the fingertip. The exercise relaxed me, centered me— readied me.

As Angelle busied herself with ice and a soda, I took in her kitchen—the pale blue wallpaper, the white lace curtains over the window, the miniature tea kettles arranged just so on a display shelf near the stove, two wicker baskets overflowing with ivy on the counter, and a clock in the shape of a rooster on the wall straight ahead. Angelle always did have a knack for warm and homey. A room left to my care was typically shit out of luck, getting stuck with same ol', same ol', like wall-mounted telephones and outdated pantries. Oddly, though, as bright and cozy as Angelle's house appeared to the eye, there was heaviness in the air. The kind of heaviness that usually followed a person through a funeral home during a wake.

"I like your house," I said, for lack of anything else to say.

Angelle joined me at the table, Coke in hand. "Thanks." She settled into her chair, then popped the top on the can and took a sip of soda. It seemed to take her forever to swallow. When she finally did, she set the drink on the table and wrapped the fingers of both hands around the can. "What happened to you back at the Bucket? Did you pick up on the kids?"

"I really don't know what happened. A lot of pain. Stuff I've never felt before. I didn't get a bead on the kids at all." I massaged my finger again, but the exercise no longer relaxed me.

"I saw how much you were hurting. You had to have picked up on something."

I gave up on the massage therapy, crossed my arms, and settled them on the table, remembering the fear that had overwhelmed me, the fear about uncovering truths. I didn't want to frighten her by trying to explain something I didn't understand myself. "Yeah, there was something. I'm just not sure what." I fought to keep my voice steady, reassuring. "Look, why don't you tell me what's been going on? Maybe that will help me make sense out of what happened back at the pier."

Angelle bit her upper lip, glanced over at the stove, then toward the archway that led to the living room where we'd entered the house. When she looked back at me, I saw anxiety flicker in her eyes. "You're going to think I'm crazy."

I grinned and tried to lighten the mood. "Girl, I've known you were crazy since we were kids."

The attempt at humor didn't work. My sister didn't laugh. Her eyes welled up with tears. Feeling like an insensitive asshole, I quickly reached across the table and placed a hand over one of hers. "I'm sorry. I didn't mean—"

"You know, me asking you to come here wasn't all about Sarah and Nicky." Angelle glanced over at the stove again, and I waited for her to continue, my stomach doing a slow roll. "It . . . it started about two and a half, three weeks ago, about the same time Poochie moved in here. I was . . . I was cooking supper, right there at that stove when it . . . it touched me the first time."

The hair on my arms jumped to attention. "When what touched you?"

"I don't know what it was."

I stared at her, waiting, suddenly fearful of what she had to say. When a long, silent moment grew into two, I prodded gently. "I don't understand."

"It . . . my . . . my . . ." She wouldn't look me in the eye, and her cheeks flushed bright pink. "Something pinched my right breast . . . *hard*."

I sat back, startled by her words. "What?"

Angelle nodded. "And there was nobody in here but me. Trevor wasn't home; he was out running crawfish traps. Poochie was in her room at the other end of the house." She drew in a shuddering breath and finally looked at me. "I was by myself, Dunny."

I gaped, then quickly scrambled for composure so she wouldn't be afraid to tell me more, even though a part of me didn't want her to. There had to be a logical explanation. Had to be. "Could you maybe have just pinched yourself while stirring something? Underwire in your bra maybe, or—"

"No!" She sobbed and pushed the soda away from her. The can bobbled, and I scooped it up before it toppled over. "Because it happened twice more, same place. And . . . and on the other side, my other breast. Then . . . uh . . . a little later, I felt something try to . . . try to . . ." She glanced at the stove again, then leaned closer to me, the tears on her cheeks fat and constant, and whispered. "Something tried to get between my legs."

"*What?*"

"I'm serious as a coronary. Dunny, it felt like a man's hands. Big hands." Her words came faster now, a tumbling avalanche. "They kept touching me, hurting me, only when I was alone, though, alone and in here. But no matter where I went—in the house, at school, the store, anywhere, I always felt like someone was watching me. All the time. Then it started happening in other places, the touching and pinching I mean. Once when I was driving back home from the store. Scared me so bad, I damn near wrecked the car."

I sat, too stunned to speak, unable to absorb what she was telling me.

"The very next day it happened at school, when I was in the middle of teaching a class for heaven's sake!" Angelle got to her feet, wrapped her arms around her chest, and began to pace. "Then when Sarah and Nicky went missing, it got worse. The kids were gone, and the touching got worse . . . *harder.* And . . . and it wasn't just a man's hands touching me anymore. It felt like it was . . . it was a man's . . . uh . . ." She gave me a woeful look. "You know . . ."

I sat bolt upright. "Are you talking about a man's *dick*?"

She nodded, a loud sob escaping her.

"Jesus, Gelle . . . Jesus . . ." My mind was a whir of mush. Nothing seemed to make sense. "Have you told Trevor any of this?"

"Oh, God, no. He'd think I'd flipped out, like Poochie. Besides, what could he do, anyway? You can't see it. There's nothing to shoot at, hit, or kick. There's just . . . nothing. Nothing, but what I feel."

I shook my head, perplexed. Beyond perplexed. Angelle was one of the most levelheaded, straightforward people I knew. Either this had to really be happening or the stress of a new marriage, a new job, and a new roommate had gotten to her. Then there were the missing kids on top of it all. I felt as though I'd walked into a bad dream. The kind where nothing linked together to form a complete story, just fragmented vignettes that circled around and around in your head, never going anywhere, never making sense.

And one you felt sure you'd never wake from.

CHAPTER TEN

Angelle stopped pacing long enough to study me.

"You don't believe me, do you?" she said, and the worry and fear on her face damn near yanked my heart right out of my chest.

I got to my feet, hurried over to her, touched her shoulder. "No . . . no, I do believe you. I do, honest. It's just hard for me to wrap my brain around all of this, that's all."

Her tears came faster. "Maybe . . . maybe this will help." She lifted her shirt, then the front of her bra, and revealed her breasts.

I gasped at the deep purple bruises covering both breasts. Rage flared white-hot through me. Someone—something had *touched* my sister—hurt her. Instinctively, I wanted to hide her, protect her, beat up, kill whatever had defiled her. "My God! How could Trevor not have seen this? You're nothing but one huge bruise!"

"He hasn't seen them because, well . . ." She pulled down her bra and lowered her shirt. "He hasn't, you know, touched me since Poochie moved in. It's almost like we've become roommates or something. He leaves to go to work at the plant early in the morning, comes home after his shift only long enough to pick up his skiff and head out to the basin to check on his crawfish traps. By the time he gets back it's real late, and he's always so exhausted . . . and angry."

"Angry about what?"

She held up her hands, shrugged, then let her arms drop to her sides. "Everything. Nothing. I don't really have a clue. He'll start an argument over the stupidest things." She returned to her chair and slumped into it. Her face held the weariness of an old woman exhausted with life. "That's why I wanted you to come so bad, Dunny. *Something* is here." She waved her hands about, indicating space in general. "I don't know if it's just in this house, in this whole town, or in the swamp. I don't know if Poochie brought it with her when she moved in or if it's just coincidence that things started at the same time she got here. All I know is it's gotten worse since the kids disappeared, and it's hidden." She looked me dead in the eye this time. "And you're good at finding things that are hidden."

I blew out a breath, scrubbed my hands over my face. "Yeah, but we're talking about . . . what? Ghosts?"

She shrugged; then her body seemed to sag with defeat.

Everything I'd found in the past had been something tangible. Water, oil, Angelle's cat, a misplaced locket, thimble, a pocket watch, a wallet. Everything had been something I could see and touch. How was I supposed to dowse for . . . for what? Air? The first time I found water, the discovery came without my focusing on it. It simply happened, as though my extra finger had taken charge of my brain to make me aware of its ability. Same thing with the oil and with Pirate. And each occurrence had produced a different sensation. Pain—extreme cold or heat—tingling as if an electric current was running through my finger. But after I'd experienced each new sensation for the first time, it never returned on its own, only when I focused on what needed to be found. What I'd felt near the swamp behind the Bloody Bucket was definitely new. The only thing it had led me to, though, was fear and pain. I didn't have a clue as to what it meant to identify.

I leaned toward her and cupped my sister's chin with a hand so she had to look at me. "Has it touched you since I've been here?"

"No. But I have a feeling it's . . . I don't know . . . it feels like it's waiting for something. Maybe waiting for you to leave?"

"Then the son of a bitch is going to be waiting a hell of a long time because I'm not leaving you until we figure out what's going on." I pulled out the chair next to her and sat. "God, Gelle, I can't believe you didn't tell me all this sooner. I don't know how you've carried this by yourself for so long. Why didn't you tell me?"

"I don't know. I guess I didn't want to worry you, and I was afraid you'd think I was losing my shit or something." She picked up the soda, sipped a little, then fidgeted with the can again. "And it's not been all by myself all this time. Last week I went to see Pastor Woodard and talked to him about it."

"You mean that preacher Poochie is always calling crazy?"

"Yeah, Sarah's uncle. I really don't think he's crazy, though. He just really gets into what he does. You know, that whole praise Jesus, hallelujah stuff. Him being a preacher and all, I thought he might be able to help. He did in a way, just by listening. He even prayed over me, said I was under attack by the devil and needed a lot of prayers. I went back to him a couple of times after that, but his praying never made it stop. I haven't been back since Sarah disappeared. I'm sure the man's under enough stress."

Sighing heavily, I got to my feet, walked over to the sink, and looked out the window above it. Preachers and demons, missing kids and swamps. It was as if I'd flown into some creepy fantasy world desperate for a hero. The fact that I was the only candidate for the position scared the hell out of me. I was as baffled by this whole thing as my sister was and didn't have a clue how to help her.

I was focusing so hard on everything Angelle had told me that it took a moment for me to realize that my eyes had trained on something. A tree, at least fifteen feet high, stood in the middle of the backyard. Its branches were filled with lush green leaves—and shoes of various styles, sizes, and colors. I remembered Poochie telling me about her prayer tree. How the shoes on one side belonged to the living and the shoes on the other belonged to the dead. *Could* she have brought a malevolent spirit here with her? Could those shoes and the souls they represented have thrown some preternatural scale off balance?

Were the shoes, the missing children, and Angelle being violated tied together somehow?

My shoulders slumped under the weight of the questions. They seemed ridiculous, too twilight zone-ish, and had no answers. In truth, I felt as useless as a rosary in a Baptist church.

"Dunny?"

I turned to my sister, the hush in her voice sending a cold chill up my spine. Her face was as white as the curtains on the window. She pointed to the archway that led to the living room—and the dark gray, wavering shadow that floated past the entrance.

There are only a few times in my life that I actually remember doing a double take. This was definitely one of those times. Unfortunately, the quick second look produced no less formidable results than the first. The shadow was tall and thick with just enough form to identify it as a person—or something resembling a person—a man from the size of it. Wide head, broad torso, arms that held only the slightest outline. Its legs reminded me of the smoke columns that had risen from the brush fire I'd witnessed back home months ago. Vacillating and dense, ever moving.

Having crossed the archway, the form paused, its uneven edges quivering as though struggling to maintain form. Then it turned. Only in profile was I able to make out the outline of a nose, thick lips, a jutting chin. I saw no eyes, only that heavy silhouette that didn't belong there.

Mesmerized, I took a step toward it, and my dowsing finger immediately grew cold. I didn't need the warning from the digit to know I was facing the dead. I felt it to my very core—that and something else. Angelle had said she hadn't seen anything during the times she'd been violated, but something in the way the shadow moved, the way its outline undulated, the way its center, its bulk wavered, was almost sensual in nature. This *had* to be it—what had been hurting her, molesting her.

"Don't . . ." Angelle's whisper came through desperate, urgent, and probably louder than she'd intended. I ignored her, keeping my eyes locked on the shadow, which was only five or six feet away. If it was looking at us, planning anything, I wanted to make sure the bastard kept its attention on me.

"Dunny, please, no . . ."

The form turned once more. It wavered, then narrowed and elongated, making itself taller, and as it did, I caught the heavy scent of musk and sweat—like that of a man who'd worked in the sun all day.

Heart clobbering the wall of my chest, I took another step toward it. It was then I realized fear had a taste. Rusty pennies. My mouth salivated with the tang and bitterness of it.

"Wh-what do you want?" I asked it, my voice sounding rusty as well. Something thunked to my left, and I shot a glance toward the noise. Angelle was on her feet, staring wild-eyed from me to the shadow, the soda can she'd had on the table now lying on its side, glubbing Coke across the blue-and-white-checkered tablecloth. The chill around my finger abruptly turned to subzero, and I clenched my teeth from the pain. I noticed tears slip down my sister's cheeks; then a strangled gurgling sound came out of her mouth. She wasn't looking at me when she did it, though. She was looking at *it*.

Reluctantly, I turned back toward the dark figure. My finger going cold had always meant I was getting close to something dead. When it got *fucking* cold, that meant I was literally within inches of the dead, damn near on top of it in fact . . . or it was on top of me—as this one was now.

In the time it had taken me to notice tears and a spilled Coke, the thing had moved closer and had done so without sound. It stood only a couple of feet away from me now, and although it was closer, its features were no more defined than they had been when it floated near the archway. A mass of dark, translucent smoke. My breath caught, and I stumbled back a step. It immediately closed the extra distance I'd created.

". . . no, please . . ." I heard Angelle begging, crying, but it sounded as if she were in another room—in another house—in another town or state. I wanted to look over at her, make sure she was okay, but couldn't take my eyes off the . . . the thing pulsing in front of me.

It drew closer . . . I couldn't move.

Drew closer still.

I squeezed my eyes shut, like a kid in a thunderstorm, terrified of what might appear in the next flash of lightning. Only I had closed mine too late. The monster was already here. A block of ice the size of a mountain seemed to hang from my finger. I cradled it blindly, heard my sister whimper, was suddenly awash in the aroma of musk and sweat and something pungent I couldn't identify. It radiated an energy that felt raw and feral, and I feared breathing lest its smoky substance, its essence find its way inside me, up through my nostrils, my mouth, into my soul.

Time seemed to fold in on itself as I stood there, waiting . . . waiting for what I wasn't sure. Teetering on flight or fight, I cracked my eyelids open to thin slits and saw it reach for me. A long, thick-fingered hand, much denser than the rest of its form, stretched, throbbed, undulated toward my face. Then its thick lips parted, and it let out a sound—the sound of crying children.

CHAPTER ELEVEN

Poochie Blackledge leaned against the wall in the hallway of her grandson's house, closed her eyes, and listened intently to the voices coming from the living room a few feet away. Something had happened to Angelle and Dunny while she'd been away. She knew it, felt it as sure as she felt they were up to something now. A little over an hour ago, when they'd picked her up at the Bloody Bucket, both had been too quiet. Even worse, neither had said a word even after she'd told them about the fight at the pier between Pork Chop and Beeno.

Ten minutes after they'd left the Bucket the first time, when Angelle claimed her sister had a headache, everyone started talking about the missing kids. Vern, Pork Chop, and Cherokee had been working to untangle the cow from the pier's pilings at the time, and as they worked, Beeno mentioned that the sheriff from Iberville Parish wouldn't be sending any more deputies to help search for the kids. According to Beeno, the parish was short on patrol power and needed everyone back in Plaquemine to work an NAACP rally. Upon hearing the news, Pork Chop lit into Beeno. He cussed and yelled about the taxes he paid and how nobody had the right to use his hard-earned money to pay cops to babysit a bunch of congregating lazy-assed niggers. The argument between them grew so heated, Vern had to let loose of the cow in order to stop the men from coming to blows. The cow floated off down the bayou, headless and gutless, and Cherokee had left without saying a word to anyone.

To Poochie, that fight had been a juicy piece of gossip. How could anybody hear that story and not ask a dozen questions? It just didn't seem natural. Of course, she was used to people ignoring her. Most folks thought she was a little off, anyway. And as much as Poochie hated to admit it, her brain *did* occasionally toss her thoughts around like the balls in the bingo machine back in St. Martinville. The thoughts would eventually settle back in the right place, but she sometimes opened her mouth while they were still in the middle of settling, which made some of her comments sound wonky, even to her.

The truth of the matter was Poochie didn't really care what folks thought. In fact, it was probably a good thing they considered her nuts from time to time. When folks thought a person had loose change jingling around in the brain, that person could do or say just about anything she wanted and get away with it. Especially if she had a good number of years under her belt, which she certainly did. But getting away with stuff was really the only benefit to getting old. Everything else that came with old age Poochie considered poop in a toilet—the occasional forgetfulness—the saggy, wrinkled body—the loss of teeth, hair, hearing, and sight. It wasn't fair that a brain could be so easily convinced it was still eighteen years old, despite its true number, but the body had no choice but to stiffen and creak with each passing year.

Fortunately, even at eighty-four, Poochie saw well enough to know adventure or trouble, which for her was usually one and the same, when she saw it, and she heard well enough to hear what she needed to hear. Like the whispering going on in the next room.

The whispering wasn't a good sign at all. Earlier, when she'd been sitting in the living room with them, Angelle and Dunny had barely spoken a handful of words, but as soon as she'd excused herself to go to the bathroom, the murmuring started. The whole time Poochie peed, she tried to convince herself they were only talking personal sister talk. After all, it had been quite a while since they'd seen each other. But the logic wouldn't stick. The funny feeling in her belly, which she believed God used as a warning device, wouldn't let go.

No matter the reason Angelle gave for Dunny being here, Poochie knew it wasn't the whole truth. She was convinced Dunny had come to help find the kids, and she'd come for other reasons Poochie couldn't quite latch on to yet. She also had a feeling she was supposed to help Dunny, but wasn't sure how or with what. Praying for the woman was a given, it was something Poochie did often and knew she did well. Not that praying was anything to brag about, just another benefit of old age. The closer a person got to the grave, the more direct she got with God.

DEBORAH LeBLANC

At her age, Poochie figured she didn't have time to mess with the repetitious hooey she'd learned in catechism. She shot straight from the hip and told God what was on her mind, and God usually returned the favor. But for some reason, He'd decided to keep most of the details about Dunny to Himself.

Since the eavesdropping wasn't working, Poochie decided to take a more direct approach. She inched her way along the wall, her walker leading the way, and peeked around the corner into the living room. The women were sitting close together on the couch, just as they had been earlier. Poochie cocked her head slightly to the left, keeping an eye on them while attempting to pick up a word or two.

In that moment, Dunny looked up, evidently sensing she and Angelle were no longer alone. Her eyes were the color of wet rust, and they held an intensity and depth that was a little intimidating. Knowing she was busted, Poochie shuffled out into view.

"Hey," Dunny said, acknowledging her with a halfhearted smile. Angelle sat back and glanced over her shoulder. Judging from the frustration that flickered over her face, Poochie figured they hadn't had a chance to say all that needed saying and wouldn't as long as she was in the room.

Poochie aimed her walker toward the kitchen. "Y'all don't pay me no mind. I'll go start supper while you two visit."

"I'll take care of supper, Pooch." Angelle glanced at her watch. "I didn't realize it was getting so late." She leaned over, ready to get up from the couch.

"No, no, stay where you at. Dere's some shrimp in

92

de icebox already peeled. I'll use dat to make us a stew. A good roux gravy over some rice, now, dat'll put some meat on y'all's skinny butts."

Before Angelle had a chance to protest, Poochie hurried through the archway that led to the kitchen. She bypassed the refrigerator and stove, fully intending to cook the stew she'd mentioned, only not now. If she couldn't get the information she needed out of Dunny and Angelle, then she'd have to get it out of God, and the one place He seemed to listen best was at the prayer tree.

After opening the back door, Poochie hobbled her way down the steps and over to the china ball tree that stood in the middle of the backyard. On the backside of the tree sat a wooden bench that Trevor had made and placed there for her. She shuffled over to it, sat, folded her hands in her lap, and sighed. Dusk was already pressing down on the day, but there was still plenty of light for her to make out the pale bricks on the house, the bayou that ran along the north end of the property, and the shoes hanging in the tree. Always the shoes.

CHAPTER TWELVE

Because of Sook, when Poochie first arrived in Bayou Crow, it hadn't taken long for word to get out that a teeaunt had moved into town. Most old folks in south Louisiana still remembered a time when a teeaunt was as common as a doctor making house calls. Now it was almost impossible to find either. In the old days, a doctor brought a little black bag filled with medicine to your house, a teeaunt, a heart filled with prayers. Both, though, carried the intent to heal. The biggest difference between the two, besides the doctor thinking he was God and the teeaunt believing *in* God, was that a teeaunt didn't take the one-shot-cures-all approach.

A teeaunt diligently prayed for the living and the souls in purgatory until he or she received a tangible answer to their prayers. That answer could come by way of a family member professing that a fever had finally lifted, or a cardinal roosting on a strand of barb-wire at sunrise, which meant a soul had found its way home to heaven. Only then would the teeaunt drop the person from his or her prayer roster. Poochie had known about teeaunts since she was a little girl, but had never really considered herself one. It wasn't as if anyone said, "Here are the rules to being a teeaunt," then trained her. She just prayed for people.

The shoes had come about out of necessity. At one point, so many people were asking her to pray for them or a sick family member or for a loved one who'd passed on and whose soul they thought had a questionable destination, Poochie couldn't keep track of them all. The shoes served as reminders, a sort of visual of the person they belonged to. Once a prayer was answered, the shoes were returned. The idea to hang the shoes in a tree came to her one day after she'd run out of places to store them in her house in St. Martinville.

To make room, she simply knotted the shoestrings together and tossed the shoes into the chicken tree that grew in her front yard. If someone brought her a pair of sandals or shoes with no laces, Poochie tied the pair together with twine. By the time she'd left her home to move to Bayou Crow, there'd been over two hundred pairs of shoes hanging in that tree. As far as she knew, they were still there waiting for her. She'd thought about taking them along, but moving them felt sacrilegious somehow, so she'd left them behind.

This tree, however, was giving her a hissy fit. The last time Poochie counted, the china ball tree held ten pairs of shoes on the left, which was the purgatory side, and eight pairs of shoes on the right, which was the living side. In fact, Sook had been the one to bring the last two pairs of shoes she'd put up on the living side—pink sneakers that belonged to Sarah Woodard and a black pair of high-top sneakers that belonged to

Nicky Trahan. Poochie had never met the children, so when Sook brought the shoes, she'd made sure to describe them down to the freckle so Poochie would have a strong visual when she prayed for them. With those babies vividly in mind, Poochie had Trevor place both pairs of shoes side by side on the same branch about midway up the tree. They were still up there, all the living shoes were. Only those two were the smallest, saddest-looking pairs of all.

But something was going on with the purgatory side of the tree that left her completely befuddled. Three pairs of shoes were missing from it. The first pair, a set of dark brown, well-worn loafers with lopsided heels, had disappeared three days ago. They'd belonged to Rospier Trosclair, a big man, according to Marie, his wife. He'd been murdered by Clarence Wallace, the father of a twenty-year-old girl whom witnesses claimed Trosclair had raped. Obviously wanting to make sure justice was properly served, Wallace got to Trosclair before the police and bashed his head in with a concrete-filled lead pipe. The loafers had been on Trosclair's feet the day of his funeral, but removed for whatever reason before the casket was closed. You couldn't get a "fresher" pair of shoes than that, right off a dead man's feet—or so Marie had claimed when she'd brought them to Poochie. Not knowing for sure if he had in fact harmed that young girl, the woman feared for her husband's soul. No one had bothered bringing shoes for Wallace. As far as Poochie knew, the man was still serving life in Angola.

The second pair of shoes, flip-flops that had belonged to a hooker named Cynthia Bergeron who'd overdosed on drugs, vanished a day after the first, and then the third pair went absent the very next day. Those had been shrimp boots, whose owner, according to the woman who'd brought them to Poochie, had killed three people and himself in a drunk driving accident. No matter whom the shoes belonged to, though, or why they'd been brought to her, Poochie couldn't understand their disappearance. Something like that had never happened to her before, and she wasn't quite sure what to make of it. Either someone was stealing the shoes, or the dead were returning to claim them. As crazy as both reasons sounded, the last one felt more probable in her belly, which really confused her.

Dropping her head back, Poochie blew out a breath and took in the expanse of sky above her. She heard the cackle of chickens coming from a neighbor's yard. A dog barking. The hum of a boat motor off in the distance. The sounds of ordinary life. She'd always found it fascinating, how chaos could swirl around a person while sameness still managed to keep its own pace, like the chickens, the dog, the sky. Chaos, sameness—two big wheels in life spinning in opposite directions, yet still capable of moving a person forward. Only the Big Man Upstairs could come up with something that screwed up and get away with it.

Lowering her head, Poochie closed her eyes and pictured the face of God. To her, he looked like an old Marlon Brando.

"God, me and you got to have us a talk," she said quietly. "I got a lot in my head, and you been leaving me in de dark too long, and I can't stand it no more. You know if you leave me wit' no answers like dat I'm gonna wind up wit' all kinds of trouble, so can you give me a break now? Let me know what's goin' on? Look here, I know you brung Angelle's sister to find dem chil'ren, and I feel in my belly dat you want me to help her find dem, but I don't know what you want me to do. I'd sure appreciate if you'd make dat clear."

Poochie paused, allowing God a chance to inter-ject. All she heard was the chickens. She pursed her lips, a little perturbed that He wasn't being more im-mediate with answers, readjusted her behind on the bench, then continued. "Okay, den here's another one. I got dis feeling dat Dunny's hands got some-thing to do with what she's gotta do for dem kids and dat don't make no sense to me. De woman wears gloves all de time. I know 'cause I seen her. Den, when we was at de Bloody Bucket, I could tell in her face dat her hands was hurtin' her real bad. Does she got a bad case of art'ritis or was dat you passing her a sign? You know, like you pass me in my belly? I'd ap-preciate if you'd let me know dat."

She opened one eye and glanced up at the sky. "And something else if it's okay wit' you . . . I know I already ask you a bunch of times about dem little chil'ren, dat somebody find dem fas' before some-thing bad happens, but you been slow answering dat, too, so I figure I bes' ask for dat again."

A soft breeze ruffled Poochie's hair and sent a chill up the back of her neck. She nodded, closed her eye, and bowed her head, accepting the breeze as confirmation of the deity's presence. "Thank you, God, for hearin' me. I know you a bit slow sometimes, but now dat I know you listenin' for sure, I'm gonna try and be patient and wait for you answers." Poochie was about to open her eyes again, then remembered an additional request. "Oh, yeah, God, if you still dere and can hear me, would you pass you hand down here and help Trevor and Angelle? Something's not right wit' dem two, no. Sometimes when I look at dem, a frisson pass t'rough me, like something bad is gonna happen in de family. So if you don't mind, please fix dat, too."

Poochie pursed her lips again, then added for good measure, "And if you got a little extra time, could you let me know what de hell's goin' on wit' de shoes on de purgatory side of my prayer tree? Dem shoes up and disappeared just like dem chil'ren, and it's makin' me cuckoo tryin' to figure out how come. So, if you would give me de answer to dat, too, I'd appreciate it. Now I'm done. Thank you."

Satisfied that she'd covered all the bases, Poochie opened her eyes, prepared to sit for a while and simply listen in case God decided to quicken His response time. That's when she saw them . . .

Three long, dark gray shapes, floating only inches from the ground, coming from the bayou toward the house. Although the forms weren't clearly defined, she could make out heads, arms, and what looked like very skinny stick-shaped legs. By the time she got to her feet, they'd already reached the house and were making their way inside by seeping through the bricks.

DEBORAH LeBLANC

Poochie grabbed her walker and made a sign of the cross. God wasn't farting around this time. He was obviously giving her some of the answers she'd asked for. The only problem was, from the looks of those things headed into the house, she wished she'd kept her damn mouth shut for once.

CHAPTER THIRTEEN

The sound of crying and grunting tugged Sarah Woodard away from a strange but wonderful dream. She'd been running through a field of purple wildflowers with a blond woman she knew to be her mother. Both of them were laughing, holding hands, exhilarated by the feel of wind and sun and freedom. Somehow Sarah knew they were headed for a flea market, one that sold magic shoes. Shoes that would fulfill their every wish, no matter how small or how big. A brand-new house with a yard as wide as the field they ran through—any car they wanted—a father who'd come home from work with flowers for her mother, one who'd gather his daughter in his arms and swing her around and around until they were both hiccupping from spinning and laughter. Anything was possible with those magic shoes, and the anticipation of reaching them and the sound of her mother's voice filled Sarah with so much happiness, she felt as if she could fly.

The faster they ran, the lighter she felt. There was no sharp pain in her sides from running, no panting or gasping for air, only joy—her mother's touch—and hope. Then, just as Sarah felt her feet about to leave the ground and her body prepare for flight, the crying tugged her down harder. The sound was faint at first, faraway, but it was loud enough to weigh her down until she felt the ground solid beneath her feet again. She tried desperately to ignore the cries, tried to run faster, to regain momentum so she could fly. But the sound grew louder, forcing her to a slower pace, too slow to keep up with her mother, who'd already let go of her hand. Her mother raced ahead, not bothering to look back. Sarah tried hard to catch up with her, but only fell farther behind . . .

Farther . . .

. . . farther . . .

When the woman finally faded out of sight, Sarah looked down at her feet and saw that she was no longer running through wildflowers. She was standing in an ocean of mud, heavy black sludge that made it impossible to run, impossible to hope. That's when her eyes fluttered open and reality hit her full in the face.

Kids were supposed to be able to wake up from nightmares, not stay stuck in them—literally. But at that very moment, she sat in a nightmare, in a hole, her hands tied behind her back, her legs outstretched and bound at the ankles. She could just see above the top of the hole, which had been filled with mud that reached the middle of her chest. The grunting whimpering sound was coming from Nicky Trahan, who sat in a hole just like hers, a couple of feet away. All she could see of him was part of his nose, his eyes, his forehead, his hair. Judging from the bobbing of his head and the grunting sounds he made, Nicky was trying to get out.

Although he was about her size, which was pretty small, and his hands and feet had been tied up just like hers, Sarah held her breath, hoping he'd find some way to break free. She watched intently as his head bobbled first one way, then the other. One way—then the other. He kept it up for quite some time; then his head bowed and stayed still. When he finally looked up and turned to her, his eyes were red and watery. He'd been crying, something she'd done quite a bit of herself before the dream.

Even at seven years old, Sarah knew that seeing a boy cry was a big deal. The boys around Bayou Crow were taught to be tough. They were conditioned to hunt, fish, play football, and no matter how hard they were hit, they weren't supposed to cry. All the boys in her class were rough and loud, always acting as if they were high school kids instead of second graders. If one of them ever made the mistake of breaking down into tears, the rest of the boys pounced on them, teasing them mercilessly. Not that it mattered to her. Sarah thought most boys were stupid anyway and, for the most part, ignored them.

Because of her uncle's constant tutoring, Sarah had started school in the second grade instead of the first, which made her a year younger than everyone else in her class. Being the only kid in school who didn't have to go through first grade was one thing; being a preacher's kid was another. Especially a preacher like Rusty Woodard, a man prone to jumping and hollering during his services as if he were being stung by a hive full of bees. Because of him and because of her age, Sarah was the target of every kid in school who wanted to move up a rung on the bully ladder.

She knew the pain that came with teasing, and even if Nicky wasn't looking at her with a please-don't-tell-anyone-you-saw-me-cry look, she would never have told a soul. Not that that mattered, either. Sarah didn't think they were ever getting out of here, not alive, anyway.

Surprisingly, the thought of dying didn't scare her as much as she figured it should have. Maybe it was because she was so tired and they'd been here for what seemed like months without any food. Or maybe anything was better than having to go back and live with her uncle Rusty.

Sarah knew her uncle did the best he could, being single and all, but she didn't think he had a clue about raising kids, much less understood how the real world worked. To the mighty Reverend Woodard, if a person didn't read the Bible twenty-four hours a day, every day, and say, "Praise Jesus! Thank you, Lord!" every other minute without fail, he was going to hell and didn't deserve to be alive on this earth. And he made a point of reminding her every day just how great a sinner her mother was. Not because she dropped Sarah off on his doorstep and abandoned her, but because she went out with a lot of men and drank alcohol and smoked cigarettes. Those things were far worse in his eyes than abandoning any child.

When Sarah had started school, her uncle, believing that fruit didn't fall far from its tree, had all but strip-searched her each day when she got home, looking for evidence that might alert him to her slipping into the *ways of the world*. He made her wear long dresses and patent leather shoes to school because that's what he felt young ladies should wear. But heaven help her if she came home with a spot or stain on that dress. Finding any smudge would usually prompt an hour-long interrogation, "How did this get here? Who were you with? Did you let someone touch you? Were you alone with any boy at any time?" This was followed by another two hours of preaching, expounding the reasons why every Christian should separate himself from the world.

She wondered what her uncle would have to say if he saw her in this hole. The pastel blue cotton shift she'd put on two days ago now looked like a muddy burlap sack, at least what she could see of it. Knowing him, Sarah figured he'd probably stand at the foot of the hole, jumping and hopping, arms waving, full of bees and the business of Jesus. All the while he'd be spitting fire and brimstone, declaring to anyone within earshot that the suffering she was going through was surely a punishment from God for all she'd done wrong. To Sarah, that was stupid, too. She knew she'd done nothing to deserve being buried in a hole. Neither had Nicky.

Two days ago she'd been walking down the levee road, heading to Dale's Trading Post, which was only two or three blocks from the Unified Kingdom of Christ Church. She had wanted a soda and was thinking about how the fizz made her nose tickle when she came upon a mewling kitten. Feeling sorry for the poor, scrawny thing, she'd scooped it up, then sat on the grassy slope of the levee and petted its soft, soft fur until its cries became gentle purrs. She'd been sitting there awhile, enjoying the feel of the kitten's trust in her, when Nicky showed up on his bike. The only reason she hadn't run off then was that he was one of the few boys from school who didn't tease her.

Nicky was asking her questions about the kitten and talking to her like a regular person when a man in a beat-up black pickup pulled off on the side of the road beside them. He stopped so short, dirt clouds rose up from the shoulder of the road, and the kitten jumped off her lap and ran away. In that moment, Sarah thought her life was over for sure. That somehow her uncle had spotted her sitting and talking with a boy and had sent someone to drag her back to the church so he could cast out the demons he was so fond of blaming for everything. Lust—greed—pride. But that didn't happen.

The man got out of his truck, talking really fast. He wore a purple ball cap that had LSU in gold letters on the brim, and it was pulled low over his eyes, so she really couldn't see his face very well. He called them by name, told them to hurry and get in the truck, that there'd been an explosion at the Dow Chemical Plant, where most of the people in town worked. He said Nicky's mother had been one of the people injured, that she was bleeding really bad and might die.

They were so shocked by the news, by his abruptness, that they only stared at him, unmoving. He got angry then, insisting they get in his truck right away. Dangerous chemicals had been released into the air, and he had been ordered by the governor to take as many people as he could find to safety. And that safety was at Fausse Point, the farthest slough south of the Atchafalaya Basin. They needed to get as far away as possible, downwind, so they wouldn't be affected by the chemicals.

She and Nicky had looked at each other then, both so afraid, not knowing what to do. The man grew even more insistent, and pounded on his truck with a hairy hand, yelling that they needed to hurry up before everyone suffocated under a huge cloud of poison. He demanded that Nicky leave his bike because there was no time to load it and had assured Sarah again and again that her uncle Rusty was already safe and awaiting her arrival.

Like idiots, they'd fallen for it.

They wound up in his truck . . .

Then in his boat . . .

Then in these holes.

The man had been right about one thing. He had taken them to the farthest slough in the Atchafalaya. The hill they sat upon was so far away from all the camps and houses, they could scream for a year, and no one would ever hear them. Everything else he'd said had been a lie.

Liar, liar, pants on fire . . .

Her uncle Rusty had always said liars went to hell. He'd obviously missed a scripture passage somewhere—because now she knew that liars sometimes *brought* hell with them as well.

CHAPTER FOURTEEN

Sarah closed her eyes for a moment, trying to re-member the feel of the kitten's fur when she'd petted it, the sound of its gentle purring, and how that sound had sent soothing vibrations all the way through her body.

"Maybe he won't come back." The sound of Nicky's voice startled her. It sounded foreign in this place, like the pound of a hammer in an empty church hall.

"Maybe," she said, opening her eyes and not feel-ing an ounce of hope that that would happen. She just didn't want to crush whatever hope he might be holding on to.

"I . . . I've been trying to get us out of here. Fig-ure out a way for us to get out, you know? But every time I pull my knees up, they get sucked back down. The stuff he dumped in here is like quicksand or something."

Sarah nodded, then considered that he might not be able to see her head move. "I know. I tried, too, and it did the same thing to me."

When the man in the purple hat had forced them into the holes, he immediately began hauling buckets of sludge from the edge of the island and dumped it over their legs. They hadn't screamed then, not like earlier when he'd tied them up and they thought he'd meant to kill them right away. She'd been too afraid he'd dump mud in her mouth if she screamed again, and although Nicky never said one way or the other, she was sure he'd kept quiet for the same reason.

After a bunch of trips to the edge of the island for sludge, the man finally stopped dumping it on them when the mud reached their waist. He'd gotten back into his boat then, leaving them there. When he returned a couple of hours later, he had a bottle of water with him and forced both of them to drink from it. After that, he dropped another bucket of mud into each hole, then left again. That became his routine.

The last time he'd come, Sarah had gathered up enough courage to ask for food. The man never responded to her question, just mumbled something about stars and the moon. She might have been young and didn't have a lot of experience with much, but Sarah knew crazy when she saw it. Living with Rusty Woodard had at least given her that advantage. It was something in the eyes, the way they talked and moved their bodies, as though something else was controlling them instead of their own brains. According to her uncle, God was the one who controlled him, but she had no idea what might have been controlling the mud man. He seemed even further removed from reality than her uncle when he was in the throes of a sermon, or filled with the spirit as he always claimed.

Why did the mud man want to harm them? What

had they done? She didn't even know him, or didn't think she did. It was hard to tell with half of his face hidden beneath that ball cap. Once they'd reached the island, he'd made sure they didn't get a good look at him by covering the lower half of his face with a camouflage bandanna, like in the old cowboy and Indian movies her uncle watched on television. The bad guys always wore bandannas over their mouths in those movies. His clothes, though, were ordinary. An oversized jacket that covered a camouflage shirt and jeans, the same clothes worn by nearly every man in Bayou Crow. He could have been anyone—or no one—or as Uncle Rusty would have said about anyone prone to lying . . . "He's got the devil in him for sure."

"I'm hungry," Nicky said. He had streaks of dried mud across his forehead and a long dollop of it along the side of his nose. Sarah wondered if it made his nose itch. How horrible to have an itch you couldn't scratch. "You?"

"Yeah," she answered.

"I wanna cheeseburger . . . no, two of them. Fries, too. Supersize—and a chocolate shake, biggest they got. Maybe an order of chicken nuggets, too. Twelve of 'em, with those little packets of barbecue sauce they stick in the bag, you know?"

Sarah held in a groan. Talking about food made her stomach hurt. It felt as if it were gnawing in on itself, desperate for anything to eat. She wanted to tell him to shut up, but didn't have the heart to. Her dream had come while she'd been sleeping. Nicky's came while he was awake. She couldn't fault him for that.

A long silence grew between them, and it seemed to

turn up the volume in the swamp. Even from an ant's-eye view, she saw nothing ahead but water and cypress trees, all brown and beige. They looked like naked old men, or what she imagined naked old men might look like since she'd never actually seen one— all twisted and lumpy, parts of them poking out at odd angles. Birds seemed to be everywhere, all shapes and colors, all of them cawing, squawking, screeching. And bugs, millions of bugs; and frogs that whined and croaked and *barrumphed*, until the sounds got all mixed together and she couldn't tell one from the other. At night, the sounds were so loud, it made her ears hurt.

She couldn't see the horizon well from where they were; too many trees were in the way. But she saw broad streaks of orange and red and purple, signs of the sun setting on a spring day. Night was on its way again. Sarah hated the night.

"I wonder what my mama's cooking right now," Nicky said, his words soft and sad. "Jambalaya maybe, with baked sweet potatoes. She cooks that so good. The jambalaya I mean. You know, with big chunks of meat all mixed in with the rice."

"Sounds great," Sarah said, trying to muster more than a halfhearted response. She didn't have to wonder about her uncle's supper menu. If she was calculating right, today was Friday, which meant greasy meat loaf, supplied by that pinched-faced old hag, Widow Costello. She had a huge brown mole under her right eye and lived down the road from the church. Her meat loaf smelled and tasted like sweaty gym shorts, and it had red things she called pimentos

111

all stuck up in the meat. On Fridays, Sarah usually settled for a peanut butter and jelly sandwich and a glass of milk, leaving her uncle and Widow Costello to the nasty meat loaf and a burbling session of "Oh, Pastor Woodard, I don't know what this town would ever do without you!" The woman's words were so syrupy, they made Sarah want to puke.

"Sarah?" Nicky's voice sounded smaller this time, as if he'd suddenly gone backward in age.

"Huh?"

A long pause—the rise and fall of chittering bug songs. "Are . . . are you afraid?"

Sarah thought about her answer for a moment, considering what might be best for him to hear—then figured it was useless to lie. "Yeah." Once the word was out of her mouth, she could almost hear her uncle shouting, "And the truth shall set you free!"

"Me, too." He let out a long, shaky sigh, then added quietly, "I want to see my mom again. I don't wanna die."

She nodded slowly, not caring this time whether Nicky saw her or not. She didn't want to talk about dying. It would make the possibility too real, turn the nightmare into a hard-core reality—one she wasn't ready to face.

"You know . . . since your uncle is a preacher and everything, you've gotta know some prayers and stuff, right? Maybe . . . um . . . maybe we could say some, ask God to help us or something."

Sarah leaned her head against the dirt ledge behind her and closed her eyes. She didn't want to talk about God either. Not about someone who'd left her without a mother or father, who'd allowed her to be raised by a weird uncle who made her wear funny clothes and treated her as if she were a contagious wart that needed to be cut off and thrown away before someone died from its disease. Who forced a little girl to desert her childhood and any hope of friends. Who demanded so much attention a person couldn't even enjoy other parts of life.

"Sarah?"

She kept her eyes closed, willing his voice away, willing herself back to sleep, back to the dream about the field and her mother and the magic shoes that would change her life forever.

"*Sarah . . .*"

Her eyes opened at the change in Nicky's voice. It had gone from soft and wishful, to whispered and urgent. She lifted her head, turned to him. "What?"

"Shhhh, not so loud. Don't move . . . don't . . . don't even blink." Nicky was looking to the right, his head straining to one side. All she could see was his hair, the streaks of mud in it. She heard him grunt and knew he was trying to pull himself out of the sludge again. Suddenly he whipped his head back in her direction. "It's coming . . . it's coming!" His eyes were still red, but no longer wet, only wide and wild.

His words seem to thrust shock-wires into her heart, tripping it into a beat so fast, it felt as if it were going to jump out of her chest. In that moment, the water the mud man had made them drink needed to come out and come out *now*. Her bladder felt stretched to capacity, ready to burst out of her body, just like her heart, thumping, hammering, determined to leave her.

Nicky bowed his head, and she heard him mumble, "God, please . . . God, please make it go away. Make it go away. . . ." His head looked like one small hill rising from a dark brown plain, and beyond it, right at the water's edge, Sarah saw the wide, thick-scaled snout of a full-grown alligator. Its mouth was partially open, its teeth a million miles long. It seemed frozen in place, watching them, sizing them up, measuring the supper that lay ahead. Then it moved forward, gripping mud and swamp grass with pointy claws and webbed toes.

Sarah felt her mouth drop open and her bladder immediately release. Oh, God, what a field day her uncle would have now with her peeing in a hole, a boy right beside her. Peeing on the pastel-blue shift so stained with grime. So many smudges. Too many. Had she not been paralyzed by the sight of the alligator, she'd probably have laughed. Laughed at the absurdity of the thought, the uselessness of it. Instead, for the first time in her young life, Sarah Woodard uttered a prayer and meant it with all of her heart. "Jesus, if you're really up there, please don't let us die."

CHAPTER FIFTEEN

The pain had been worth it. Olm just wished his ancestors would have given him some kind of warning. It had all come so unexpectedly. The dark form in his truck, the way it had moved over him slowly, almost seductively, before it bit into his chest. The pain had been fierce, like two rows of sharp thick sewing needles clamping down on him at the same time. He'd gone blind with agony for a moment, nearly driving his vehicle off into the bayou that ran alongside the road. It had taken mind over matter to keep that from happening. Mind over matter—his mind over what mattered.

Once *they* released him, the form disappeared, leaving him stunned, bruised, and questioning whether he was going mad. It soon became clear to him, though. He wasn't going insane. He was evolving, and Olm was stunned that he hadn't caught on to that fact sooner. Logically, it was simple really. If a person invoked every ancestor from the Great Spirit World that had come before him, surely some significant, physical manifestation had to come with that invocation, right? Of course. And how better to get a person's attention than to back him into a corner and cause pain?

Thinking through it now, Olm realized that the attack hadn't been an attack at all. It had been an initiation of sorts, which meant that the dark form had to have been one of his ancestors. Possibly his great-grandfather or his great-great-grandfather, the latter a man he envisioned to be one of the most powerful leaders in the Skidi tribe, in the entire Pawnee nation. It had to have been him, for it was only after that attack—that initiation—that Olm's mind blossomed, opening up to a new idea that would enhance his ceremonial sacrifice to Tirawa. He would never have come up with a plan like that on his own. Just as he'd suspected from the very beginning, the collective knowledge of his forefathers, every leader, warrior, medicine man, and ceremonial priest, was slowly but surely becoming his own.

The first idea had come to him the moment he spotted the old woman with the pinched face and the mole beneath her right eye. Olm knew when he saw her that she was to be part of the ceremony. Not as a sacrifice, for she was far too old and ugly for that. But her blood poured around the fire that would consume the children's hearts would cause a savory scent to rise up to the heavens, like exotic incense strategically placed on an altar. How could Tirawa not be impressed with that?

Luring the woman to him had taken very little effort. Olm knew her to be lonely and always eager to serve, to please. As soon as he had her alone, he wasted no time. He took an electrical cord from a nearby lamp, wrapped it around her neck, and cut off her air supply. The woman's struggles had been feeble, her death relatively quick. Once her body quit twitching, he carried her to the bathroom, leaned her body over the edge of the bathtub at the waist, then waited twenty minutes to make sure her heart and brain were as lifeless as her limbs. Only then did he puncture the right side of her neck with a screwdriver, boring into her carotid artery. Her blood flowed thick and easy, like rich red wine into the plastic gallon jug he'd brought along to capture it. Once the jug was filled, he left the woman hanging over the tub, allowing the remaining blood in her body to gurgle down the drain.

Although Olm had made sure to be meticulous in the cleanup, the tricky part came when he had to load the woman into his vehicle, then into his boat. His plan was to dump her somewhere near Gro-beck Point, which was a stretch of marsh thick with buttonwood trees and water lillies, and it was en route to the children. No one would ever find the old woman there, and even if they did, there wouldn't be enough of her left to identify. Once her body was exposed to the elements, the raccoons, birds, alligators, and other swamp scavengers, they'd be lucky to find matching bone fragments.

The entire time Olm worked to move her out of the house, into his vehicle, into the boat, he felt sure he was being watched and kept glancing over his shoulder every few seconds. He'd felt someone hiding behind a tree, the corner of a house, behind a car door, waiting to catch him in the act. The paranoia did nothing to stop him, though. He'd doggedly pressed on. If anyone got too nosy, he'd just have to make sure they met up with the same demise as the old woman.

Twisting the throttle, Olm set the skiff's motor into high gear. He was anxious to see the brats' faces, the horror in their eyes when they saw him. Night was a challenge since he had to depend on the aid of a flashlight, which was fine, but it didn't provide him near the satisfaction of seeing those young, terror-stricken faces in the white light of day.

Olm lowered his head to cut the wind from his eyes and pushed the point of the skiff even faster down the lower Grand River. He veered right through Flat's Cut, taking note of the giant willows, cypress trees, and tupelos, each dressed in new spring greenery and most accessorized with gray Spanish moss.

The whine of his motor echoed through the darkening passages. Beavers and nutrias scrambled up nearby banks while egrets with three-foot wingspans skated over the surface of the water. Blue herons flew a few feet ahead of him, and a barred owl swooped overhead, then roosted on a nearby treetop. There were alligators, some ten, fifteen feet long, poised like felled logs, watching as he zipped by. No wonder his ancestors took to this place so easily. The Atchafalaya—the name alone carried the strength of the Native American, with its thousands of acres of swamps, lakes, and water prairies, each rich with wildlife, both in land and water; its very soil capable of nurturing any seed.

Olm pulled back on the throttle, slowing, and took a left into Rooster Shoot, a narrow waterway that led directly to Gro-beck Point. When he reached the mouth of the point, he hooked a hard right into an inlet stuffed with water lilies, puttered through the bramble about a hundred feet, then tossed the old woman out of the boat. Very few people set crawfish traps or ran trout lines in this area because it was so clogged with vegetation. He felt confident no one would happen upon her body here.

After making sure the boat was free of evidence, Olm turned on a small headlight that was perched on the bow and steered his way out of the inlet. He veered back into Gro-beck Point, where he quickly circled into an offset bayou that brought him to a straightaway that led to Fausse Point. Along the way, he heard bullfrogs croaking, locusts and mosquitoes whining, and he soon joined their chorus, humming to himself, content with his progress and the bright future that lay ahead of him. Night was falling and the great moon was rising. That huge white orb had the power to stretch its light to the four corners of the earth. He felt its illumination fill him, and it made him want to dance, stomp, whoop in victory.

Suddenly a flash of mustard-yellow light, caught out of the corner of his eye, stole Olm's attention. It was the size and shape of a basketball, had a tail like a comet, and hovered over the water a few hundred feet to his right. He blinked, and in the fraction of a second it took his eyelids to flutter, the ball of light was beside him. It circled his boat, rushed out a couple hundred feet ahead, then stopped and hung in midair—pulsing—pulsing.

Olm had been so shocked by its abrupt appearance that he'd let go of the throttle, which killed the engine. While he was gawking, it suddenly dawned on Olm that he was looking at a feux fo lais, something he'd heard about since childhood but had never seen before. Fishermen and trappers spoke of them often, eerie, illusive swamp lights that taunted and mesmerized boaters to follow them, then lead them into the deepest parts of the swamps, where they kept them until daybreak . . . if they survived the night . . . if they didn't wind up lost forever. As legend had it, the only way to outsmart a feux fo lais was to stick the blade of a knife in the ground or in the heart of a tree at the time it was spotted. Supposedly this would send the light dancing around the blade instead of around its intended victim.

And there was little question in Olm's mind that he was indeed this *thing's* ultimate target.

CHAPTER SIXTEEN

Watching the yellow sphere, Olm felt himself being drawn into its dance—the swirling, whirling, so beautiful, so brilliant—its tail wavered and flickered like a silk scarf in a breeze. Although it emitted no sound, he could have sworn on anything and everything holy that it spoke to him. Called to him seductively— "Follow me . . . follow meee."

That call tugged at something deep in Olm's chest, making him want to, ache to respond. Every nerve ending in his body felt awakened by the glow before him, and he found himself desperately wanting more of it. On a barely conscious level, he knew he was coming dangerously close to the point of no return, falling under the feux fo lais's spell. He gripped the throttle hard, then purposely snapped his teeth down on his tongue to regain charge of his senses.

As soon as Olm broke eye contact with the feux fo lais, he felt stronger, more in control. He leaned over toward the back of the boat to a tool chest, opened the chest, and grabbed the utility knife he kept inside. He opened the knife and cranked up the motor again.

Seemingly perturbed by the sound of the engine, the feux fo lais did a furious twirl about the boat, then stalled and floated up closer to him. Keeping one eye on it, Olm aimed the bow of the skiff toward a cypress tree and inched the boat forward a foot or two. The twirling ball of light followed, maintaining only a slight distance. For a moment, Olm feared they might collide before he reached his destination.

Holding his breath, he counted to three, then cranked the motor up to wide open. In an instant, he slalomed right, skimming the side of the cypress tree, and as he flew by it, Olm jammed the pocketknife deep into its soft bark. A second later, the feux fo lais hit the right side of the boat, nearly jostling him off his seat, then flew in an arc over his head toward the knife. The cry that followed sounded like a thousand female cats in estrus, and as soon as the feux fo lais hit the handle of the knife, it burst into a million tiny embers that fell to the water and died.

With a nod of satisfaction from a job well done, Olm revved the motor up again and shot off toward the knoll. He made it there in record time. As soon as he nosed the skiff onto the bank, he grabbed the gallon of blood near his seat, got out of the boat, then secured the skiff to a nearby cypress tree with a rope. Adrenaline had his blood racing, his heart knocking out of its natural rhythm. The contentment he'd felt only a short time ago had been replaced with a growing anger and agitation. Nothing was going to stop him from his mission. Not the feux fo lais, not the swamp, not the universe itself. *His* destiny was all that mattered.

Gritting his teeth, Olm hurried to his special hiding place behind a giant willow, where he kept the mud bucket and the other tools he knew he'd need for his sacrificial ceremony. Once there, he placed the gallon of blood near the base of the tree, picked up the bucket, then marched over to the side of the knoll and filled the bucket with sludge. Ignoring the painful weight it placed on his arms, Olm stormed over to the foot of the hole where the boy sat. Even in the deep purple haze of dusk, he saw fear in the children's eyes. That pleading, desperate look infuriated him all the more.

"You *will* die," he said, then dumped the bucket of mud into the boy's hole. It moved the level of sludge higher up on the kid's chest—but not high enough. The girl whimpered, the boy let out a sob.

Determined, Olm did an about-face, went back to the edge of the knoll, scooped up another bucket of sludge and carried it back. That one he dropped over the girl, which moved the level of sludge just under her breastbone. She let out a bloodcurdling scream, so satisfying to his ear. Looping his arm through the handle of the now empty bucket, Olm stood before the kids and pointed to each in turn.

"You will go down in history as the ones chosen for the Great Olm, his first and final sacrifice to the Great Tirawa. I am Skidi bred, of the Pawnee nation. My people are a great people. My fathers, grandfathers, great-grandfathers, all strong leaders. So magnificent will be this offering that the Morning and Evening star will bow before me as they bowed before my forefathers."

"I wanna go home!" the boy cried. "Please, don't hurt us . . . Mama! I want my mama!"

Olm snorted. "So pathetic. Here you have a chance to go down in history books, and what do you do? Cry for your mother's tit. You're a pathetic little shit, a sad, sad—"

"Stop!" the girl suddenly yelled. "Leave him alone! You're a horrible man, and you're the shit! You're the shit! Nicky didn't do anything to you. Leave him alone!"

Taken aback by the girl's outburst, Olm stood silent for a few seconds with his head cocked. When he finally got his wits about him, he clenched his teeth and said, "Brazen little bitch, huh?" With that, he did another about-face, went back to the edge of the knoll for more sludge, then returned to her.

"No, please, she didn't mean anything," the boy cried. "Stop! Don't hurt her, please! No more— please, no more!"

Ignoring his pleas, Olm dumped the mud directly over the girl's head. She gasped, immediately shook her head to fling off the muck, her mouth hinged open so she could breathe.

"No!" The boy's scream was so loud and shrill it sent a covey of quails whooshing out from nearby brush.

Olm grinned, watching the sludge ooze down over the girl's face, down her shoulders, settle into the pool already at her chest. When he was sure she was able to breathe normally, he set the bucket down on the ground and did a series of little hops and steps, turning in a circle as his people would have done during a victory dance.

Feeling as if he could bend iron with his bare hands,

Olm lifted his arms in the air and let out a triumphant whoop. Then he lowered his arms, clapped his hands to make sure he had the children's full attention, and pointed to a nearby hollow, cypress stump and the thin shoots of green sprouting from its middle.

"Do you see that? That dead, rotted cypress tree, that hull of nothing? It holds *nothing* in and of itself. There's nothing left of it but a shell of its former self. Yet within its center grows new life, new birth. Do you see that? *Do you see it*? That new life is called an Olm." He slapped a hand against his chest. "I am Olm, that which is born from what was once thought dead. I *am* like that new growth within that old dead stump. I *will* be reborn. That is the power of my ancestry, of my tribe, of my people!"

No sooner did he finish his proclamation than Olm saw a flicker of yellow off to the east. He froze, watching. The kids were crying, screaming, slobbering all over themselves now in pathetic, useless supplication. He hated their crying.

"All good," Olm said. "All good. It will all be good." And it would be because they were so very afraid. That's what he needed—he needed them to be afraid. He needed that fear for Tirawa. He desperately wanted to add more mud—*now*.

Turning his eyes from the orange light in the distance for only a second, he glanced down at the kids. He couldn't add more sludge. Not now. It would take him too far into the process too fast. Now wasn't the time to offer them. It wasn't time for their deaths. He had to wait. He *had* to. Or all that he'd worked so hard for would be stolen from him. Everything in the ceremony had to fall in just the right order with the apex of Brother Moon as it swelled to glorious fullness.

Olm peered up, saw the dot of orange light suddenly blink out; then before he was able to draw his next breath, more lights appeared. Feux fo lais? Dozens more. Some much closer now. They were the size of marbles and glowed like gator eyes in the dark—yellow-orange, steady, intense. But the lights couldn't be the eyes of alligators. There were too many of them, and they were too high off the ground. And they began to dance for him—call to him—were circling him.

He forced himself to look away, down at the ground, forcing his thoughts to the number of buckets he would need to complete the ritual.

Six buckets . . . six each. Six more buckets and the kids would be gone. . . .

Before Olm knew it, he was scooping sludge up from the edge of the knoll. He ran back and dumped it over the boy, his mind spinning. *Don't look at the lights! Don't look!*

He ran back for more mud, sweat trickling down his face, heard the kids crying—the whine of insects around his ears. "Five, just need five for the boy, six for the girl . . . six."

The bucket seemed to fill on its own. He didn't remember dipping it, scooping up anything, yet he was already running back toward the kids, grunting, panting, sweating, the bucket full.

He threw the sludge over the girl. "Five more! Five!"

Again he found himself racing to the edge of the

knoll, only this time his brain seemed to hook on to a different frequency in order to admonish him, *You're going too fast. It's not time for them to die, stupid! Wait for the moon! Wait!*

But he couldn't wait—couldn't.

Insects whining—kids crying . . .

"Four buckets now, four!"

Four . . .

CHAPTER SEVENTEEN

Poochie had made good on her promise, serving up a shrimp stew that would have made Paul Prudhomme envious. Although it was the best thing I'd tasted in years, getting it past my throat and into my knotted stomach had been a chore. But then again, the simple task of breathing had become a chore since my encounter with the dark figure earlier. Even now, sitting at the dinner table with my sister's family, thinking about it, the sound the thing made—those crying children—haunted me, made my breath catch. I still heard those children so clearly in my mind, vividly remembered the thick, dark hand reaching for me. I don't know if it was my loud gasp that caused the entity to vanish or the fact that my eyes went from slits to saucers, but vanish it did, almost as quickly as it had appeared. Had it not been for Angelle assuring me over and over that she'd seen it, too, heard it, witnessed everything I had, I would have thought I'd gone bonkers and hallucinated the whole thing. Both of us had been so shaken by the incident, Angelle had to pull out heavy artillery to calm our nerves—a bottle of Jose Cuervo. Two shots each eventually did the trick. And I could have used another one right about now.

Although a few hours had passed since the shadow episode, and I hadn't seen the thing again since we'd returned from collecting Poochie at the Bloody Bucket, I still couldn't keep from looking over my shoulder—like now.

My next breath was one of relief. Still nothing. I felt wired for sound. Not only was I anxious over some goddamn *thing* suddenly popping up in my face out of nowhere again; I was worried about the covert operation Angelle had concocted while downing tequila. She'd hinted at it again on the drive over to the Bucket, then haphazardly fleshed it out when Poochie wasn't underfoot, which was hardly never.

The plan was to get a skiff, which I learned was an eighteen-foot aluminum boat with a pointed bow, and take that boat out into the swamp. According to Angelle, it was crucial to have a pointed bow. Otherwise they'd never get the boat through the flats, which were filled with water lilies and marsh grass—whatever the hell that was. And it was important that we waited to run at night. There was too much activity in the bayous during the day, men crawfishing, trapping, checking trout lines, and she was sure they'd get nosy seeing two women out in a boat alone and undoubtedly ask questions or follow them out of blatant curiosity. With that in mind, Angelle planned to wait until Trevor fell asleep tonight, then take his boat. It didn't matter that the man was her husband; being an accomplice to grand theft, much less thieving something I knew nothing about, like boats, made me nervous.

Poochie slapped a hand on the table, startling me out of my reverie. "And you should've seen dat cow," she said, then whisked a hand through the air. "It just took off down de bayou like somebody was reeling it in wit' a fishing pole. No head, its belly all open and its guts hangin' out. Talk about something to see, yeah."

"So you've said . . . again," Angelle mumbled.

Trevor shook his head. "All kinds of crazy people in this world, Poochie." He picked up the plate he'd filled and emptied twice, got up from the table, and walked over to the sink. "Doesn't make sense that somebody'd throw away a perfectly good cow."

"Dat's what I'm sayin'," Poochie said. "Imagine all de good barbecue we could've got outta dat?"

Trevor grinned, set his plate inside the sink, then walked back to the table, rubbing his belly. Watching him, I couldn't help but wonder, as I did during Thanksgiving, when they'd visited me in Cyler, and as I did on their wedding day, what spark of passion my sister had caught from this man. Ever since she was little, Angelle had buzzed with life, so curious about everything, wanting to touch and learn and be everywhere at the same time. Trevor on the other hand reminded me of a plow horse, steady and reliable, not easily excited by much. In the looks department, Angelle carried the same height and slender build I did, but her heart-shaped face and flashing brown eyes were exquisite and never failed to turn a man's head. Trevor was of average weight and height as well, only with light brown hair and eyes. He'd fit into an average slot, along with every other average Joe, in any place America. If ever there was a case of opposites attracting, those two were it. I didn't understand it, but then again, I didn't need to.

"Plant's shorthanded again," Trevor said to Angelle as he settled back into his seat. "I'll be pulling the eleven-to-seven tonight."

Angelle frowned. "You've been here over an hour and a half and you're just telling me that now?"

"Since when does it matter when I tell you?"

Glancing down at her plate, Angelle picked at a grain of rice with her fork.

"Poo-yi," Poochie said, then got up from the table, collected her plate and glass, and brought both over to the sink.

Feeling a bit of steam rise between Angelle and Trevor, I took Poochie's cue and silently excused myself from the table. After picking up Angelle's plate, I carried it over to the sink, then went back for my own dirty dishes. It was awkward clearing a table with one hand stuck nonchalantly in your pocket, as if doing so were natural. Natural for a one-armed paperhanger maybe . . . On my second trip back from the table, I spied a pair of yellow rubber gloves near the sink, grabbed them, and quickly put them on. There. Anonymity.

As Trevor kept pressing Angelle for an answer, Poochie came up beside me, rolled her eyes, then plugged the drain in the sink with a stopper and turned on the faucet. I shook my head and mouthed, "Let me, please." She'd done the cooking; I wanted to do the dishes. Besides, it would distract me from the argument that was brewing at the table. Poochie nodded, then reached for a dry dishcloth and pantomimed that she'd dry.

With our roles established, Poochie and I went to work. Behind us, the tension grew thicker than the roux that had been in the shrimp stew.

Trevor let out a heavy sigh. "If that's all it takes to upset you, then this should really piss you off . . . I'm taking Bullet and leaving in a few minutes to check traps before my shift. I've got fifty of them down on the west end of Point Coupee Lake and put out seventy-five more at Flat's Cut. Those are both new areas, so I need to make sure nobody's out there messing with those traps. Make sure beavers haven't gotten to the bait."

Angelle cleared her throat, and I knew that was her way of trying to maintain composure. I didn't know what a Bullet was, but if it had anything to do with checking crawfish traps, there was a good chance it resembled a boat. If so, that meant our plans were fucked, and she didn't want to overreact to the news. I glanced over my shoulder toward her, and sure enough, there was frustration etched all over my sister's face.

"Why should taking your boat out piss me off?" she said. "You're always checking traps. Are you . . . did you plan on bringing it back before you go to work?"

"No," Trevor said, leaning back in his chair. "Too much crap. It'll be easier to load the boat back on the trailer and haul it to the plant with me."

I chewed my bottom lip as I washed the last glass. Bullet was indeed a boat—a boat we wouldn't have— which meant we'd have no way to go look for the kids.

"So do you have to work the night shift tomorrow night, too?" Angelle asked, the question sliced with sarcastic overtones.

"What the hell's your problem?" Trevor asked.

"I'm just asking."

"I don't know what shifts I'll be working tomorrow. Like I said, they're shorthanded at the plant, and I'm going to go work when they tell me to work. Damn, Gelle, you know we've got bills to pay, a mortgage on this house. What do you want me to do when the foreman calls? Tell him, 'Wait, I've got to check with my wife to make sure it's okay for me to work that shift'? I mean, goddamn!" Trevor shoved himself away from the table and got to his feet.

Poochie and I took turns peeking over at them from the sink. I wished there were more dishes to wash.

"I never said you had to do that." Angelle tossed the napkin she'd been mauling in her fists onto the table.

"Then what's with the forty goddamn questions?"

"I was just asking!" Angelle's voice clipped up an octave and about two more decibels. "What the shit's wrong with a wife asking her husband when he's going to be working?"

I found myself mesmerized by the argument. It was like getting caught up in a soap opera. The plot might be predictable and the acting bad, but you managed to get hooked on it, anyway. I had to force myself to turn away again and act as if I wasn't listening. I wiped down the counter, even though it was spotless—and that's when I saw the toaster on the counter near the refrigerator slide over about five inches—on its own. In the next second, my extra finger turned to ice, just as it had earlier today. Cold meant dead. Somehow that had to be tied to whatever made the toaster move because the rest of the people in this room were very much alive.

The lights overhead flickered, and Poochie let out a little gasp. "Good Lord be wit' us."

I couldn't help but say a silent prayer that whatever god Poochie believed in had heard her.

CHAPTER EIGHTEEN

"Probably just some weather stirring up," Trevor said, glancing up at the flickering light. "Best get out the flashlight and candles just in case the lights go out for good. You know how it is around here, a mouse pisses and Bayou Crow loses power." For someone who'd just been barking words out at his wife, his voice seemed carefully controlled as he spoke to Poochie.

"Dat wasn't no weather done dat." Poochie propped a hand on her hip. "Dey don't got not one cloud in de sky. Just a big full moon and de stars. De closest rain right now is prob'bly on de other side de world. It's a ghos' dat did dat."

Trevor scrubbed a hand over his face. "Poochie, you know there's no such thing as—"

"Oh, no, don't you *even* go tellin' me what dere is or dere's not. I'm a whole bunch more years older den you. I wiped you butt and you snot when you was a little boy, remember? I t'ink I know what I'm talking about. I'm telling you, I was out to de prayer tree earlier before I come in here to cook, and I seen dem come into de house."

"You saw what come into the house?" I asked,

glancing over at Angelle. Her face had turned pale again.

"Dem ghos'. T'ree of dem. Slide right t'rough de bricks like dey was nothing but a screen door."

"What . . . what did they look like?" Angelle asked quietly.

My heart thundered in my ears. I was anxious to hear Poochie's answer.

"Y'all don't get her started," Trevor said. "Don't encourage her. There's no such thing as ghosts, and that's the end of it."

"Puh! You can make all de end of it you want, Mr. Big Britches, but what I'm telling you is de trut'. I was out dere by de prayer tree having me a little talk wit' God 'cause Him and me, we not been understandin' each other too good lately. De las' thing I told Him about was de shoes dat's gone missing from de tree; den I saw de ghos'."

"If there are any shoes missing from that tree it's probably because some bum came in off the street and took 'em," Trevor said.

"Yeah? Den how come dat bum was too stupid to grab de good pair? He took de ones all busted up and old."

Trevor muttered something unintelligible and slouched in his seat.

"Dey was all gray-lookin'," Poochie said, looking from me to Angelle, "and came from 'cross de bayou, all de way up to de house. Dey float low to de ground, flat, like dey was laying down, you know? Dey had a head, some arms; dey legs look funny, though, kind of like a baseball bat, skinny like dat, and dey didn't have no feet. Dat don't make no sense, huh? If dey de ones stole de shoes, where dey gonna put 'em if dey don't got no feet?" She paused for a moment, then shook her head as though to whip her thoughts back into line. "Anyways, like I said, dey come from de bayou to de house right after I talked to de good Lord. I said, 'Show me de sign, God. Give me de answer for what's going on round dis place.' Dat's when I saw dem, and dat's how I know dey for real ghos' 'cause de answer came straight from de good Lord, and He don't lie."

"Would you just stop talking about stupid shit like that?" Trevor bellowed.

Poochie took a step toward him, her face turning bright red. "You t'ink you jus' found a fancy way to tell me to shut up? Huh? Come on. Be a man. Tell me dat again straight to my face and see if I don't pass you a slap on de other side of you face."

Angelle held up a hand. "Y'all stop, please."

Feeling like a voyeur in a PG-13–rated ménage à trois, I took off for the bathroom to get away from the fighting and to grimace in pain in peace. The ache in my finger was overwhelming. It was so cold it burned. Way beyond excruciating.

As I walked down the hallway, I could still hear Angelle, Poochie, and Trevor pitching words back and forth, all of them getting louder. A few feet ahead on the left, I saw the dim glow from the night-light Angelle always left on in the bathroom. I couldn't wait to get in there and close the door, shut out the anger from the kitchen, react to my pain in private. The intensity of it was evidently affecting my eyesight, too, because with every step I took, the glow from the night-light seemed to grow brighter and brighter, then suddenly dim to near darkness. It did that twice, and was on the upswing to brightening again when something dark and oblong suddenly bolted out of the bathroom, then flashed across the hall into a bedroom. I rocked to a stop, heart thudding. Had I just seen that? It had happened so fast—optical illusion caused by a blink? Caused by the night-light brightening—darkening? Bright—dark—dark, just like the form in the kitchen that smelled of musk— just like the shapes Poochie said she saw slipping into the house through the bricks. There was only one way for me to know for sure. . . .

Tucking my left hand under my right arm, I realized I was still wearing the rubber gloves. I slipped them off, stuck them in the back pocket of my jeans, clamped my teeth together, then headed for the bedroom—praying nothing was in there.

As soon as I reached the room, I flipped on the light switch, squinted against the sudden brightness, and flinched as if expecting a blow. The pain in my finger didn't intensify, but it didn't decrease, either, which meant . . . what?

A twin bed with a plush pink bedspread and metal side rails sat against the back wall. Beside it was a nightstand that held a pink plastic cup, a small wooden cross perched on a round base, and a tiny statue of an angel wielding a sword. On the other side of the room near a window was a narrow dresser with a framed eight-by-ten portrait propped on top of it. The photo was of Angelle and Trevor, she in a wedding dress, he in a tux. Taking in the cross and statue again, and knowing that neither my sister nor Trevor was overtly religious, I figured this had to be Poochie's room. If something had come in here, it wasn't in here now . . . unless it was hiding under the bed. And I wasn't about to look and find out.

Despite the pain in my finger, I was too nervous now to lock myself away in the bathroom—especially after what I'd seen, or thought I'd seen—so I headed back to the kitchen. Halfway down the hall, I heard the arguing still going on and made a quick detour into the living room, then out the front door and into the yard.

As soon as I got outside my finger began to warm up. Whatever had caused it to act up was obviously in the house—the toaster, the flickering lights, that racing shadow that may not have been a shadow at all. What the hell was going on here? If all of this was caused by some spirit—or three of them, as Poochie claimed, what the shit was I supposed to do about it? My finger might be alerting me to the dead, but that didn't do me any good if there wasn't a body involved. What was I supposed to do with air, smoke? Even if I could identify a spirit, how was I supposed to capture it? What the hell was I supposed to *do* with it?

Frustrated by too many questions and not one decent answer, I began pacing the front yard, my left hand tucked safely away in my pants pocket. The evening was warm, the air abuzz with mosquitoes. I swatted a couple away from my face, and in that movement my eye caught the glimmer of water about five hundred feet ahead. I walked toward it, saw the reflection of the moon on its flat gray surface, felt anticipation swell in my chest. So much craziness had gone on in the short time I'd been here that I hadn't had time to get a bead on the kids. No matter the reason, it seemed utterly pathetic given they were one of the biggest reasons I'd come here in the first place. I might not know what to do with ghosts and ghouls, but I knew what to do with the missing, and it was time I did it. The only thing different in this situation versus anything else I'd ever hunted for was the swamp. I'd never worked through water before, but that didn't mean I couldn't. All I had to do was focus, maybe harder than usual, really zero in on those kids. I didn't know what Sarah and Nicky looked like, but that truly didn't matter. It wasn't outward appearance my finger connected to; it was energy.

I walked to the edge of the water, glanced about to make sure the coast was clear, then pulled my left hand out of my pocket. It felt weird standing out here without my gloves, without my finger tucked into my palm. Hiding, I was always hiding. Throughout dinner, I'd kept my left hand hidden under the table; later it went into my pocket, then inside rubber gloves. Out in the open this way, I felt vulnerable, naked, as if I'd literally stepped out into the world without a stitch of clothes on.

Gritting my teeth, I curled my left hand into a fist, then held it out at arm's length. If this was going to be anything like at the Bloody Bucket, I was in for another serious round of ouch. But that's why I was here, right? The kids. The kids and Angelle.

After glancing around once more to make sure no

one was watching, I unlocked my fist and splayed my fingers, stretching them out wide. I closed my eyes and focused on Sarah first—that little girl, only seven years old—what it must have felt like to be that small and lost in such a big wilderness, in the dark—how afraid she must be. I did the same with Nicky—only eight years old. Then, without any conscious effort on my part, their energies merged in my mind, and those assumed fears became one huge, living, breathing terror. The power of it rolled over me in waves, cutting my breath.

Within seconds, my extra finger reacted—violently. Burning, biting, as if a firecracker had blown off the tip. Then the digit pulled itself up—up as if meaning to point to the sky—then it jerked over to the right, overlapping the two fingers beside it. Fire raced through the finger, down through my hand, my wrist, up my arm. I gasped from the intensity of it. I'd never felt anything like this before.

Heat normally came when I hunted for inanimate objects—keys, a watch, a hairbrush. But this wasn't normal heat. It was explosive, intense, and I didn't understand it at all. The only thing that did make sense was the steady point of the finger. From where I stood, it was telling me to head east.

Despite the pain, I forced myself to calm, concentrate, clear my mind so I could understand and interpret what I was experiencing.

Time . . . something to do with time . . .

The more fierce the heat, the pain—the shorter the time . . . the less time we had to find the kids? The less time the kids had to live? Which was it? Both?

141

. . . shorter the time . . . shorter the time . . . I rolled the words over and over in my mind, concentrating hard on the kids, desperate for a clearer interpretation.

Suddenly I heard the slight clearing of a throat, then, "I'd be careful with that if I were you."

Startled, I whirled about. A man was walking past me, already fifty or so feet away—a man wearing a black Stetson, a long black coat. Cherokee. How long had he . . . son of a bitch—my finger . . . he'd seen it!

CHAPTER NINETEEN

I felt anesthetized, too stunned to move or speak as I watched Cherokee's tall silhouette meld into the dark distance until there was no discerning his black coat from the cloak of night. He'd seen—seen *me*. Not even Angelle had ever witnessed my finger reacting with such intensity. What would he do? Who would he tell? Would I walk into town tomorrow morning and find every head turning my way, every expression screaming, "Freak!"? Or would it be like before, people following me everywhere, wanting, begging, nagging, never giving me a moment's peace?

A sudden squeal of tires on pavement broke my train of worry, and I glanced toward the sound. It was Trevor's truck, peeling down the highway in front of the house. Even with his boat in tow, he managed to pull smoke from the asphalt. Evidently, the tiff he'd been having with Angelle and Poochie hadn't ended on a warm and fuzzy note. *Great, something else to worry about.* Tucking my left hand into my pocket, I headed back to the house, still trying to come to terms with the fact that I'd been *seen*.

When I walked into the kitchen, Poochie was rambling about the absurdity of men, while wiping down already clean countertops. Sometimes that's what women do to work out anger or frustration, we wipe things, clean things, scrub things. Right now Poochie looked angry enough to scrub somebody's face off.

Angelle was sitting at the table, her head in her hands. She looked up as soon as I walked in. "You okay? Where'd you go?"

"Went for a walk."

"You look . . . I don't know . . . frazzled?" She peered at me intently, and I saw the questions in her eyes she obviously didn't want to ask aloud. *Did something happen to you out there? Did you see . . . something?*

In that same momentary eye contact, I tried relaying my own message. *I'll tell you later.* Then I said audibly, "I'm fine."

Her brow furrowed, and her eyes flickered to Poochie, then back to me. "Sorry you had to hear that big mess earlier."

I gave her a half smile. "No worries." I pulled out a chair and sat beside her at the table.

"If it was up to me," Poochie said, tossing her dish towel into the sink, then coming over to join us, "I'd take all dem men and put dem in one big trash pile 'cause dat's all dey good for. Or put dem all back in diapers 'cause most de time dey act like babies anyway."

"Trevor isn't usually like that," Angelle said. "He's been putting in a lot of hours at the plant and with those new traps . . . he's probably just really stressed out."

Poochie harrumphed. "You can make all de excuses you want. I know you trying to be nice, but I know dat boy. Dat's my grandson. I can say he's a piece of shit when I need to, and right now I need to 'cause he's acting like a piece of shit." With that, Poochie aimed her chin at me. "And you, you got you a man?"

Slightly taken aback by the question, I shrugged, then shook my head.

Poochie cocked her head, her eyes flashing with curiosity. "Mais, how come? You pretty and you smart. How come you don't got a man?" Before I could answer, she stuck out a hand and wiggled it from side to side. "You one of dem . . . what you call dat? A lessbean?"

"Jesus, Poochie," Angelle said, her head snapping to attention. "Dunny is *not* a lesbian."

Poochie tsked. "You don't gotta get you drawers all tied up you butt. I was just asking."

I grinned, relieved that the conversation had turned down a less serious road for once. "It's all right. I date men, Poochie. I just haven't found one worth keeping is all."

She nodded. "I know what you sayin'. Like I say, dey just babies dat never grow up."

Angelle opened her mouth as if to say something, then closed it, evidently changing her mind. Seeing that, I scooped up the conversation so Poochie wouldn't zero in on her.

"Talking about men, I saw Cherokee outside a moment ago. That's his name, right? The guy who wears the black cowboy hat and the long coat?"

"Yeah, dat's Cherokee. Where you saw him like dat?"

"Out on the other end of the property, near the bayou."

Poochie frowned. "Huh . . . I wonder what he was doin' out here dis time of de day? He lives all de way down de Plaquemine Highway, pas' de big bridge. He makes a little pass into town every once in a while, goes eat at de Bucket, you know? But I don't remember de last time I seen him come out dis way. What he was doin' out dere?"

Folding my hands under the table, I quickly sorted through words I might be able to use that wouldn't incriminate me or create a lie. "I don't know. He just sort of showed up. Talked to me for a couple of seconds; then he was gone again."

Poochie's brows peaked. "He talked to you?"

"Well . . . yeah," I said, a little surprised that she seemed surprised.

"Huh, dat's something. Cherokee hardly don't talk to nobody even when he knows dem. Stays to himself most de time; you know what I'm saying?"

"He's a little weird if you ask me," Angelle said. "Wearing black all the time. The only time he takes off that coat is in the dead of summer, and even then he still stays in black. It's always so hot around here I don't know how he stands it."

"Dat's not really too weird, no. Some people get cold all de way down to deir blood, so it's hard for dem to warm up. Either dat or dat's jus' what de man likes to wear. From what I can see, he's not too bad. Kind of nice in his own way, you know? At leas' he's not stupid like dat retarded Pork Chop over to de Bloody Bucket."

"Is Cherokee from around here?" I asked.

"I don't know much about him," Angelle said with

146

a shrug. "He's been around here as long as I've been here. That's about it."

"Oh, dat man's been here since he was a baby," Poochie said. "Sook tol' me."

"Is there anything Sook *doesn't* tell you?" Angelle asked.

Poochie pursed her lips, glanced up for a moment as if contemplating the question, then said, "Non. Sook's pretty good about dat. She tells me what I gotta know, about Cherokee, about a lot of people around dese parts."

"What'd she say about Cherokee?" I asked.

"Dat his mama and daddy was quiet like him. His mama was part Cherokee, dat's how he got his name. His daddy, I t'ink Sook said he was part Sioux or Chitamachi, I'm not too sure. Dey got a lotta injuns round here. Sioux, Cherokee, Pawnee, all dat. Some of dem full, some of dem mix up wit' de Cajun people."

"Is Sook part Native American?" I asked, remembering the woman's broad features.

"Non. Part Sook's people's from Mississippi, part's from New Orleans. Dat's how come she got a funny accent. Dem people from Mississippi, dey nice, yeah, but when you mix dem wit' de people from here . . . it's like puttin' turnips in a gumbo. It might taste good, but it's gonna look funny."

I grinned, not sure I understood the reference, but getting a kick out of her own accent. Then something dawned on me from earlier. "Why does Trevor call you Poochie like everybody else? How come he doesn't call you Grandma or Granny?"

Poochie crossed her arms over her large, sagging

breasts. "Because I said so, dat's why. I tol' his mama and daddy de day he was born, have dat boy call me Poochie. I didn't want no name like Grandma. Dat makes me sound like a old woman ready for de nursing home, and me, I was far from goin' to de nursing home den. I'm still far from dat, you know?"

I nodded in agreement. I couldn't see Poochie in a nursing home.

"Okay, let's hol' up a minute. . . ." Poochie settled into a chair and tapped the tabletop with a finger. "I wanna put something on dis table right now. We got to quit dancing around Trevor, Cherokee, all dat. We got to get some serious business down now."

As soon as Poochie said "down now," my finger began freezing up again. I gritted my teeth, trying to keep my expression neutral.

"What are you talking about?" Angelle asked.

"You know what I'm talking about." She turned to me. " 'Specially you. I know you seen dat toaster move, huh?"

I sat back, surprised. I thought I'd been the only one to see it happen.

"What about the toaster?" Angelle asked.

"You was too busy fussin' with Trevor to see, but dat toaster over dere, it moved by itself. I seen it. And you sister, I know she seen it, too." Poochie drilled me with a look. "You might think I don't know nothin' 'cause I'm too old, but I seen how you went out de kitchen before. You was hurting. You hands was hurting. How come dat is? You feel dem ghosts with you hands or what?"

Angelle's eyes went wide. She looked ready for a panic attack. "Poochie, there's nothing—"

"Look, don't play crazy with me, no. I know better. And you know better, you, too."

Besides curiosity, I saw determination and honesty in Poochie's bright green eyes. Seeing that, I felt something spontaneously unlock inside me. Like an old forgotten closet door, it creaked open slightly, and I suddenly found myself wanting to tell Poochie Blackledge everything. My mouth went dry. I licked my lips. Then, without any explanation, I pulled my hands out from under the table, stretched out my fingers . . . and laid both of my hands palm down on the table.

CHAPTER TWENTY

Angelle let out a breathless "*Dunny . . .* "

Poochie's eyes settled on my left hand. She pursed her lips and nodded. "Uh-huh, I knew it was something." She looked up at me. "So, what you can do with dat?"

"Mostly find stuff."

"Like dem little chil'ren?"

"Maybe."

Angelle looked as if she'd just seen a UFO, mouth hanging open, eyes wide with that deer-in-the-headlights look.

"It's okay," I said to her. "I really don't think she'll say anything to anyone."

"You talkin' about me sayin' something? Ha! Not me, no." Poochie pinched her thumb and forefinger together in front of her mouth, twisted them as if turning a key, then made a tossing motion over her left shoulder. "You see dat? I locked dat all up and t'row away de key. Whatever you got to say gonna stay right here."

As simplistic as the gesture was, it opened that closet door within me even wider, and I soon found myself telling Poochie everything, starting with the water found on Frieda Hughes's property. By the time I reached the part about finding Pirate, Angelle had evidently warmed up to my exposing the *secret* because she started adding little comments. About how much she loved that cat. How devastated she'd been to discover he'd died such a horrible death. How she'd kept my secret all these years and never once told a soul, not even her husband. I followed up with more stories, moving through all the years and incidents that had involved that extra finger.

As amazed as I was at how easily the words spilled out of my mouth, I was even more amazed that Poochie never stopped us once to comment. She listened intently, nodding or shaking her head in commiseration, especially when I told her about the kids who'd teased me at school, calling me Freak and Water Witch—about the men who'd come into my life pretending love, but actually meaning to use me for their own gain.

When I finished, I felt purged, as if someone had lifted a forty-pound sack of wet concrete off my back. The three of us sat in silence for a moment, Poochie studying my finger as if it were a puzzle piece and her responsibility was to find out where that piece was supposed to fit.

Her tone was almost reverent when she finally spoke. "It's hurtin' you now, huh?"

"Yeah, a little. Cold, but not a hard cold like earlier today." I volleyed a look between Poochie and Angelle. "When I was outside, near the bayou a little while ago, I picked up a different kind of pain, not cold at all."

Angelle sat bolt upright. "The kids?"

"I'm not sure. Possible, though, because I was concentrating on them when I felt it."

"What did it feel like?"

"Fire. You remember that Fourth of July when we were kids, the time that Black Cat exploded in your hand?"

"God, do I ever!"

"Sort of felt like that, only in the tip of my finger. Weird. Then it pulled up and over, pointing east."

"So we gotta go find dem in de east?" Poochie asked, leaning closer to me.

"The direction I'm sure about. What'll be found in that direction is what I can't quite figure out. I couldn't really interpret what was happening or what it meant because I've never felt it do that before. Heat usually means I'm getting close to finding a lost object, like jewelry or something. But this wasn't just heat. It was *fire* hot. And there's so much . . . *energy* in the bayou, the swamps, that Lord only knows what I might be picking up."

"But at least it's something," Angelle said. "Some place to start, right?"

I shrugged, afraid to give her too much hope.

"So what de cold means? Dat what you gonna find is dead?"

"Usually, yeah."

"So de cold in you finger now, it's tellin' you we got a ghos' in de house?"

I shrugged again. "That's the only thing I can figure. Cold always means dead. Even though it's not as cold as before, maybe that just means there's one here now, whereas earlier it was more. Maybe the three you saw coming in here through the bricks."

I'd never seen a look of relief wash over a woman's face as purely as it did on Poochie's in that moment. "Mais, I can't believe . . . somebody finally believe what I gotta say." She sat up tall in her seat, face beaming. Then she pointed to Angelle. "Okay, before we go sidetrack again, it's you turn."

"What do you mean?"

"I know you got a story to tell you, too. You don't have a extra finger like you sister, but you got something in you, I know."

"I . . . I don't under—"

"Tell her, Gelle," I said softly. "Tell her about the touching."

Angelle's face turned five shades of pink before rolling into brick red. I reached over and squeezed her hands, wanting to encourage her. When she finally spoke, her voice was hesitant and soft, and the tears began almost immediately. With absolute detail, she recounted the pinching, the bruising, the invasion of hands and other male body parts. By the time she was done, all three of us were crying.

"Poo-yi." Poochie pushed away from the table, sniffled hard, and hobbled to the sink. She grabbed a fistful of paper towels and blew her nose.

It was then I realized she'd not been using her walker. "You seem to get around pretty good without that metal contraption of yours."

Tossing the paper towels into the trash, Poochie tsked. "I don't have to use dat all de time. Sometimes my balance goes a little cuckoo, so I have to use it to hold myself up. Don't want to fall on my face in de public, you know? And over to de Bucket, I ride my scoot 'cause I'm too lazy to haul my big butt from one of dem aisles to de other."

I smiled, and it felt good to release some of the tension that had hung in the kitchen for so long.

Poochie suddenly closed her eyes for a second, waving a hand in the air. "Okay, hol' up, hol' up, we goin' sidetrack again." She pointed at me. "Now, let's see . . . you feel de ghos' wit' you finger, and you t'ink you know de direction we supposed to go for de chil'ren. . . ."

I nodded.

She pointed to Angelle. "And you, dem ghos' been messin' wit' you. A bad ghos', so we gotta figure out how to turn dat off." She brought her finger to her mouth and tapped it against her lips for a moment. "Hmm . . . hmm." She dropped her hand. "Okay, de bes' I can understand from de good Lord is dis. De ghos' in de house, de ghos' dat touch her, de los' babies, all dat's mixed up together."

"That doesn't really make sense. How would they all be connected, especially the kids?"

She shrugged. "I'm like you, me. I don't understand too good. My finger don't hurt like you finger, but He put a picture in my head. It don't make no sense, dough."

"A picture of what?" Angelle asked.

"A cypress tree."

"One?" I asked.

"Non, and it's not de regular tree. It's de stump. Old, rotted stump and de new tree growin' inside dat."

"Huh?" Angelle and I said at the same time.

"A new tree growin' inside a old stump dat's rotted like dat, dey call dat a olm tree. I know dat much, me. But I don't know what He's trying to tell me wit' dat. He show me de tree . . . you finger . . . de ghos' . . . what de ghos' was doin' to Angelle's tee-tons—"

"Tee-tons?" I asked.

Poochie gave me a bewildered look, as though she'd never met anyone who'd never heard the word *tee-ton* before. "Yeah, tee-ton . . . you know, you two breasteses."

Angelle blushed hard and looked away.

Now that definitions were cleared up, Poochie shook a finger at me. "You know, I don't know what we supposed to do to stop what's in dis house. I don't know how we supposed to stop dem from takin' de shoes out de prayer tree. But something's tellin' me, and I think it's de good Lord, dat if we find de chil'ren, den all de rest is gonna be fix. We just gotta find dem."

"We were planning to go look tonight," Angelle said, "but since Trevor isn't bringing back the boat, we won't have any way to get into the swamp."

"Poo-yi, girl, you must be crazy! Even if you had de boat, you can't go out in dem swamps in de middle of de night. Dat's too dangerous. And would you even know what to do wit' de boat?"

"I've been out with Trevor checking traps before. He showed me how to run the boat. Start it, steer it, everything. All we'd have to do is bring a flashlight or a headlight, and I could find my way around . . . I'm sure."

"Den thank de good Lord Trevor took de boat! You two don't got no business bein' out dere by youself. Dat's cuckoo. Don't you know what's out dere? If de ghos' come from de bayou up in dis house, den what else you think is out in all dat big swamp? Not Santy Claus, no. De feux fo lais might get you out dere."

"What's that?" I asked.

She leaned close to me again. "A lot of people believe de feux fo lais is different things, but me, I know dat's not true. A feux fo lais, dat's a los' soul from purgatory. When dey get los' dey float around in de swamp until dey find where dey supposed to go. Some of dem souls get mad 'cause dey los', den all dat mad turns into a big ball of light. Dat light tries to trick you, lead you way, way out in de black, black swamp." Poochie sighed. "Den it leaves you dere, so you los' forever. Can't ever find you way back."

"Then if we see anything like that, we just won't follow it," Angelle said matter-of-factly.

"It don't work like dat. I think de feux fo lais uses gris-gris or somethin' 'cause it makes you follow it whether you wanna go or don't wanna go." Poochie pursed her lips for a moment. "Mos' do dat, anyway. Dere's a few feux fo lais dat might be close to figuring out where dey supposed to go, and dose don't get so mad. Dey not gonna make you get los'. Dey gonna help you get home. De trouble is, you never know which one you got when it shows up, de good one or de bad one. Wit' all de stuff dat's been goin' on around here, I think de bad would come. And dey would lead y'all way out dere where nobody, not even de game warden, is gonna find y'all. Non, y'all bes' wait for de day. In de daylight y'all can go look."

"I can't go out during the day," I said.

"Mais, how come?"

"Everyone would see what I showed you, Poochie. That extra finger. They'll find out what it can do. I don't need that kind of hassle in my life again. You have no idea what it was like having people follow me around everywhere, always wanting something from me. People get greedy. They want me to look for oil and gold, and they get desperate."

Angelle nodded. "It's true. I saw it. I remember all those people."

"Yeah, I can see how dat would happen. Dere's greedy all over de world. Everybody's got dat today." Poochie rubbed her forehead with three fingers for a long moment, then finally looked over at us and said, "Oh, yi, dat's not good, no."

"What?" Angelle asked.

"What I just seen."

Poochie looked up at the ceiling as if watching an overhead screen. I felt Angelle's leg jiggling nervously near mine.

"What, Pooch?" Angelle asked again, an impatient snap in her voice.

"Y'all in a big fight . . . in de dark . . . in de boat. Poo-yi, out in de water . . ."

"A big fight?" I said.

"With who?" Angelle chimed in.

Instead of answering, Poochie stood up, leaned over me, and made a sign of the cross on my forehead with her right thumb. Then she walked over to Angelle and did the same thing, only after crossing her forehead, she said to her, " 'Scuse me, cher," then quickly made the same mark of the cross on each of Angelle's breasts. Once that was done, Poochie lifted her hands up high, palm up, as if she expected the ceiling to fall and planned on catching it. "God, if you ever listen to me, Poochie, den you need to listen to me now. Please take care of us and please—"

Poochie never got the chance to finish her prayer. For in that moment, the light fixture hanging over her head exploded, and the kitchen went dark.

CHAPTER TWENTY-ONE

Nicky Trahan hated the dark, even more than he had at any other time in his life. In the dark, back home, he always imagined *things* hiding under his bed. In the dark—hiding in the closet, waiting to attack him every time he had to go to the bathroom in the middle of the night. In the swamp, where he and Sarah were, the dark was different. It had sounds that frightened him because he didn't know what they belonged to. For all he knew, that chittering, squawking, croaking, grunting could belong to a bear. Like those giant brown ones he'd seen during a field trip at the zoo in Baton Rouge. Then again, maybe it was a wild hog or a bobcat. It could even be another alligator.

They'd been lucky with the first alligator. Way lucky. They'd been so frightened by it, he and Sarah had screamed at the top of their lungs, until no sound would come out of their mouths anymore. The screaming must have scared the gator because it let out a loud hiss, then flipped itself backward into the water. It hadn't come back . . . yet. But the gator knew where they were, and Nicky feared it would find its way back to them. And if it did, he didn't think they'd be able to scream loud enough to scare it away again. Not only was he hoarse from all the yelling, but there was so much mud pressed against his chest it made it difficult to draw in a big breath. There was no way he'd be able to pull in enough air to scream loud enough to even scare away a mosquito.

He swallowed, forcing down the little bit of saliva he was able to gather in his mouth. He was so hungry, and so scared of all the shadows moving around them. Even a little breeze made a branch look like a monster's arm raking across the ground, creeping toward them. He tried to be brave, tried not to cry. It was so hard. He imagined what it would be like if he had a dad right now. Imagined him out in the swamps, looking for him and Sarah this very minute. His dad would be the kind of person who would never go looking for just one kid when two were missing. He'd want to find both.

In truth, Nicky didn't know who his father was. Each time he tried talking about it with his mother, she'd cry or get angry and drink more whiskey. Because of that, Nicky had no idea who the man was, what he looked like. Didn't know the color of his hair or eyes. Didn't know how tall he was, or if he was strong or skinny. In a way, that was good because it allowed Nicky to imagine his dad any way he wanted to.

At that moment, he pictured him to be Superman: tight-fitting shirt over a broad muscled chest, and the shirt had a big red S on it. He'd be able to pick up buildings and move them sideways to check and make sure his son wasn't under one of them. He'd bat cars out of the way with one hand. He'd be able to grab alligators with two hands and rip their mouths apart for even thinking about eating his son for supper. Then, with one finger, his dad would pick him up by the back of his shirt and simply lift him out of the thick, stinky mud.

Even better, if his dad was Superman, then that would make him Superboy, and Superboy didn't cry. Superboy was strong. Not as strong as his dad, but close to it. Close enough to rescue people. And he wanted to rescue Sarah.

Girls weren't supposed to be treated the way that man had treated her. Girls were supposed to be taken care of and given presents. That's what his mom had told him, anyway. And that must have been the truth because every time he looked over at Sarah, all he wanted to do was take care of her. Nicky had never been in a fight before, but he knew if he had the chance, he'd fight that bad man, the one pouring the mud. He'd punch him in the nose, make his mouth bleed, put a sleeper-hold on him the way the wrestlers did in WWF. He'd take care of her. Yes, sir, he would.

"Hey . . ." Nicky called out to Sarah as loud as he could, but the word came out sounding like a warbled croak. He tried again. "Hey, Sarah!"

She didn't move. Maybe she was afraid to move. Afraid the mud man was nearby and would dump more stuff on them. As far as he could tell, though, they were alone for now.

"Psst!"

She still didn't move. He turned his head toward her as far as he could and squinted.

The moon was big enough and bright enough for him to see that her head was leaning forward, not back the way it had been before, when she was sleeping. Nicky knew the man had put more mud in her hole, too. What if he'd put too much? Sarah was a little smaller than he was; suppose the mud went up to her neck and when she dropped her head, she drowned? Maybe she drowned in the mud . . . and if she drowned, then that meant she was dead . . . and if she was dead, then that meant he was alone. He didn't want to be alone.

Nicky tried forcing her name out of his mouth with all his might—with Superboy power. "Sar—ah!" Once again, it came out choppy and crooked, but at least it sounded a little louder than what he'd managed before.

Not loud enough, though . . . Sarah still wasn't moving. Her head was still flopped over, like a rag doll's.

Feeling lonelier than he'd ever felt in his life, Nicky lifted his head, looked up to the stars, and sobbed, "Mama! Mama, please, please come and get me. *Please*, Mama."

Somebody had to save them. Someone had to come. He didn't care if the whole school heard him crying. If every boy in his class teased him for the rest of his life, he didn't care. As long as someone came and got them out of the mud. Came to save Sarah first, then him. She was smaller, and she was a girl, so he'd go second. It was only right that she'd go first.

Nicky thought of his mother and wept even harder. He wanted so much to believe, so much to wish that she was out in the swamps looking for him. That she was the first one in a mega line of people who were hunting, searching for a little boy and a little girl. But no matter how hard he tried to imagine it, the only thing Nicky saw in his mind's eyes was his mother lying on the couch, a half-empty bottle of Jim Beam on the coffee table beside her, and the slack face of drunk.

As Nicky lowered his head, wishing his hands were free so he could wipe the snot from his nose, he heard a loud *plop!* in the mud. After the plopping sound, all he heard was *ka-thunk . . . ka-thunk . . . ka-thunk* in his ears. It felt as if his heart had moved from his chest to his head, and it wasn't allowing him to hear anything else but its rapid beat. Fear felt like a burrowing animal in the pit of his stomach.

Wanna be Superboy . . . need to be Superboy . . . Mama . . .

He squinted and strained his eyes to see what might have fallen in with him. Even with the light from the massive moon, there were so many shadows everywhere that they overlapped to make more darkness.

Nicky caught the glimpse of something . . . something silver? But not silver.

It moved in a curling, wiggling, sliding motion. If

he turned his head just right, Nicky was able to see mud stirring around his chest. He bowed his head and leaned forward slowly as far as he could. He didn't have to lean very far before he saw an arrow-shaped head slither through the mud, heading for his face.

CHAPTER TWENTY-TWO

Sook aimed a pair of tweezers at the cut just below Poochie's left eye. "Sugah, you wigglin' like a worm fixin' to be stuck up on a hook shaft. If you don't hold still, I'm gonna wind up pokin' your eye plumb out. Now put your head back and be still so I can get a good look-see."

Sitting in her scooter, Poochie tsked and leaned her head back against the top of the seat. "I don't know what you poking around in dere for. I tol' you I took all de glass out last night."

"I just wanna check and make sure."

Poochie sputtered through pursed lips, then closed her eyes and let Sook get on with her business. She'd been lucky. The night before when the light fixture had exploded right above her, Poochie'd had the good sense to shut her eyes a half second before the shards of glass rained down over her. She hadn't been able to move out of the way fast enough, though, to escape total damage. Tiny slivers of glass had jabbed her in the face, the two worst being in her forehead and in her left cheek. It felt as if she'd been pelted with BBs.

The second after the light fixture had shattered, Angelle and Dunny had sprung into action. Angelle had raced off for a pair of tweezers, then hurried back and began plucking out glass slivers. As she operated, Dunny stood watch with a dish towel, dabbing specks of blood as they appeared. Funny thing was not one of them questioned the explosion. They hadn't even talked about. It was as if they understood collectively that whatever was in the house had overheard their plans to find the children—specifically after Poochie had mentioned that she'd suspected finding the kids might cause a chain reaction that would send the spirits back to where they belonged. Evidently, those spirits didn't want anything to do with being sent back, and Poochie figured the shattering light fixture had been another attempt to scare them away from their plans. How wrong they were. If anything, it made Poochie more determined than ever to put an end to all of this nonsense.

After spending the night huddled together in Angelle's bed so they could watch over one another, the three women had gone through the motions of breakfast with very little appetite. Trevor had made it home about seven forty-five, looking like something that had been dragged behind an eighteen-wheeler for twelve hours. He didn't even comment on the fact that they no longer had a kitchen light fixture or say a word about the small cuts on Poochie's face—if he'd even noticed either at all. All he'd done was sit at the table, shovel in his breakfast, and gripe. In between bites of scrambled eggs and biscuits, Trevor had grumbled about having to work the three-to-eleven shift today, which meant he'd get only five hours of sleep before having to run back to the plant. Angelle, obviously trying to play nice after the spat they'd had the night before, had offered a few commiserative comments, but Trevor had been in such a foul mood, her words only solicited another argument.

No sooner had Trevor stormed off to bed than Angelle and Dunny began making plans to commandeer Bullet later that afternoon, after Trevor left for work. Poochie had been in the middle of trying to talk them out of going into the swamp alone again, when Sook called, asking her to come down to the Bloody Bucket and lend a hand. Fearing that Angelle and Dunny might head out to the swamp despite her warning, or even worse, leave without her if they decided to really go, Poochie had been hesitant to agree. The fact that neither Angelle nor Dunny could take the boat as long as Trevor was home had offered a little reassurance, but not much. As soon as the women had dropped Poochie off at the Bucket, which had only been a little over an hour ago, she'd been fidgety with worry. No telling what those two girls were up to left to themselves like that.

Poochie had promised Sook she'd stay at the Bucket until two, but right now she was so uneasy, so nervous it felt as if ants had collected under her skin and were scurrying about. She wished she'd told Sook no and stayed with Angelle and Dunny instead. *Something* was going to happen. Poochie felt it in her bones—under her skin—in the very roots of her hair. The problem was she didn't know what that something was or where it was going to happen, or when, how, or to whom, which made her want to be everywhere at once.

Everywhere at once meant next to Trevor, even though he was probably still drooling on his pillow right about now—with Angelle and Dunny—even with Sook and Vern, even though they were only distant relatives by marriage. That was the problem with being the oldest in a family, especially the matriarchal root. The need to protect the family flock was inherent, but hard to do when your body was sliding into the shitter at warp speed.

"What happened to you?"

Poochie opened her eyes and saw Cherokee standing in front of her. The poker face he normally kept well intact had slipped aside, revealing concern. "Looks like you've been in a catfight."

"Non, not no cat." Poochie flinched—"Ay-ii!"—and batted Sook's hand away. "Stop dat!"

"Sorry 'bout that. I'm just tryin' to help."

"How? By peeling off de rest of my face?"

"It looked like a piece a glass."

"Dat was skin, cuckoo! Now leave dat alone like I said!"

Sook threw up her hands and stepped back. She shook her head "All right, you go right on and be hardheaded, then. It's your own business. But you needa think on it twice before you go climbin' up on another stepladder again. Leave the lightbulb changin' to Trevor, you hear?"

Poochie made a *pfft* sound and waved her away. The stepladder-lightbulb story had been a bald-faced lie, and lying was something she rarely, if ever, did. She was always afraid of the repercussions. If a person lied, she got a lie back, or the lie told would end up coming

true. Under the circumstances, though, Poochie figured God would understand the need for the fib. She'd
given her word to Dunny and Angelle not to tell a
soul about what they'd shared, and as far as she reck-
oned, there was no way to tell the story about the light
fixture without discussing all the details that made it
happen. And Poochie didn't trust her brain not to slip
up if she tried to tell part of the truth mixed in with
part of the lie. Best to keep things simple.

"*You* were changing a lightbulb?" Cherokee asked.
He tipped his hat back, and his dark eyes glinted with
mischief.

"What? You don't think I can change me a lightbulb? You bes' think again. Jus' 'cause I'm old don't
mean nothing but I might gotta do it a bit slower den
you, dat's all. Me, I can for sure change a stupid bulb."
She harrumphed, then gave him a stern side glance,
wanting to reiterate the seriousness of the matter.

"So I see."

"You see, huh?" Poochie pursed her lips and bobbed
her head slowly. "Tell me what you see, den. What
you was doing over to Angelle and Trevor's house
last night? Dunny tol' me she saw you out by de
bayou."

Cherokee's grin faltered. He pulled the tip of his
hat back down with a finger, then turned away and
headed for the swinging doors that lead to the bar.

"Where you think you goin'?" she called after him.

He didn't respond, his black coat swishing gently
against the back of his black jeans.

"Hol' up," Poochie called again. When he didn't
turn back, she cranked up her scooter and hurried

after him. He made it into the bar before she could reach him, so she butted the doors open with the nose of the scooter. It took a moment for her eyes to adjust to the dim room, but she soon spotted him settling into a chair at his favorite table. She shook her finger at him. "Don't you think you can jus' run off and ignore me, non."

"Who spit in your Cheerios?" Vern asked. He was wiping down the bar, moving ashtrays, saltshakers, and napkin dispensers around as if someone were timing him with a stopwatch.

Pork Chop was perched on a stool across from Vern, Bud Light in one hand and a bowl of chili in front of him. He snorted. "What're you talkin' about? Poochie spits in 'er own cereal."

She whirled her scooter about. "Guess dat's better dan pissing in my own boots like you, huh, Pork Chop?"

Vern guffawed.

Pork Chop grumbled. "Ain't funny."

Poochie turned her attention back to Cherokee. "You gonna tell me, or you gonna make me sit here all day waiting for you mout' to move?"

Cherokee sat back, stretching his long legs out in front of him. The grin on his face clearly said, *And what if I do?*

"Quit bustin' his chops, Pooch," Vern said.

"I'm not bustin' nothing, me. I asked de man a question, and he won't give me no answer."

"Then there's your answer. The man don't wanna talk." Vern aimed his chin at Cherokee. "I got some chili out back in the kitchen. Want some?"

"Sounds good," Cherokee said. "Coke, too."

Poochie gave Cherokee a stern look. She intended to have the last word, even if no more words were spoken.

He winked at her and grinned.

With a *tsk*, Poochie aimed her scooter for the bar and Vern. "And you, how come you rushing around like you drawers on fire?"

"Gotta get outta here while there's still light." Vern flipped the cleaning rag over his right shoulder. "Since Iberville ain't sendin' no more dep'ties to hunt for them lost kids, Barry Ancelet and me's takin' one of my boats to go look for them out by the back passes. Can't keep sittin' here hopin' they'll turn up."

"Hoping who turns up?" Beeno Leger pushed through the bar doors. He was dressed in his gray police uniform with its frayed cuffs and shiny black shoes. His salt-and-pepper hair was slicked back with enough oil to fry a batch of chicken gizzards. The man's head had always reminded Poochie of a football that sat aslant on a trophy stand. The point of his crown and chin were so prominent it obscured the rest of his face. Prop that head on a pudgy body and you had an overweight Barney Fife with a birth defect.

"Them two kids," Vern said. "Gettin' ready to go out to Slack Lake to look for 'em. Don't think anybody's been out that far yet."

"Figured you was heading out. Saw your boat hitched to your truck out front." Beeno walked over to the bar and claimed a stool next to Pork Chop. "No use going out that far, though. We already been out there, even ran the dogs. Nothing."

"Y'all tried the Flats?" Pork Chop asked. "Out by Turtle Bayou?"

"Yeah. Even had divers work Whiskey Bay."

"What about Rooster Shoot and Gro-beck Point?" Vern asked.

"Iberville guys went out there day before yesterday. Still nothing." Beeno motioned toward the bowl sitting in front of Pork Chop. "Chili?"

"Yeah."

"Caught a whiff of it when I was driving by. Thought I'd stop in for a bite before going over to Woodard's place."

"What's de matter wit' de preacher?" Poochie asked.

Beeno gave her a sideways glance, then did a double take. "What happened to you?"

"Huh?"

"Your face."

"Oh." Poochie touched her forehead absently, then swatted the air with a hand. "Nothing. Ran myself into a lightbulb, dat's all. Now, what you was sayin' about goin' to Woodard's?"

Beeno shrugged as if the whole matter was nothing but a bother and he had better things to do. "I don't know, said somebody made a mess in his church last night. Probably kids out pulling a prank."

Poochie sighed. "Yeah, mais, we know for sure what two kids wasn't out dere fooling around in de man's church." She shook her head and tsked softly. "You know, it's a sin and a shame, yeah. I been meanin' to go back and see Larissa Trahan. You know, Nicky's mama? She was tore up bad de day her boy went missin'.

I need to go back dere and see how dat poor woman's makin' out."

"Don't bother," Beeno said. He nodded a thanks to Vern, who'd placed a bowl of chili in front of him. "Larissa left town."

"Left?" Poochie asked, dumbstruck.

"You're shittin' me!" Vern gaped at Beeno.

"Nope," Beeno said. "Went out there the other morning to get one of Nicky's shirts for the track dogs and the neighbor said she'd left. Had a suitcase with her and everything. Didn't say where she was going, and nobody knows where she went."

"What kind of woman leaves town without knowing where her kids are?" Cherokee asked, his voice rumbling deep and low with incredulity and disgust. Even though he was cloaked in shadows, Poochie sensed his body tensing with anger.

"A drunk one, I s'pose," Beeno said. "I guess the stress of Nicky being gone was too much for the alcohol to handle, so she took off. Who knows?"

"Man, that ain't right," Pork Chop said. He shoveled a spoonful of chili into his mouth, then immediately spat it back into the bowl, sending a shower of meat sauce across the counter. "Ughh!"

"Je-*sus* Christmas!" Beeno jumped up, checking his shirt and the front of his uniform pants for splatter.

"What the hell'd you do that for, Pork Chop?" Vern asked.

Pork Chop swiped his tongue with a napkin, then gagged out, "Tasted funny."

"Damn, boy, kill a man's appetite, why don't you?"

Beeno said, his face screwed up with revulsion. He stuck a hand in his pocket, pulled out a couple of dollars, and threw them on the counter. "Remind me not to sit by your nasty ass next time I come in here to eat, a'ight?" He stormed out of the bar, shoving against the swinging doors so hard they bounced back and nearly hit him in the face.

Vern slapped a hand on the counter and leaned toward Pork Chop. "There ain't a damn thing wrong with that chili, and you know it. I had me a bowl earlier, and it tastes fine, like it always tastes."

Pork Chop was too busy guzzling beer to respond.

Shaking his head, Vern untied the half apron he'd been wearing and tossed it behind the counter. "I swear, man, you 'bout as dumb-ass as dumb-ass gets." He rounded the counter and motioned to Cherokee. "Bar's all yours, buddy. Keep dumb-ass there out from behind here while I'm gone, okay? I should be back by suppertime."

"No problem," Cherokee said, and got to his feet.

Pork Chop slammed his beer can down on the bar. "Hey, where you get off callin' me a dumb-ass? I'm a payin' customer."

Vern stopped in midstride and eyed him. "My bar, my business. 'Sides, you got a tab bigger'n my house mortgage. When you pay it, then you get to be a customer. Till then, you a dumb-ass." With that, he stormed off toward the swinging doors.

Feeling a sudden, unexplainable arc of panic when Poochie saw Vern heading out of the bar, she trailed after him on her scooter. "Hol' up. Why you still going out dere? Beeno said dey checked everywhere already."

"In case they missed somethin'," Vern said, then with a wave of his hand, disappeared beyond the doors.

As Poochie watched the doors wobble to a close, a picture abruptly filled her mind's eye. It made her shudder, stole her breath. She whirled her scooter about. "Pork Chop, you need to come and take me over to my house right now."

Pork Chop cocked his head, gave her a you've-got-to-be-kidding look. "What I look like to you, a taxi?"

"What's wrong, Poochie?" Cherokee asked, having already taken his place behind the bar.

"Don't know yet." She zipped her scooter over to Pork Chop and slammed a fist down on his left knee. "I said you gonna take me to my house, and you gonna take me right now!"

Pork Chop yelped, cupped his knee with a hand. "What the hell—"

"I said now!" Poochie hammered the hand braced over his knee.

"Stop, goddamnit!" It took a few more knee hammers before Pork Chop finally gave up and did as he was told.

Ten minutes later, when Poochie was finally sitting shotgun in Pork Chop's old black pickup and they were barreling down the highway toward Angelle and Trevor's, she crossed her fingers and said a silent, persistent prayer.

Please, God, let dem be dere . . . please let dem be dere . . . please let dem be dere. Please . . .

After what seemed like days, Pork Chop finally pulled into the driveway behind Trevor's truck. Poochie didn't wait for him to help her out of the pickup. As soon as Pork Chop pulled to a stop, she flung the door open, crawfished her way out of the truck, then pulled out her walker and headed for the prayer tree in the backyard—where she felt called. Where she hoped *not* to verify the picture she'd seen in her head.

As Poochie hobbled around the house, she heard Pork Chop yell after her. She ignored him, the same prayer playing over and over in her mind . . . *Please, God, let dem be dere. . . .*

When she finally reached the prayer tree and rounded it to the bench where she normally sat, a little gasp escaped her.

There it was, just as she'd seen in her mind's eye back at the bar—an empty spot on the prayer tree—where the pink sneakers had been—the ones that belonged to Sarah Woodard. Gone . . . they were gone.

And, *oh, God*, if the dead had come back for their shoes that had hung on the purgatory side of the tree—did missing shoes on the other side mean the living were now dead?

CHAPTER TWENTY-THREE

Olm stood in front of his bathroom mirror and slowly unbuttoned his shirt. The idea for what he was about to do had come to him only moments ago. Another brilliant idea that had seemingly come out of nowhere, only proving once again that he was being led down the path to rebirth. He planned to execute the idea to the letter and make it as ceremonious as the sacrifice that would be offered tonight.

As he moved from button to button, Olm thought of his ancestors. Their skin had been such a luxurious brown, much darker than his own. He pictured their long black hair, some with lengths that reached the middle of their back. Unfortunately, his hair was collar-length and cropped close to the ears. He didn't have time to grow it out.

However, he could rid himself of something his forefathers hadn't possessed. Chest hair. Although his was sparse and only traveled from nipple to nipple and down the center of his belly, Olm felt it was a barrier between him and the great warriors in his linage. He didn't want anything to hinder what the great Tirawa might send his way.

DEBORAH LeBLANC

Once his shirt was completely unbuttoned, Olm shrugged it off his shoulders and hung it neatly on the hook behind the bathroom door. Then he took a bar of soap that sat at the corner of the sink, turned on the faucet, wet the soap, and began to lather his chest.

He grimaced as his fingers moved over his left breast and the bruise that sat just below his left nipple, where he'd been bitten. Another bruise, this one the size of a baseball, marked the upper part of his right arm. The surprise attack in the truck, the bites and bruises, were a small price to pay. A man headed for greatness should be willing to give his all, no matter what. And he was willing. He would gladly have offered his entire right arm if it had been required of him. Bruises were nothing, almost shamefully insignificant for what he would soon be given. By ten o'clock tonight, he would possess power not yet experienced by any other man on earth.

With his chest now completely lathered, Olm rinsed his hands, grabbed a disposable razor, and held it poised at his chest.

"You have done well," he murmured. "You have performed better than expected, holding patient, determined. It's no wonder you were favored and chosen."

With that, Olm ran the razor down the center of his chest. When he reached his navel, he rinsed the hair and soap off the blade, then aimed for another strip of hair.

"Did you see, Tirawa? Did you see the fear in the children's eyes when I was last with them?" Olm

178

spoke softly, as if the great deity were sitting behind him on the toilet, listening. "Even without the help of all the great leaders that came before me, I was able to build an altar of terror for you in these children such as you've never seen. If this is indeed what feeds you, Great God of the Universe, Creator, Leader of the Morning and Evening star, then certainly you must already be pleased with my efforts. Certainly you find me worthy."

With half of his chest free of hair, Olm stood a moment and contemplated what the great deity might look like. Did Tirawa possess the eyes of a wolf, cunning, sharp, ever seeing? Did he have the ears of a fox, so keen they could pick up the sound of a feather floating its way to the ground? Were his limbs like that of the bear, massive, destructive, and powerful? And did he boast the wings of an eagle, able to soar up into the heavens, then swoop down on his prey?

It excited him to think that Tirawa might grace him with a physical presence, appear before him to personally place upon his shoulders the mantle of supreme power. An extra reward for all the work he'd done over the last few days, all of it geared toward this purpose. There was no way Tirawa could turn his back on him now, not when he'd exemplified such devotion and meticulous work. In fact, was it not Tirawa's hand that had stayed his own from ending the lives of the children too early? Before the apex of the full moon? In his exuberance and enthusiasm, he'd almost been swept away, bringing about their deaths far too soon.

Another swipe of the razor—more hair gone—another rinse of the blade—another run, this one the last one, from nipple to nipple.

Smoothing a hand over his chest, Olm smiled at the slick, hairless feel of his body. In the mirror, he no longer saw the face of an average man. The Olm before him had a strong jaw, prominent brow. He envisioned himself standing around a campfire in full, brilliant headdress, felt the heat of a fire against his skin, heard the first beat of a ceremonial drum.

Olm dropped the razor and lifted his arms up high, his feet already beginning a steady *thump, thump, thump—thump* in time with the drums. Then, in the distance, like a cloud of smoke suddenly forced his way by a mighty wind, he heard the cry of a thousand men, medicine men, warriors, priests. They whooped and clicked their tongues, proclaiming in unison the start of the Spirit Dance.

"Hey-nah-hahna-hey-nah-hey. Untah-atah-atah-a. Oonah -untah-hey-nah-hey. Hey-nah-hey. Hey-nah-hey."

The chanting grew louder, louder still, and soon Olm was prancing in place in front of the sink. Back and forth, in a circle, watching his chest slick with water as he moved in and out of view in the mirror. The roar of the fire he'd imagined seemed to be roaring in his blood now, boiling it, infusing it with adrenaline. He felt weightless as his feet pounded the floor in rhythm to the chant.

"Hey-nah-hahna-hey-nah-hey. Untah-atah-atah-a. Oonah -untah-hey-nah-hey. Hey-nah-hey. Hey-nah-hey."

Olm wanted to *feel* the chant, wanted to feel the drums in his soul. Wanted to *be* the beat. Wanted to be one with Tirawa so his own spirit would dance the Spirit Dance on the floors of heaven. Wanted to see the great Tirawa, touch the headdress of the mighty warrior.

Oh, yes, what he planned to offer this very night would be the greatest sacrifice of all time, in all the history of his people. For generations to come, the name Olm would be remembered, revered. *He* would be known as the Great Warrior, the mortal man who'd touched the priestly dress of the mighty Tirawa. His name would be synonymous with that of Tirawa, for he would be considered mighty, too.

So much to do, so much. He wanted to make sure that the climax of the sacrifice tonight would be the greatest tribute that Tirawa had ever known.

He'd pour mud over the boy first . . . slowly, slowly, heightening his terror . . .

. . . and force the girl to watch . . .

Mud rising up over the boy's bottom lip . . .

. . . rising up to his nostrils . . .

Then past his nostrils, just far enough so even if the boy tilted his head back, he'd find no air.

He'd do the same with the girl next. And neither child would have the leverage to lift their bodies above that fraction of an inch that would give them life . . .

Both would struggle and fight for air . . .

. . . sludge filling their lungs. The mud—the merging of water and land that had once been owned by his people.

Once that part of the ceremony was over and their spirits had been released, Olm planned to remove the children from their holes. First the girl, then the boy—he'd lift each slowly from the mire, lay them on dry ground, then rinse their bodies with clear water. Then, with the skill of a surgeon, he would cut open their chests and remove their hearts. Even now he could feel them in his hands, each still warm and slick with blood, so perfect. So ready.

He'd lift his hands up high, revealing the hearts to the million stars above, making all of them a witness. Then he'd carry the hearts over to the wooden mantle he'd have waiting and place them side by side atop it. When that was done, he'd begin the Spirit Dance, offering the hearts to the Morning and Evening stars—to the face of Tirawa, which came by way of Brother Moon. Soon afterward, those two powerful sacrifices would be set ablaze in a sacrificial fire, in the same sacrificial circle where he'd offered his father's body. As they burned, he would sing praises to Tirawa. Yes—oh, yes—all of it done at the apex of Brother Moon's fullness.

With sweat running down the sides of this face, his shoulders, and the small of his back, his chest glistening, Olm forced his mind to quiet, forced the rush of adrenaline to calm.

Calm . . . quiet . . . shhhh . . . soon . . . very soon . . .

Slowly, the weight of his body returned to him. His feet slowed, slowed, then finally stopped their steady pounding. He took a long, deep breath, held it, and lifted his chin and looked in the mirror. He saw the eyes of a great warrior staring back at him and nodded an acknowledgment. This was to be his transformation—this the man he would become by the end of tonight.

Satisfied, Olm released his breath, reached for a towel, and wiped down his chest, his arms, his face. Once dried, he folded the towel and placed it neatly on the side of the sink, then headed out of the bathroom.

So much left to be done . . . so much . . . and time was running short.

CHAPTER TWENTY-FOUR

We drove along in silence, each lost in thought. Angelle watching the road, me peering through the side passenger window not seeing any of the landscape.

It hadn't taken much to convince my sister to bring me to the Unified Kingdom of Christ Church. All we'd had on our hands that morning was time, anyway. At least until Trevor left for work and we were able to commandeer his boat. I figured it was just as good a time as any to see Woodard. Maybe he'd have some answers, some spiritual insight into everything that had been going on around here. Not that I was particularly interested in religious hoohah.

In truth, I was probably more curious about him than anything, wanting to meet Sarah's uncle, see for myself if the man was just zealous in his faith or nuts, as Poochie claimed. I truly hoped it was the former. Even in the throes of fervor, he might still be able to shed some light on things, and since Angelle had already confided in him about the touching incidents, he could very well become an ally to some degree. Either way, I didn't want to discount the possibility of his help, even if we had to be cautious about the kind of help he might offer. I doubted seriously I'd reveal my secret to him the way I'd done with Poochie, but if Angelle had trusted him enough to tell him hers, then I figured he couldn't be all bad.

A small brick building suddenly loomed in my line of sight. We were already in the church parking lot, which was empty save for an old pickup parked under an oak a couple hundred feet away. Angelle pulled the car up close to the building and cut the engine.

"It's bigger inside than it looks out here," Angelle said, as though having to excuse the church's meager structure.

We got out of the car, and as I scoped out the surroundings a wet, warm breeze touched my face. I shivered, even though it was far from cold. I wasn't used to the humidity . . . hell, I wasn't used to a lot of things around here . . . the accents, the food, most of all the weirdness.

The church looked a little like a drugstore, only smaller. Redbrick—glass front doors, and instead of a steeple it had a high-pitched roof. The sign on the front lawn that read THE UNIFIED KINGDOM OF CHRIST CHURCH was probably the only thing that kept visitors from stopping in, thinking they'd find tampons and nasal spray inside. Behind the church stood a small brown clapboard, which I suspected was the preacher's house.

"Over here," Angelle said, then led me to a side door near the back of the building.

We walked into a short nondescript hallway that smelled of cinnamon, fresh-brewed coffee, and something musty that made me want to sneeze.

Halfway down the hall, Angelle motioned to a door on the left. It held a narrow gold placard that read OFFICE. "Here," she whispered, then knocked on the door.

"Come!" someone called out from inside. Whoever it was made it sound as if they were granting lowly peasants entrance into a royal chamber.

Royal chamber indeed. The room was only twelve by fourteen and held a small metal desk, two ladder-back wooden chairs, and a framed picture of the church on the right wall. Below the picture was a corkboard with blue letters near the top that read SAINTED SOULS OF UKCC, and beneath the title were numerous Polaroids of men and women of various ages. Behind the desk sat a man I assumed to be the preacher. He looked like the Pillsbury Doughboy with a bad comb-over. His gray suit was ill-fitting, and his emerald-green tie did nothing to help the ensemble.

We walked into the office, and the preacher leaned back in his chair and grinned. Crooked teeth—thin lips—eyes the color of dirt.

"Sistah Angelle!" he said. "How *good* to see you. Glory to Gawd, you're lookin' well today."

Angelle smiled. "Pastor Woodard, this is my sister, Dunny. Dunny, Pastor Rusty Woodard, Sarah's uncle."

I walked over to the desk and offered him my hand. "Pleased to meet you."

He grabbed my hand and held on to it with both of his. I felt trapped and immediately wanted to yank out of his grasp. Something about his greasy smile already had me doubting Angelle's trust in the man.

"So pleased to meet *you!* Sistah Angelle has told

me so *much* about you. I'm so *glad* you've come to visit us in our little town of Bayou Crow. You'll find our *congregation* and our *people* some of the best in this state." He looked down at the glove on my left hand. "It's awfully warm for those gloves, don't you think, sistah?"

"Well . . ." I pulled my hand out from between his. "I—"

"Oh, I do apologize for using such familiarity. You see, here at the Unified Kingdom of Christ, we believe we are *allll* the brothahs and sistahs of the Lawd, and I have a tendency to gather in whatever part of the flock comes to my door. You do *believe* in the Lawd, now, don't ya, Sistah Dunny? I'm sure being a relative here of Sistah Angelle that you must be close to the Lawd."

I glanced over at my sister and arched a brow. Looking back at Woodard, I said, "Well, yeah, I believe in God—"

"Halleluiah! Thank ya, *Jeee*-sus! As usual, the *good* fruit doesn't fall very far from the tree. You don't mind me callin' ya Sistah Dunny, now, do ya? Especially considerin' that you are indeed in the *family* of Gawd."

I had to work hard not to snicker. He sounded like a radio evangelist who was only seconds away from asking some new church member for his weekly tithe. "Feel free to call me whatever you'd like."

"*Thank* ya, *Jeee*-sus. *Thank* ya, Lawd. Now, then, tell me, sistah, what is it with your gloves?" His grin broadened. "Sistah Angelle doesn't have you pullin' weeds out in her garden while you're here visitin', does she?"

"No,"Angelle said, quickly jumping in. "Dunny has a condition with her hands. The gloves protect her skin from the sun. She can't have them in bright sunlight, things like that."

I smiled and nodded to confirm Angelle's lie. Such a natural thing to do . . . smile. Nod. Agree. Hide. Anything but let people know what was hidden in my left glove . . . what was hidden inside me.

"Ho! Hallelujah, I do understand. You know Sistah Gloria, don't ya, Sistah Angelle? The one who comes out here every Sat'dy night? I'm sure you've seen her here. Well, she wears gloves on her hands, too, but they're the lacy kind. Poor thing, bless her heart, she got the dermatitis so severe that any kind of sunlight exposure just makes her blister all up. We're *prayin'* for a healin'. We *believe* the Lawd will bring about a healin' that will set her *free* from that terrible affliction. If ya'd like, Sistah Dunny, while you're here in town, come on to one of our prayer meetin's, and we'll put you down in a prayer circle, call the *glory* of Gawd down on ya, ask the Lawd to heal ya, take your affliction from ya."

I stood there, blinked, a bit stunned from his barrage of words. Woodard pressed his palms on the top of his desk and stared at me, obviously expecting a response to his oh so generous offer.

"Um . . . thank you for the invitaton," I said. "But I . . . I don't think I'm going to be in town for very long."

"Of course we're hoping she changes her mind and stays much longer," Angelle chimed in.

I shot her a look. Was she *trying* to get me stuck in one of Woodard's prayer meetings? As soon as I saw the expression on her face I felt ashamed of myself. She looked sad and lonely, with only the smallest spark of hope still in her eyes. It felt backward to me. I thought I was supposed to be the lonely one, feeding stray dogs apple fritters and beef stew, all that old spinster shit. It was then I realized the preacher had addressed me again—twice.

"What?"

"I was sayin' that I'm sure you'll agree to allow your sistah here to sit in proxy for you. You would, wouldn't ya, Sistah Angelle? Sit in proxy for your sistah so the Lawd will heal her condition?"

Angelle frowned slightly. "Of course . . . I mean, I guess so. I—"

"Halleluiah! *Thank* ya, *Jeee*-sus. Now please, both of you ladies sit down and rest yourselves a spell. . . ." Woodard pointed to the ladder-back chairs across from him.

Although I would have preferred getting run over by a Mack truck, I sat in one of the chairs, then grabbed Angelle's arm and pulled her down to the one beside me.

"Can I get ya'll coffee or juice, sistahs? We have some wonderful, wonderful cinnamon rolls, too, that Sistah Betty brought in this morning. In fact, I was just gonna heat one up for myself in the microwave out in the kitchen. Would y'all like one?"

"No, thank you," I said. I glanced over at Angelle, who was shaking her head. When she looked at me, I gave her a quick eye roll to say, *Does this guy ever shut up?* Her lips tightened slightly, which in sister-speak meant, "Chill!" We both turned to face the preacher.

He jittered in his seat like an engine about to rocket off a launchpad. "Sistah Angelle, I know it's been some time since you and I have had a chance to talk, but tell me, how is your . . . um . . . er—umm . . ." He glanced at me, then did a slow rolling glance back to Angelle. "Your *condition*? If I'm remembering correctly, the last time we talked things had not been completely resolved. I know we prayed for ya, prayed for your deliverance and healin'. Unfortunately, things went bad with my niece shortly after, and we didn't have a chance to follow up. Sad to say, sometimes things like that do come up just to hinder the Lawd's work."

I knew he was referring to the touching incidents that Angelle had told me about, and I inwardly cringed for my sister. I felt embarrassment bouncing off her beside me. In that moment, any thoughts I'd had about this man possibly helping us flew out the window. He was too crass and obnoxious to be worth a shit. The only benefit he could possibly provide was maybe more information on Sarah.

Angelle cleared her throat. "No, Pastor Woodard. There haven't been any more reoccurrences of that since Dunny's been here."

The man threw his hands up over his head, fingers spread wide. "*Hallelujah*, praise *Jeee*-sus. We have a healing to confess! The Lawd sent an *angel* by way of your sistah. It comes from the presence and power of the blood of the Lamb that sits in your family, comin' all the way from your grandparents, your parents, and the love the two of ya share. That love broke the spell cast by that evil spirit and sent 'im back to the pits of hell where he belongs."

"So you think what happened to Angelle was caused by a spirit?"

"Yes, sistah, I most certainly do, praise Jeee-sus."

"How can you be sure that's what it is? I mean, Angelle didn't see or hear anything. Has it happened to anyone else in town that you know of? How can you—"

Woodard held out a hand as though he meant to stop traffic. "Just look at the *evidence*, sistah. Just look at the evidence. The spirit of the Lawd is a good and *healing* spirit. Demons only come to confuse and *destroy* those of us who are true believers. They aim to take us down to the fiery pit with 'em."

"Yeah, okay, but did you consider anything like psychological trauma? I mean, my sister was really affected by the fact that your niece and that little boy disappeared. They were in her class. Don't you think that could have something to do with it?" I peered over at Angelle. She was staring at her hands, obviously not liking the bend in the conversation. I turned back to the preacher. "Do you have any training at all in psychological matters? Do you have a Ph.D.?"

He let out a throaty chuckle. "Oh, Sistah Dunny, the wonderful thing about servin' the Lawd is that He provides His shepards with *alll* the degrees they need to take care of His flock. Your sistah didn't suffer from any psychological issues. It was the *deee*-mon that went after her—"

"Pastor Woodard, I—" Angelle began, but Woodard was too cranked up to be stopped now.

"—such a *good* woman. Such a *pure* woman. Such a bighearted and *givin'* woman. Why, it's no wonder the demons wanted her. They wanted to take away that innocence."

I realized I'd jumped onto a merry-go-round I had no business riding on. The guy was definitely a Froot Loop. I'd have to grab Angelle later and whack some sense into her for ever getting involved with the guy. However, judging by her increased squirming, I figured she was already kicking herself in the ass—and wishing she could kick his.

CHAPTER TWENTY-FIVE

"I'm sorry to hear about your niece . . . Reverend," I said, intentionally changing the subject. "I'm sure her disappearance has been very difficult for you."

For the first time since we'd arrived, the man held silent. He nodded slightly and lowered his head. When he looked back up at us, a tear ran down his right cheek. "It's been one of the most challenging things I've come upon in this lifetime, Sistah Dunny. I'm tellin' ya, I'm in my prayer closet almost twenty-four hours a day, prayin' for that child's soul."

"Has anyone come up with any leads on either of them?" Angelle asked.

"The only evidence found for either of them was that young man's bike. It was parked on the side of the levee. I just feel in my *spirit* that since those children went missing together, they were *together* when they were abducted."

"Who's searching for them now?" I asked. "I haven't seen a lot of activity going on around town, not like search parties or anything."

"I don't know who's searchin', but I'll tell ya how I see it, sistah, the way I *believe*. If it's the Lawd's will to bring her back, then the Lawd will bring her back.

There are times in life when we've got to stand tall, no matter the tender age, and take Gawd's punishment as it comes. I believe this is her *punishment* for being with that young man. Heaven help us, glory. *Glory* be to Jeee-sus. Yes, Lawd. If those two children were involved in any kind of *sin* of the flesh, then Gawd will dispense His *punishment* as He so sees fit. It's not my business to step in the path of the Lawd. If they are dealt *punishment* for sins of the *flesh*, so shall it be His will. If they are innocent they will be brought *back* to the fold."

I gaped, unable to believe what I'd just heard. "Wait . . . wait just a minute. Are you saying you haven't been out searching for your niece because you think she was . . . what? Messing around with that little boy?"

He lifted his chin. "I'm sayin' it's all in Gawd's hands, sistah. What better *warrior*, what better *police officer*, what better judge of sinner and saint than Gawd Himself?"

"Whoa," Angelle said, sitting ramrod straight in her chair. "Straight out, Preacher—are you saying you think there was something going on between Nicky and Sarah, and that's why they're missing? Because God wanted to punish them for being together? You actually think that's why they're missing?"

"That's it exactly, Sistah Angelle. That's what I'm saying. The Lawd will punish without favor. No matter if she is the niece of one of his *shepherds*, He punishes without favor."

"That's a crock of shit!" Angelle jumped to her feet, her chair rocking back, nearly tipping over.

Woodard gasped so loud, had the window been open, people from the next parish would probably have heard him. "Sistah Angelle! I can tell by the *filth* comin' out of your mouth that the demon who defiled you previously is still *present*. We will pray, sistah. We will pray for your *deliverance* from this demon, pray for the town's deliverance, for it runs amuck with the devil's own. There's evidence of it everywhere! *Everywhere!* Even in this church." Breathing hard from his fervor, he leaned over as if to relay confidential information. "Why, early this morning I found where someone had actually *ur-in-a-ted* on the foot of the pulpit! Can you believe the blasphemy? Can you *believe* it? Even worse, glory to Gawd, they'd stuck a knife, a knife mind you, plunged it right in the middle of the cross on the altar. Blasphemy, I tell ya! A demon from hell was trying to stab the very heart of *Gawd*. Let's pray, sistahs. Let us pray for the *deliverance* of Sistah Angelle and the *deliverance* of this town!"

"You're the one needin' the prayers, Preacher," Angelle said. "I've had enough of this bullshit." She signaled to me that it was time to go.

Way past time, I thought, gladly getting to my feet. Just as we turned to leave, a policeman walked into the office, almost colliding with Angelle. He maneuvered around her without bothering to excuse himself and walked up to the preacher.

Angelle signaled for me to follow again, and I mouthed, "Wait up." I recognized the cop from the Bloody Bucket. The metal name tag over his left breast pocket read Officer Leger, but I remembered Poochie calling him Beeno. I wanted to hear what he had to say. If there was anything he'd found out about the kids.

This time Woodard got to his feet. "Officer Leger, thank you so very much for coming to our aid. It's always a pleasure to see you and know—"

"What's been going on in here, Woodard?" Beeno said. "I heard you yelling all the way out in the parking lot."

"Officer Leger, I was just . . . I was just commenting on the attributes of Gawd. As a preacher, as a *shepard* of his flock, I have a tendency to get a little carried away in my zeal, as you well know."

Beeno drummed an impatient beat on his right leg with his fingers. Something about the cop's attitude, the way he held himself, the condescending look in his eye, urked me. Cocky. Full of himself, like a Chihuahua that thought it was ten feet tall and bulletproof. "Yeah, yeah, I know, carried away. Look, I've got a lot of irons in the fire and don't have time for one of your sermons. Just cut to the chase and tell me what you called in about earlier."

"Ab-so-*lutely*, brotha . . . oh, I mean, *Officer* Leger." Woodard hurried around the desk and motioned Beeno to follow as he headed out of the office. He took quick, tiny steps, almost as if he was running on tiptoe.

Beeno let out a frustrated breath and followed him.

I immediately started after them, and Angelle grabbed my arm, yanking me to a stop. "Let's get the hell out of here, Dunny. I can't believe what that son of a bitch said about Sarah." Her face was red with anger. "I don't want to be anywhere near that guy or this so-called church. Not now, not ever again. If I'd known he was anything like that, I'd never have come to see him in the first place."

I put my hand on her shoulder. "Don't beat yourself up about it. Sometimes it takes a while for shit to float to the surface. Hang on a sec, though. I want to take a peek at what's going on. Asshole or not, he is Sarah's uncle. Maybe there's something going on that could give us a heads-up before we hit the swamp, you know?"

"Then you go. I can't stomach being around that bastard another second. I'm going to go sit in the car." With that, Angelle turned on her heel, left the office, and stormed down the hall toward the exit.

I watched her leave, then hurried down the hall in the opposite direction, where I'd seen Beeno and Woodard head. The preacher's constant chatter made finding them easy, and I was soon peeking around a doorway into the belly of the church. Woodard was pointing to a dark circle on the floor next to a lecturn.

"This is the first of the sacrilegious acts I found this morning, Officer Leger. Imagine it, someone standing right here, ur-un-a-ting in the house of the Lawd! Can you believe it?"

"How do you know it's piss?" Beeno asked.

Woodard's double blink was obvious even from where I stood. "I would ask you, Officer, to please use the appropriate terminology in the house of Gawd. Such crass language is quite offensive to the ear."

Beeno, who was standing with his back to me, shifted his weight. The body language equivalent to an eye roll. "Fine, Woodard. How do you know that it's *urine* on the floor?"

"Why, from the smell."

"I don't smell anything."

"You've got to get up close, brothah . . . I mean, Officer Leger. You've got to get up close."

"You mean to tell me you stuck your nose down in it?"

"Now, Officer, how else would I be able to figure out what some heathen put around this lectern?"

"Well, you either smelled it or you stuck your fingers in it, then stuck your fingers in your mouth. That's what I'm thinking, anyway."

I put a hand over my mouth to keep my laugh in check.

"No, sir, no, sir. It was the smell, I'm tellin' ya."

"Fine." Beeno walked over to a wooden cross that hung on a backdrop behind the altar. There was a red-handled knife stuck in the center of the cross. After pulling a handkerchief out of his back pocket, Beeno used the cloth to work the knife out of the wood. Once it was freed, he held it up and examined it with what seemed like avid appreciation. "A Koji . . . Man, I haven't seen one of these in years. I don't know anybody around here who's got one like this."

I'd never heard the term Koji before, so I assumed he was referring to a brand name. To me, the knife looked like an exclamation point with a blade stuck on the end of it.

Beeno shook the knife in Woodard's direction. "I'll find out more from this knife than I will that piss . . . I mean that *urr*-ine. So you can go ahead and clean up around your lectern. I'll take the knife with me and see if I can come up with anything."

"Sure, Officer, whatever you need. You do your work for the good state of Louisiana, and I do my work for the good Lawd."

Beeno shifted his weight again. "Yeah, okay . . . look, did you hear any strange noises out here last night? Maybe real early this morning? Dogs barking all of a sudden, anything at all? What about strangers walking around the church parking lot or around your house out back? See anything like that at all?"

"Not a soul save for the *precious* lambs from the Lawd's flock."

Beeno blew out another exasperated breath. "Fine. I'll get in touch with you if I come up with anything." With that, he turned, so quickly I couldn't duck out of sight fast enough for him not to see me. He paused for a half beat when he spotted me watching them, then headed for the front doors of the church without saying a word.

I stood dumbstruck, watching him retreat, back military-straight. His investigation had to have been the oddest in police procedural history.

"If you will excuse me, Sistah Dunny." Woodard's voice was too close to my ear. I turned, nearly bumping into him. I hadn't even seen him walk my way. He put a hand on my back, as if to encourage me out of the building. "This way, sistah."

I was more than happy to oblige.

As Woodard led me outside, he babbled on and on about the *Lawd*. To my surprise, he followed me all the way to the parking lot. Pesticide probably couldn't get rid of this guy. I'd had enough of him, wished him away, wished I hadn't hung around just to see some stupid knife stuck in a cross and piss on the church floor.

He stayed by my side as I approached Angelle's car. I saw my sister sitting in the driver's seat, watching as I approached. Her face darkened when she saw Woodard. If her anger was any greater, she'd be spitting fire and brimstone all over the preacher's ass.

Woodard continued to ramble, but my attention was drawn to Dale's Trading Post a couple of blocks away and the tall man walking out of it, carrying a grocery sack. There was no mistaking the black Stetson and long black coat. Although he walked alone, it was as if someone had nudged him to let him know I was watching because he stopped, turned, looked my way, and nodded a greeting.

". . . and the Law will provide to those who . . ."

I offered Cherokee a quick nod in return, and for some odd reason, suddenly became aware of how dressed-down I was in jeans and a T-shirt. What did it matter what I was wearing? He'd seen my hand. In fact, I could still remember the strange comment he'd made as he passed me . . . "I'd be careful with that if I were you." Even stranger was that he hadn't stopped to ask a single question, never followed me to find out what the finger was about or what I was doing out by the bayou. The warning he'd given me had been more matter-of-fact than ominous. Like someone saying, "If you aren't careful playing with that fire, you might get burned." What a strange man . . .

". . . power of the *blood* of the *lamb* . . ."

I heard the engine to Angelle's car roar to life, so I hurried to the passenger door. The look she shot Woodard's way could have peeled varnish off a roomful of furniture.

"—and again, sistah, you're welcome to our humble church any time during your visit here in Bayou Crow. Now if you will please excuse me, I must take leave and ready myself for tonight's service. Our little congregation is at this very moment preparing for a series of services. *Deliverance* services to cast out the demons that might have infiltrated our little Sarah's soul. Should she be returned to us by the grace of Gawd, we need time to be spiritually *prepared* for those deliverance services. The demons are always at the ready to attack, and if they've gotten their hands on her, things will only get worse. This is urgent business, sistah, urgent. But, oh, what a friend we have in *Jeee*-sus! *Thank* you, Lawd! Praise you, *Jee*-sus." With one hand held skyward, Woodard turned and headed back for the church, all the while waving and shouting about the glory of *Gawd*.

Without a doubt, Poochie had been right. The man was a cuckoo—fruitcake—a serious lost cause. And there was little question that if Sarah was found and returned to that man, she'd need a series of services—psychiatric services.

CHAPTER TWENTY-SIX

As far as I was concerned faith and Woodard's Gawd were the only things that kept us from careening off the highway into the bayou. Angelle was so infuriated with the preacher when we left the church, she took a left out of the parking lot when she should have taken a right, and we wound up ten miles out of Bayou Crow before either of us realized it. She was still cursing a blue streak by the time we finally reached home.

"I swear to God, could I be any goddamn dumber?" Angelle fumed as she stormed up to the house, me at her heels.

"Stop being so hard on yourself. You were going through a tough time. Hell, you still are. I should never have asked you to bring me there. I'm sorry."

"There's nothing for you to be sorry about, Dunny. That fucker should be sorry." We'd reached the front door by this time, and Angelle grabbed the knob, turned it, and kicked the door open. "Goddamn, I still can't believe I ever asked that low-life son of a bitch for help!"

Poochie was sitting on the couch when Angelle burst into the living room, and she gasped in surprise.

"Lord of Mary, what's de matter? You scared me so bad my heart almost bus' out my ches'. Which sumabitch you talking about?"

"Sorry, Pooch, didn't mean to scare you," Angelle said, closing the door with a lot less force than she'd used to open it.

"So, what sumabitch?"

I started to say, "That wacko preacher," but Angelle beat me to the punch.

"Woodard," she said. "You should've heard what that bastard said about those kids. About his own niece, for heaven's sake! He was talking about that sweet little girl like she was some kind of prostitute or something."

Poochie's mouth fell open. "He called his niece a pew-tan?"

Angelle gave her a puzzled look. "I said he talked about her like she was a prostitute. Not a . . . whatever you said."

"Pew-tan, dat's de same thing as a ho. I can't believe he called his own blood dat. He said dat? She was a ho?"

"Yeah!" Angelle said.

"To be fair, Woodard didn't exactly use the word *whore* when he talked about Sarah," I said. "But he just as soon have."

"You've got that right," Angelle agreed.

"I tol' y'all he was cuckoo, didn't I say dat?" Poochie looked over at me. "I said dat, huh?"

"Yep, you were right, crazy," I said. "He ranted and raved so much he could've held church right there in the parking lot." I shook my head. "And he thinks demons took over the town because Sarah was messing around with Nicky. How crazy and pathetic is that?"

Poochie tsked. "Bad."

Angelle tossed her car keys on the coffee table. "He's the demon if you ask me. I swear if that man is treating his niece that way, he should be brought up on charges. Child neglect or child endangerment, something. Whatever they can stick on him for screwing up that poor kid." She cocked her head suddenly, and it was then I noticed all the shoes on and around Poochie's lap. "What are you doing with all those tennis shoes, Poochie? Aren't those my Skechers?"

"Yeah, dem's you shoes. Y'all come over here and grab each of y'all a pair. We gotta go do—"

"Wait a minute," I said, something else suddenly occurring to me. "What are you doing here, Poochie? Aren't you supposed to be at the Bucket?"

Angelle's head snapped back in surprise. "Yeah . . . we were supposed to pick you up at . . . How did you get here?"

"Pork Chop. I had him bring me back to de house."

"You did *not* have that alcoholic drive you over here!" Angelle said incredulously.

Poochie batted the air with a hand. "Aw, de man wasn't too poo-yiied when he drove me out here. He made de truck go pretty straight."

"Damn, Poochie," Angelle said. "Like we don't have enough stuff—"

"Look, y'all need to stop running off at de mout' and listen to what I gotta say. Y'all come see. I wanna show y'all something."

Knowing we were probably going to be racing along the same old track until we did as she asked, I stepped over to Poochie. Angelle followed reluctantly.

"What?" Angelle asked, frowning.

With her lips folded in tight over toothless gums, Poochie handed me a pair of sneakers that looked very much like the Jordans I'd packed in my carry-on bag, only the laces were knotted together. She gave Angelle the Skechers along with a pair of large, dirty black tennis shoes, both pairs with knotted laces.

"Okay," Poochie said, "here's what y'all gotta do, and y'all gotta go fas' about dis business. Bring dem shoes outside and put dem up in my prayer tree. I can throw dat myself, but I can't throw too good. We gotta get de shoes all de way to de top in de branches. Dat's where dey need to go."

Angelle's shoulders slumped. "Just put the shoes back in the closet, Poochie. We don't have time for this."

I saw steam building in Poochie's eyes and decided to jump in before she exploded. "Why do you want us to put the shoes up there?"

"Dunny . . ." Angelle snapped a hard look my way.

Taking advantage of the opening and opportunity to make her point, Poochie said, 'Cause I said to, dat's why. We gonna need it." She handed me a pair of faded, open-back house slippers. A hole had been bored through the side of each, and a piece of twine bound them together. "Here, take dese, too. Dat's mine. Now I need for you to throw dis one all de way to de tippy-top of de tree if you can. *All* de way to de tippy-top, you understand?"

Angelle held out the black sneakers. "If Trevor sees how you've screwed up his shoes, he's going to have a fit."

"Trevor don't need to know nothin' dat Trevor don't need to know. And he's not here anyways."

Angelle glanced at her watch. "It's not even one o'clock. His shift isn't until three. Where'd he go?"

Poochie shrugged. "He said he was gonna pick up Allen, de man he was workin' wit' tonight, and dey was goin' to check traps before work. Said he was gonna come back here before his shift and drop off de boat. He didn't say, but I bet he's bringing de boat back because de big boss over to de plant tol' him he couldn't bring Bullet back dere no more."

Slightly confused, mostly because of her accent, I asked, "So, *is* he bringing the boat back here?"

"Dat's what he said. But you know how dem men are. Sometimes dey say one thing and do something else. So in case he don't come back, I already got us another plan."

"A plan for what?" Angelle asked.

"Listen up, and you gonna see. Now, de first thing we gotta do is pack us some stuff that we gonna need out dere in de swamp. You know, a flashlight, some rope, a knife in case we got to cut something. When we get de boat, I'm gonna ride in de middle, and, Angelle, you gonna drive de boat. Dunny, her, she's gonna sit up to de front and hold de flashlight so—"

"Whoa, whoa, whoa!" Angelle said. "What are you talking about? Poochie, you aren't coming with us."

"Oh yeah, I'm comin'. If you think you gonna leave me here while y'all two go get youselves killed

206

out in de bayou, you cuckoo. We got to go together to find dem babies, and we gotta go fas'. Dat's why I came back here from de Bucket. When I was over dere I saw me a picture of de prayer tree in my head, so I made Pork Chop hurry me back here to see if de picture was true. And it was true. I come back here to look and sure 'nough, just like de picture. Dat little girl's shoes was gone. Gone out de prayer tree."

"You mean, Sarah Woodard's shoes?" I asked.

Poochie nodded. "Yeah, de little pink ones dat was up dere. Dey missin' just like some of de shoes on de purgatory side of de tree is missin'. I'm scared for dat little girl bad. Somethin' in my belly is sayin' if her shoes is gone, maybe her life is gone, too, you know?"

Something about the conviction in Poochie's eyes, the way she kneaded her fingers as she spoke, made her words ring too true. It sent a chill up my spine. Angelle must have felt something similar because her face went pale.

"When did Sarah's shoes disappear?" Angelle asked. "How long ago did you notice they were gone?"

" 'Bout a hour maybe. All I know is we gotta get outselves out dere fas'. Dat's why I got dis plan. You see, if people see me in de boat, dey gonna think y'all just taking me for a little ride out to de bayou. Dey already know how much I like to go fishing." She nodded at Angelle. "You, dey know you go help Trevor wit' de traps sometimes, so de already know you can drive de boat, but what you need is de reason to drive de boat. Dat's why I'm gonna go me, so you can use me as de excuse."

"But—"

Poochie didn't let Angelle finish; she nodded toward me "And you, people gonna think you just wanna ride in de boat 'cause you from out dere in Texas, and dey don't got all dat water in Texas." She held out her hands. "So you see how dat's gonna work? You riding in de boat 'cause you wanna see de water, me, I'm in de boat 'cause I like to fish, and Gelle, her is in de boat 'cause she's drivin' de boat. Dat way it's gonna make sense to any of dem hard-legs dat want to stick dere nose to our business."

"Whether it makes sense or not doesn't matter," Angelle said. "You can't come with us. It's too dangerous and—"

"No, no, hol' up and let me tell you somethin'." Poochie sat tall, her eyes snapping bright green fireworks. "Look here, I cut sugarcane for twenty-five years out in de middle of de Louisiana heat, and I can bus' me a nutria trap faster den anybody in dese parts. I know dangerous, me. I can work wit' dangerous. But you, you too soft."

"Now, wait just a minute—"

"Non, you wait a minute. I'm not saying you soft like dat's a bad thing You teach school. Me, I don't. So dat means y'all can't go out in de swamp by yourself. You don't know de bayou like me."

"It doesn't matter—"

"Look, we don't got no time to fuss about dis. I'm tellin' you. I got me a feeling right in de middle of my belly. Dat little girl is in some serious trouble. We got to go find bot' of dem fas'. If we not too late already." Poochie looked at me. "And you, I know you understand what I'm sayin'. I know you feelin' dat it's coming close."

Reflexively, I glanced at Angelle.

"No, no, I'm talkin' to you. You got to look at me."

I turned back to Poochie. "All I know is the direction we're supposed to head, Poochie. I don't have a handle yet on whether the kids are alive or dead."

"We don't need no handle, we need de boat. You hear what I'm sayin'? Dat's de other side to my plan. You see, if Trevor don't bring de boat back to de house, I know where we can get another one. Vern's got a second boat over to de Bucket. I'm just gonna go borrow it."

"What makes you think Vern or Sook's going to let you borrow their boat?" Angelle had her hands on her hips. She looked completely exasperated.

"Dey don't gotta know I'm gonna borrow it right den and dere. I'll let dem know when we get back."

Angelle's mouth fell open. "What?"

"Are you saying steal their boat?" I said, arching a brow. "You're worried about us going out into the middle of the water but you're not worried about grand theft?"

Poochie shrugged. "Vern's boat's not but eighteen foot, if dat. Dere's nothing grand about dat. Now, if we was talkin' about takin' somebody's shrimp boat, dat would be different. Dem things is almost forty foot—"

"You know what she's talking about, Poochie!" Angelle snapped.

"Don't you get loud wit' me and—"

"You can't steal a boat! And even if we get Trevor's you still can't come with us. Look, think about it. Those skiffs hold three people at best, and even then it's a tight fit. If you're with us and we find those kids, how are we supposed to get everybody back? Or what if we find the kids and there's somebody around we have to deal with, like the person who took them? Then what are we supposed to do with you?"

"Dat's easy. If we find de chil'ren, all you gotta do is set me out by a cypress tree somewhere; then y'all come back and get me after you bring de babies back to de landing. And if somebody out dere gives us some trouble like you said, I can fight 'em me too."

Angelle threw a hand up in exasperation. "That's ridiculous. As if I'd leave you stuck on some small piece of dirt out in the middle of the bayou."

Poochie stuck out her chin. "You don't got no choice."

"Oh, I've got a big choice." Angelle combed a hand through her hair rapidly. "I just don't have to take you."

"Yeah, you do got to take me. How you—"

"Listen to me, Poochie . . ."

As their argument grew more heated, I detoured around Angelle and went into the kitchen to get a glass of water. There was an empty feeling growing in my chest that although I didn't get the significance of Sarah's missing shoes, Poochie was right about the need to hurry. In fact, we might already have missed the proverbial boat. So much time had been spent waiting for the perfect time, because I didn't want anyone to see my extra finger and what it could do, that those kids could already be dead.

Having reached the kitchen, I got a glass out of the cabinet, then went over to the sink and filled it with tap water. Instead of drinking it, I set the glass on the table, walked over to the back door, opened it, and looked out at the prayer tree. It struck me that as ridiculous as it looked with Dockers, flip-flops, sandals, shrimp boots, and sneakers hanging from its branches, that tree was doing exactly what it was created to do: simply be. I studied it, letting my thoughts gather speed.

It didn't make a bit of difference to that tree how ridiculous it looked. It didn't cringe in embarrassment or hide in fear. Poochie was out there in the living room, wanting to throw another four pairs onto its branches, and that tree couldn't care less. Shoes or Christmas ornaments made no difference. They could all hang from its long, leafy branches.

That's because it's just a goddamn tree, my brain argued. *A tree doesn't know pain, doesn't feel it.*

It was easy to fall into the logic of that, but I knew if I did, I'd only be hiding again. Making excuses for myself. And my excuses had already wasted enough time. Because of them, those kids probably suffered more than they had to—or worse.

The weight in my chest dropped to my stomach, deepening, widening. Shame will do that to a person. That tree, as simple and insignificant as some people might consider it, didn't care whether somebody called it a freak or called it anything at all. And here I was, hiding. Over a stupid finger. While two kids sat, we hoped, out in the middle of nowhere, crying for their parents, both of them probably hungry and thirsty. And God only knew what other horrors they were going through.

"You dumb fuck," I muttered.

My voice reverberated in my ear. I *was* a dumb fuck. I couldn't believe I'd let so much time go by without doing anything.

Turning on my heel, I marched back into the living room, a surge of adrenaline heating up my feet, working its way up my legs, into my belly, across and through my chest, up to my face, making it burn. I felt as if I were on fire. Burning . . . burning.

By the time I reached Angelle and Poochie, I must have looked like a madwoman because they turned to me, eyes widening.

"Poochie, give me all the shoes you've tied together. We're going out back and toss them up into the tree."

She looked stunned. "We are?"

"Yeah, and—"

"What's gotten into you?" Angelle asked, frowning deeply.

"Sense. It's time to stop dicking around."

"But—"

"No 'buts,' Gelle. I came to help, and you let me come here on my own terms, and I appreciate that, but as of now, those terms have changed. I've got to get off my ass."

Poochie clapped, her face beaming. "Now we talkin'!"

"Gelle, get a flashlight, some bottled water, rope, whatever else you think we'll need out there."

Angelle nodded hesitantly. "What about a boat?"

"If Trevor was to bring his back after work, what time would you expect him to get here?"

"By two thirty at least."

"What time is it now?"

She glanced at her watch. "One forty-two."

"Okay, we'll give him another half hour, forty-five minutes tops. If he's not back by then, we get Vern's, just like Poochie said."

Poochie nodded vigorously. "Dat's right."

"We can't just steal Vern's boat, Dunny," Angelle said. "What if we get caught?"

"Then we get caught."

"Just like that, huh? What about that whole grand theft thing you were griping about earlier?"

"I thought about that and figure with Sook and Vern being Poochie's relatives and all, we shouldn't run into a problem. I mean, do you really think they'd press charges?"

"Does it matter? It's still—"

"Do you? Seriously, do you think they'd have us arrested?"

"No . . . but somebody will see your—"

"Stop with the buts already, will ya?" I stripped off my gloves and threw them on the couch next to Poochie. "I don't care whose boat we use or how we get it. And I don't give a fuck who sees my hand!" The expletive flew out of my mouth before I could catch it. "Sorry, Poochie."

"Don't be sorry to me," she said. "I say dat bad word me too sometimes."

"Good, 'cause I'm sure I'll let loose a few more before this is all over. And it will be over, got that? Both of you? It *will* be over." I held out my left hand and splayed all six fingers. "However we find them, dead or alive—those kids are coming home tonight."

CHAPTER TWENTY-SEVEN

Somebody shut the dog up . . . all that barking, loud barking . . . and the cat, too much meowing . . . way too much meowing. Call the neighbor. Call them and tell them to turn off the lawn mower. I have to sleep, have to go to sleep. School tomorrow . . . school. Don't they know I have an important spelling test? If I don't get a good night's sleep, I won't pass the test. Big test . . . Applesauce—a-p-p-l . . . somebody stop the cat from meowing, okay? Please! The dog barking . . . barking. Somebody check on him, see what's wrong. Barking too loud. The lawn mower, the buzzing. The barking. The meowing . . . stop all that noise! I have to sleep . . . sleep! Test tomorrow . . .

"Sarah?"

I'm trying to go to sleep, Uncle Rusty. I really am. But there's so much noise. The dog, the lawn mower. I promise, I'll be a good girl, though. I'll get a good night's sleep and pass the test tomorrow. I'll make a hundred, you'll see. Applesauce—a-p-p-l—

"Sarah!"

Sarah Woodard opened her eyes only to find the sky on fire. No . . . not fire.

Painted.

The horizon was swathed in orange, red, yellow,

DEBORAH LeBLANC

deep purple, all of it swooshing back and forth, broad
strokes tipping up to the right, up to the heavens,
then shooting off in another direction, like a forked
tongue. Like a painter who had too big a brush and
no idea what he wanted to paint. Angry, angry
strokes, so much color. Deep, brilliant color that
seemed to soak into her skin, into her eyes, into her
heart. Was God mad? Was that what her uncle Rusty
meant by God's wrath? Did He burn the sky before
He burned your soul?

"Sarah . . ."

She blinked at the sound of her name and turned
toward the voice.

Nicky Trahan. He was in a hole.

She was in a hole. Felt mud up to her neck, nearly
to the top of her throat. Then she remembered the
man had come back. He'd been so angry. He kept
throwing buckets of mud on top of them and saying
they were going to die. Watching him, she'd been
so afraid. He'd seemed angry and happy all at the
same time.

Sarah remembered seeing fire in the man's eyes.
The same fire her uncle had when he preached in the
church on Sunday mornings. With his hands raised
up in the air, his feet stomping, yelling at everybody
about how they were going to go to hell if they didn't
repent. Repent and be saved. The man with the mud
had had that same fire. But his god must have been
different because what god would let any man kill
two children? Tell him to smother them? Make them
so afraid they wound up peeing in their pants? So
afraid they cried no matter who was watching?

With her eyes still locked on Nicky, Sarah leaned her head back, felt the mud ease up around her ears, and considered that the mud man's god and her uncle Rusty's god might not be so different after all.

She refocused her eyes on the boy just a few feet away. Nicky was crying openly, not bothering to hide his tears. His seemed to be trying to look everywhere at once, his eyes darting here, there, here, there, snot running out of his nose and over his lips, both of his cheeks wet. Sarah felt a weight on her own face, as if something heavy had been glued to her chin and left cheek. She couldn't see if it was dried mud, and there was no way for her to touch and feel it to make sure.

"I . . . I thought you were dead," Nicky cried. "I thought you were so dead! I kept calling you and calling you, and you wouldn't open your eyes. All day. All day I kept calling you. I thought you had drowned. I thought you had drowned because you'd put your face in it, and you didn't pick it back up and . . . and . . ." His sobs grew louder until he was wailing.

Sarah had heard people cry that hard before, but only at funerals when her uncle stood at the pulpit and talked about the dead person. About how good he was, and how much he was going to be missed. She'd heard that crying in the church. She wanted to tell Nicky not to cry. She wasn't dead. She'd only been . . . what? She couldn't remember anything between the time the man had dropped more mud on them and right now. She couldn't have fallen asleep, could she? Maybe she'd passed out, although she didn't know how she was supposed to tell if she had. She'd never passed out before. Not that she knew of, anyway. Was it like sleeping? Was it like dying a little bit? How could she just fall asleep in all this mud, especially being so hungry? So thirsty? Maybe that was it. Maybe that's what was happening. She was dying of starvation. They hadn't eaten in so long. She couldn't even remember the last thing she'd eaten.

She glanced over at the burning sky again and tried to remember if it was the sunset or the sunrise. What day was it? How long had they been there?

". . . and then there was this snake, and I had to hold really still 'cause its head was back like it was going to bite me, so I had to hold really still. Like on television, you know? How the crocodile man said if you come up on a snake, you've gotta hold really still, and I did. And I closed my eyes, and I held my breath, and . . . and . . . it came up on my neck. The snake crawled up by my ear, and then it went out the hole, and you wouldn't wake up. I called you and called you, but you wouldn't wake up. I was so afraid, Sarah. I was so afraid!" Nicky's sobs turned to hiccups and gasps for breath.

She wanted to pat him on the back and tell him everything would be okay. But that would have been a lie. A big fat lie. And her uncle Rusty said liars always go to hell. But weren't she and Nicky already there? Wasn't this hell? Was this the pit her uncle talked about in his sermons? No . . . no, he'd said fiery pit. Fiery pit. But the sky—the sky was on fire. And she was in the pit. Nicky was in the pit, too.

"Then I wished . . . I wished . . . then I wished I

was dead," Nicky wailed. "I was so scared that I wished that. I wanted the snake to go ahead and bite me and get it over with. I know we're gonna die, Sarah. I know it. That man's gonna come back and put more mud in here, and I don't want it to go up my nose! I don't want that junk in my eyes and my mouth so we can't breathe and we can't get up, and I don't want that! So when the snake came, I really wanted it to bite me but I was too scared, and you were there, and you'd be all by yourself if I died, and . . . and . . ."

Sarah wanted to tell Nicky thank you for not leaving her alone, but she was too tired to make her mouth move. She knew what he meant, though, about wanting to die. She would have wanted to do the same thing, bring in the darkness on her own terms instead of having someone force her into it. She studied the mud streaks on his face, the darker tracks on his cheeks made by the tears, the mud that made his hair stand up in little peaks on the top of his head. He'd stayed alive for her. Just for her. No one had ever done anything like that for her before.

In that moment, she wanted more than anything . . . more than getting out of the mud, out of the swamp, out of life . . . to buy Nicky a present. Do something really nice for him. Something that would give him a warm feeling the way she had right now; the feeling of being hugged by somebody big and strong who cared about her a lot. But there was no way for her to buy a gift, no way to get out of this pit. No way to open her mouth and say thank you.

It took all the energy Sarah had just to blink,

which she did once . . . twice. Then she watched curiously as Nicky's eyes suddenly seemed to grow bigger and bigger, as if something had clamped onto his upper and lower lids and was pulling them as far apart as possible. His mouth opened and closed as if he were talking, but she couldn't hear him. Then his mouth opened really wide. . . .

Was he yelling?

Her name maybe?

All Sarah heard was a whining noise. The lawn mower? Where was that cat?

"Sarah, look out!" That time sound came out of Nicky's mouth when he moved it. His eyes were stretched far to the left, as if he was trying to look behind her. His mouth opened wide again. "It's back! Look out!"

Gathering all the willpower she had, Sarah was able to turn her head ever so slightly. This would be her gift to him, reacting to his voice. Acknowledging that he'd called her name. That would be her present.

She turned her head a little more . . . a fraction of an inch, a mere fraction; then she saw a flash of movement. Something odd appeared in her line of sight, and it seemed to freeze there, as if the earth had suddenly quit moving. Gravity quit working. Time had grown tired and simply stopped.

Inches away, a small, open mouth . . . two needle-length fangs . . .

Nicky screamed.

The earth moved again, only now it folded time into milliseconds . . .

The small mouth jerked—Nicky wailed—needles flew—

So much pain in her right cheek . . . fire . . . her face was on fire . . . just like the sky.

CHAPTER TWENTY-EIGHT

"I can't believe we stole a fucking boat," Angelle said as we pushed against the nose of the skiff to move it off the trailer and into the water.

"Hey, you were the one who started talking about stealing boats in the first place." I blew a shock of hair out of my eyes.

"I did not! That was Poochie."

"Huh-uh, you wanted to take Trevor's boat first thing, remember?"

"That's different, and you know it. He's my husband."

"Technicality." I gave her a little smile to let her know I was teasing. "Doesn't really matter. Everything worked out okay. I mean, it's not like we really stole this boat."

"Close enough, though. I lied through my teeth, telling Pork Chop that story," Angelle said. "Vern's going to come back, see his boat's missing, and Pork Chop's going to tell him what I said. Vern's going to know right off it's a bullshit story and probably call Trevor. I'll never hear the end of it."

"Nobody's going to give two shits about any boat when we get back with those kids."

Angelle stopped pushing and stared at me for a moment. "What makes you so sure now that we're going to find them?"

"Bottom line? 'Cause this stupid finger's never failed me when I really needed it. Now come on and push so we can get out of here. People are going to start paying attention if we don't get our asses in gear."

She nodded and started pushing again. "After we get this thing launched, I'll go park the car and trailer back in that grove we passed a couple hundred yards back. Less chance of somebody I know seeing them."

"Good idea." As eager as I was to start the hunt, I felt weird out in public without my gloves and kept glancing around. My paranoia wasn't only about the boat not belonging to us; a lot of it had to do with how vulnerable I felt. I remembered the tree, the conviction, the heat of shame I'd felt, and took a big breath to calm and control the fear.

When it was obvious that Trevor wasn't returning home with the boat, we'd headed right over to the Bucket, not wanting to waste any more time. As soon as we got there, Angelle laid out a story that sounded plausible enough. She told Pork Chop and Sook that Vern had asked Trevor, who also worked odd jobs as a mechanic, to fix some doomathingy on his boat. Since Vern had asked for a stat job, according to Angelle, and Trevor was working late at the plant, she'd been asked to pick up the boat for him. That way he'd be able to start working on it as soon as he broke shift and got home. As she spun the tale, Poochie had sprinkled in a few "Dat's right!" and "Yep, he said dat," while I just hung back and nodded.

Luckily, Vern still hadn't returned from his scouting trip, so Pork Chop had no way to verify the story, and since Trevor had worked on Vern's boat before, few questions were asked. Sook had simply said, "Sure, go 'head. Don't make me no never mind." And Pork Chop added, "Tell Trevor he can slot in my Evinrude when he's done with Vern's and has time." I didn't know what Pork Chop meant by "slot in," but Angelle quickly agreed to pass along the information.

Cherokee had been standing behind the bar while the production unfolded, and I saw in his eyes that he thought the whole boat repair story was a crock of shit. Still, he said nothing, only stepping outside to watch with Pork Chop as we drove away, boat and trailer fishtailing behind the car.

The most difficult part of the plan so far had been Poochie, when we'd insisted she stay home. She'd screeched and hollered, cried and wailed, insisting that since she'd played such an important *and* convincing role in getting the boat, she should be allowed to go.

It had taken over an hour to calm Poochie down and convince her that she was needed at the prayer tree with their shoes. Someone had to stay and pray to make sure everyone came back home safely. We reminded her, too, that five people wouldn't fit in a boat designed for two. If she came, she'd wind up endangering the kids' lives—all of their lives, actually—by overloading the boat.

That last part eventually sank in because she suddenly became as docile as a kitten, saying, "I didn't think about it like dat." But she'd looked so hangdog when she said it, I felt sorry for her. Angelle must have felt the same because she'd gone out of her way to make sure Poochie was comfortable before we left. She'd settled her onto the couch, placed an afghan over her lap, left a sandwich and a glass of milk on the coffee table for her, then turned on her favorite movie, which happened to be *GI Jane*, something Poochie claimed she'd seen forty-two times already. She also swore she'd seen the scene where Demi Moore struggles to her feet, all bloodied in the face, and yells for her master sergeant to "Suck my dick!" at least a hundred times. Poochie recounted that scene so many times that by the time we finally did leave the house, I couldn't get those three words out of my head. I think Poochie just liked saying the word *dick*.

At first, I'd been a little worried about leaving Poochie alone in the house, what with all the weird things going on lately—Angelle being violated, the dark fucker that had gotten in my face, the one that had slipped across the hall from the bathroom, the moving toaster, shattering light fixture. So I'd suggested we bring Poochie back to the Bucket and have her stay with Sook while we were gone. But Poochie wouldn't hear of it. She'd insisted that if we were leaving her behind to pray, then she had to be by her tree. No argument there, but it was the *way* she'd said it that troubled me. There'd been hard-core mischief in her eyes at the time, and her demeanor had gone from wildcat to pussycat to Cheshire cat. A sort of put-on-Demi's-uniform-shave-my-head-and-get-to-the-business-of-kicking-ass look.

It was hard to tell whether Poochie was slipping

off the deep end or if she had something brewing in the back of her mind. The latter felt probable because concocting adventure seemed to be an abstract hobby of Poochie's, one she was very good at. Regardless, we'd left her sitting on the couch, movie already playing on the television. The perfect picture of an elderly woman settling in early for the evening. Poochie played the part so well, Norman Rockwell would have been impressed—grossly naive and more than likely in for the shock of his life, of course—but impressed nonetheless.

"Here," Angelle said, startling my thoughts away from Poochie. She handed me the towline. "Hang on to this while I go park the car and trailer." Then she hurried off to do just that.

As I watched my sister drive away, I noticed that the horizon had become a vacuum cleaner, sucking the sun down to its borders, soon to leave Angelle and me with darkness and disadvantage. The moon was already out, a huge gauzy, translucent ball, waiting patiently for its turn to take center stage. Wisps of clouds floated across its face.

A late afternoon breeze carried with it a fecund odor swaddled in humidity. I'd never been anywhere that felt so damned wet. My clothes stuck to me, my hair stuck to me, gnats stuck to me. It was as if the air were made of some kind of glue.

The steady *shhoop . . . shhoop, shhoop* of water lapping against the aluminum hull of the boat made my eyelids heavy. I imagined schools of fish swirling close to the bank to check out the sound, saw them serpentine through labyrinths of vegetation, some of them predators, some prey, all of them constantly on the move. They had no knowledge of me, of my problems, or of the danger Angelle and I might be headed for. In that moment, I envied them their mindless, singularly focused life, to search for food and shelter. Perhaps they had their own horrors to deal with. Perhaps life was one game of eat or be eaten for them. Perhaps I was envying the wrong things.

The water that lay ahead, whether swamp, bayou, river, I couldn't tell the difference, looked like a tarnished silver highway that stretched on seemingly forever. Along its roadside were cypress trees, many of them heavy-laden with moss that hung from their branches like clumps of coarse gray hair. Some were only stumps, jagged knees and fingers that rose from the water like gnarled, brown body parts refusing to die. Amongst them were willows, tupelos, maples, and cottonwoods, all of them a perch for singing, twittering birds. The shadows created by the lush forest life that packed both banks seemed to converge down the middle of the highway, bringing darkness before the death of the sun.

It would take a lifetime to absorb the richness of this place, but as beautiful as it was, there was no mistaking the underlying sense that came with it—these waterways might be able to nourish and sustain life, but they could also take it away.

I turned my gaze back to shore. Having come from a dustbowl, all of this water—so much of it— was daunting and intimidating. And it didn't help that I couldn't swim for shit, nor could Angelle as far as I knew.

I had every excuse I needed to be scared shitless, turn tail, and run. To go back to that dry hole I called home, where all I had to worry about was a mangy old dog scratching on my back screen door and the deadlines from the newspapers I wrote for. Life was easy and quiet back there—as long as I didn't mind the memories—as long as I didn't mind the loneliness. And I didn't. Not really.

Sighing, I wiped sweat from my forehead. Here I was, holding on to a rope tied to a boat, getting ready to fuck all that easy, quiet life. Maybe Poochie wasn't the only one with a few cogs slipping.

When Angelle returned moments later, her expression was somber, her face slick with sweat. She climbed into the boat and went straight to the motor that sat on its squared-off back end.

"Get in," she said, squatting near the motor. As I did so, she pulled her hair back in a ponytail with a rubber band from her wrist, then grabbed a red rubber ball that sat in the middle of a rubber hose, which ran from the gas tank to the motor. She began squeezing the ball rapidly, as if working an exercise ball.

"Do you have any idea what you're doing?" I asked, wondering if she'd have to keep pumping the ball the entire time we'd be moving through the bayou.

"Yep. Just priming the motor." She gave the bulb a couple more squeezes, then hit the start button on the throttle. The engine sputtered . . . coughed . . . roared to life. A plume of gray smoke rose from the back of the engine, filling the air with the scent of gasoline. Angelle smiled, then motioned to the bench seat near the bow of the boat. "Sit there."

As soon as I plopped my butt in place, she revved up the motor, and the boat began to inch away from the landing and farther out on that tarnished silver highway.

This was one road trip I wasn't looking forward to.

CHAPTER TWENTY-NINE

"Unload the supplies from the bag, will ya?" Angelle shouted over the roar of the engine. "We're going to need the flashlight pretty soon. Don't want to be searching for it once it gets dark. And check under the seat you're sitting on. There're two paddles under there. Pull 'em out. We'll need 'em if we get stuck in a patch of water lilies. Those things get tangled up in a prop, it's major shit to cut 'em loose. Have to paddle your way out then."

Paddle our way out? Shit . . . great.

"O–okay . . . there any life jackets in here?"

"Should be. Probably in the seat compartment under me. I'll look in a minute. Don't worry, I won't go fast."

I wasn't worried about going fast. I was worried about falling into the water. But I kept my mouth shut and searched through the supplies we'd brought along. Within minutes I had the flashlight in hand and two bottles of water were rolling around on the floor of the boat. As we puttered along, I turned in my seat so I faced the front of the boat instead of my sister and tried to relax. I wondered how different this would be had I come here on vacation instead of on a mission. I'd probably be taking pictures right about now, catching the sunset over the water, laughing with Angelle, maybe getting a lesson or two on how to cook shrimp stew. I wasn't so sure I'd want to be headed where we were headed, though, even on vacation. All those shadows. The dark water. The hanging moss. Snakes—alligators. Shit . . . I hadn't thought about the possibility of snakes out here. There were probably tons of them . . . big ones. Poisonous ones. I felt my butt cheeks tighten on the seat.

True to her word, Angelle kept the boat running at a snail's pace for quite some time. When we came upon a fork in the waterway, the whine of the engine quieted to a soft putter, and the boat slowed even more. I turned back toward Angelle. She was standing now, lifting the top of the seat she'd been sitting on with one hand. After looking into the compartment beneath it, she looked up at me with pursed lips.

"No jackets," she said.

"Great."

She let the seat drop back into place. "It'll be okay. I'll be careful. Just make sure not to stand up in the boat while we're moving."

"Yeah, like that's going to happen."

Angelle shrugged apologetically. "Sorry. Didn't think about bringing some because Trevor always keeps two in his boat." She aimed her chin in the direction of the fork. "It's your show now. Which way do we go?"

Trying to still the gnawing concern in my chest over not having any life jackets, I turned to face the fork—and a decision. Now or never . . .

I thought about the kids, focused on how frightened they must be, then held out my left hand. The reaction was immediate and painful, as if someone had grabbed hold of it and yanked hard, pulling it sideways toward my wrist. I glanced over at my sister. The direction was clear; there wasn't a need for words.

I saw fear flicker in her eyes, and I could only imagine what she saw in mine. So many emotions were rolling through me, I couldn't stick a label to just one. Panic—excitement—anger—fear . . . fear. Okay, so I could label one.

Angelle nodded once, inferring "Ready?"

I returned the nod. This was as ready as I was going to get. The whine of the engine returned, and as the boat veered left, I hunkering back into position, faced west, keeping my left hand out in front of me.

The burning, firecracker sensation in my little finger intensified as we pushed through the darkening water, this channel much narrower than the one behind us. Still holding the flashlight in my right hand, I clicked on the switch and used the beam of light to direct Angelle. Right, into another chute—right again into a wider bay—left, quick left into a much darker slough.

So much of my attention was focused on the kids that I barely noticed the scenery. An occasional houseboat, an egret the size of a snow goose, things I would normally have gawked at only irritated me, distractions that caused my finger to go dead and me to regroup my attention. Worse than the distraction, though, was the length of time this was taking. Already it felt as if we'd been sloshing around the swamps forever, going around in circles. Everything looked the same. Green—dark—wet.

A time or two we'd happen upon what looked like a field of grass, which was actually the water lilies Angelle had warned me about earlier. It was slow going through those patches, Angelle working the throttle, fretting every time the engine sputtered. The lilies were bad enough, but the darkness . . .

Night didn't fall upon the swamp, it collided with it. One minute shadows were gently merging over the water, and the next, I could hardly see the front of the boat, even with the flashlight and the glow from the moon. I slapped at a mosquito whining in my right ear, surprised I could hear it at all.

Although we seemed to be the only humans on some watery planet in a lost universe, we were far from the only creatures here. The collective sound of what must have been a bazillion insects, and God only knew what else, was so loud I could hardly hear myself think.

Following the pull and pain in my finger, I aimed the flashlight to the right. "Turn there, between those two big cypress trees." I glanced back to make sure Angelle had heard me.

She nodded, then batted a hand across her face, swatted the left side of her neck, her ear. "What's with all these mosquitoes?"

"I said to turn right—right—you're going to miss the turnoff." I aimed the flashlight at the opening of the slough, and she quickly banked right. The passageway was narrower than any we'd traveled through so far. A little over twenty-five feet from bank to bank. The brush and thicket of trees were much heavier, too.

"Jesus!"

Hearing the surprise in Angelle's voice, I jerked the flashlight beam in her direction.

It looked as though a light gray veil had settled over her head and shoulders. Her left arm flailed about. "Jesus . . . God, look at all these fucking mosquitoes!" She spat, spat again. "Ugh!"

The beam from the flashlight acted like a sword, cutting through the gray veil, splitting the swarm of mosquitoes that covered her in half, sending them off in another direction. They swooped up, around, and behind until they'd settled on top of me. I barely had time to close my mouth before I felt the sting on my lips, them drilling into my nose, my ears. A mass of buzzing, whining, flitting gray matter that clouded my vision. "Shit," I muttered through clenched teeth, lowering my head, batting the air around me. I felt tiny pinpricks on my face, my neck, my arms.

I braved a glance at my sister through slitted eyelids. She was still doing the batting, swatting mosquito dance, all the while sputtering and spitting, swinging her head from side to side. She finally let go of the throttle to use both hands, and the engine sputtered twice, then died. She stood up, arm still swinging, turned toward the motor.

I held the crook of my left arm over my mouth to minimize the number of bloodsuckers I'd have to eat, and started to yell at Angelle to get us out of there, but all I got out was "Get us—" before something hit

the left side of the boat, jostling me hard in my seat.
I dropped the flashlight. "Fuck!"

Something hammered against the boat again, nearly
knocking Angelle overboard this time. "Shit!" She
grabbed on to the throttle for balance. "Shit . . . shit!"

"What the hell's doing that?" I yelled, scrambling
for the flashlight.

She didn't answer. Her back was to me now, and
she was leaning over, evidently meaning to restart the
motor.

The boat bobbled in the open water as I chased the
rolling flashlight on the bottom of the boat. As soon as
I got a grip on it, I shot the beam over the side of the
boat, aiming it into the murky water—and on an alligator with a head the size . . . of a fucking Camaro.
The moment the light hit it, the gator opened its jaws
wide and snapped at the thin wall of aluminum, our
only protection.

"Go!" I yelled to Angelle. "Get us the hell out of
here now! *Now!*" I didn't want to take my eyes off
the alligator, as if that would make any difference on
the timing of its attack.

"I'm trying!" The engine coughed, sputtered—died.
Sputtered again, then chugged, the sound of a motor gasping to turn over but flooded with too much
gasoline.

"Gelle, get us the fuck—"

"I'm trying, goddamnit, I'm trying!"

The engine whined, then revved, chugged, and died.

Suddenly, another *thunk* on the side of the boat.
The attack came so fast and hard, my butt slipped off

the seat, and I fell onto the floor of the boat. That time, though, I kept hold of the flashlight. No way was I going to let it go again. If I was going to die, they'd have to bury me with the son of a bitch.

Whine—chug—whine—*grooommmm* . . .   the engine finally caught, and in the next moment, Angelle had us flying down the slough as if the boat were propelled by rockets. She yelled something to me, but her words were snatched away by the wind.

I held on to the side of the boat, squinted, aimed the flashlight ahead, hoped she could see where she was going.

Too fast . . . too fast. We were going way too fast for oncoming cypress stumps—oncoming cutoffs we needed to take. I yelled over the rush of wind, "Slow down! Slow down!"

Whether it was from the speed of the boat or our location, I couldn't tell, but my finger suddenly became multidirectional. My entire hand vibrated with fire and electricity, and my finger waggled as if wanting to point in every direction at once. North—east—south—it was as if the kids had exploded, and my hand meant to find every molecule that floated back down to earth.

I shouted to Angelle again, "Slow down! I can't pick anything up. I don't know where we have to go. You're going to slam into something!"

Evidently figuring out that I was trying to tell her something, Angelle geared back the throttle, and the roar of the engine quieted. The boat slowed. "What did you say?"

"I said slow down."

"I got that, the other thing."

"I'm not picking up anything specific. Not sure where we're supposed to go."

Her shoulders slumped.

On trembling legs, I got to my feet and carefully made my way back to the seat at the front of the boat. Grimacing, I aimed the flashlight out over the water, trying to get a feel for our surroundings. My right hand shook so violently from the pain in my left that the beam of light jittered and jumped. A giant firefly on amphetamines.

I patted the air with my hand, signaling for Angelle to slow down even more. I didn't feel certain about our direction anymore. Just as before, everything around me looked like everything else I'd seen since we'd left the landing. Left looked right, and right looked absolutely wrong. I threw nervous glances over both sides of the boat to make sure Crocodile Dundee's mascot hadn't followed us. Seeing all was clear, I started drawing in long, deep breaths, attempting to refocus. Slow . . . easy . . . breaths.

Calm . . . calm . . . think about the kids . . . the kids . . . kids . . .

"Which way?" Angelle asked.

I shook my head, still not feeling a clear direction. It was as if my entire left hand had been forced on top of a hot plate that had a short in it. At least the beam from the flashlight was growing steadier by the second.

"Which way?" Angelle asked again.

"Not getting anything specific."

"Still?"

"I can't help it. It's not doing like it was before."

"God, Dunny. It has to. I don't know where the hell we are. I don't even know how far out we've come."

I looked back at her sharply. "I thought you knew these swamps."

"I said I got out in the boat sometimes. I didn't say I knew all the sloughs and flats and lakes around here or how one turns into the other. I was only following your direction, and I figured if you could get us out here, you'd get us back." She was nearly panting with panic now. "You *have* to do something!"

"Do what? I can't *make* it do anything, Gelle, you know that."

"Jesus . . ." Angelle shook her head, fiddled with her ponytail, swiped the back of her hand over her mouth. "Fuck . . ."

While she fretted and fidgeted, I turned back to the front of the boat, squinting to figure out what lay ahead of the flashlight beam, beyond in the path of moonlight.

Trees and more trees—water and more water— turtles slipping off logs on the nearby bank—the plop of fish leapfrogging from their schools—and something else . . .

"Still nothing?" Angelle asked.

Instead of answering, I trained the flashlight beam on something pale near a clump of cypress trees lining the bank a couple hundred feet or so ahead on the right. It looked like a white seven. . . .

My interest piqued, I pointed to it. "Go that way. Slow, though. Go slow."

"What is it?"

"Just go."

No sooner did Angelle aim the boat in that direction than the fiery hot sensation radiating through my extra finger did an about-face. It turned cold. Antarctica cold. And cold meant dead. Oh God . . . cold was dead. Whatever was sticking up near the gnarled base of the largest cypress tree was dead. I was sure of it . . . stone-cold dead sure of it.

"Please don't let it be one of the kids," I whispered. "Please, not the kids."

"What did you say?" Angelle called over the sputter of the motor.

"There . . . that white thing by the trees." I struggled to hold the flashlight beam steady.

Angelle pushed the boat forward a little faster, moving us up closer . . . closer still.

I leaned forward, squinting.

"It looks like a seven . . ." Angelle said, directing the comment more to herself than to me.

"Yeah. I . . . wait . . ." Either I'd cocked my head the right way, or the beam of the flashlight managed to slice through just the right shadow, because suddenly that pale silhouette came into stark view. It was a seven, all right . . . created by a human leg and foot. And we were coming on it too fast. *God . . . shit . . .* I threw my left hand up. "Stop! Stop the boat!"

Angelle immediately killed the motor, but not soon enough. The boat continued forward until the bow

hit the large cypress, dislodged the leg, and sent it sliding under the water. After regaining my balance, I
held my breath and pointed the flashlight over the
bow and peeked over the edge, not wanting to see, but
needing to.

"What was it? Did you see?" Angelle asked, clam-
bering toward the front of the boat.

"Stay back," I said. And of course she didn't.

"What is it?"

The flashlight suddenly blinked off, then on . . .
off, then on. Then off, and we were left to the milky
hue of moonlight. I beat the head of the flashlight
against my left palm. "You have extra batteries for
this thing?"

"I put fresh ones in before we left the house. It
can't be the batteries. Maybe when you dropped it
earlier . . ."

I tapped the flashlight again, harder.

"What was it?" Angelle asked again. "Did you
see it?"

In that moment, the flashlight chose to blink back
on, and its beam ricocheted from the cap of aluminum on the bow, into the water, and right into the
eyes of death. Angelle must have spotted the dead
woman at the same moment I did because her scream
rang out so loud and long it made my ears sting.

There was little question it was a woman. Her face
and torso bobbed to the surface, tapped against the
boat as small waves sought the shore of the bank. Her
face was narrow with a pointed chin, and a mole sat
high on her right cheek . . . right below an empty eye
socket.

"God—oh, God . . ." Angelle scrambled for the back of the boat, causing the skiff to rock, jerk from side to side.

The flashlight blinked off again. No light—no life jackets . . . "Calm down or you'll flip the boat!"

"How the hell you expect me to calm down! It's a dead woman, for heaven's sake! A dead woman right up against the boat!" She stomped her feet in fear, her shouts echoing through the swamp.

"Stop it, Angelle!" The flashlight beam jiggled on again. Off, then on. I aimed the light in her face and saw welts from the mosquitoes on her neck, her cheeks, her forehead.

She threw a hand over her eyes, turned around, and stooped to grab the fuel bulb from the gas tank. "We're outta here. Poochie was right, we've got no business here. You grab—"

Thwump! A shudder ran through the floor of the boat.

Gasping, I aimed the flashlight at the floor.

Angelle caught sight of it first and screamed as if somebody were gutting her. The light blinked off again, flickered on. Angelle's arms were pinwheeling now, trying to move her body away—away from the large brown water moccasin that lay coiled near the supply bag on the floor of the boat.

I stood like an idiot, unable to move. I looked from the snake to my sister, who was scrambling backward so quickly she didn't notice the wooden bench coming up behind her knees.

"Gelle, watch out!"

Too late. The back of Angelle's knees caught the

bench, buckled, and sent her careening out of control. Her head bounced against the boat motor, and a loud *crack!* reverberated through the dark as her skull made contact. In the next instant, I saw her body tumble over the side of the boat, then heard a splash—a *thunk* . . .

I was so stunned it took a second for me to react. And when I did, my reaction was soaked in panic. "Gelle!" I hurried toward the back of the skiff, the flashlight blinking off . . . on . . . off. I beat it against my palm. "Gelle!"

She couldn't swim. I couldn't swim . . . what the hell was I supposed to do? The snake . . . I didn't care about the fucking snake. My sister . . . in the water . . . couldn't swim. *She's gonna die—can't swim—*

Swim was the last word that went through my mind as I dropped the flashlight and dove into the inky black water—headfirst.

CHAPTER THIRTY

The first mistake I made was trying to open my eyes underwater. I saw nothing but a canvas of black. It was as if the water below and the sky above and everything in between had vanished. I blinked to make sure my eyes were really open. Still nothing, nothing but a burning in my eyes that I had to ignore.

The second mistake was trying to scream for Angelle before I broke the surface of the water. I tasted gasoline, mud, and stagnant decay. My lungs felt ready to burst. The need for oxygen, to cough and gag, was so strong it nearly overrode common sense. *Stay calm! Calm!* I thought of the dead woman. Wondered if some of her hair had gotten into my mouth, any of her sloughed-off skin, fingernails. The thought made me retch, which brought another wave of water into my mouth.

I heard nothing but the gurgle of water, the *whoosh* of my frantic movements. The absolute assurance that I was about to die in some disgusting swamp overtook me, and I screamed inside my head, screamed with my mouth closed, my eyes opened wide.

But if I died, who'd save Angelle? Who'd get her away from the dead woman? I could see it, plain as

day . . . the dead woman taking my sister into her a
floating off with her. Going down . . . down
together. My sister. The dead woman. My sister
empty eye sockets.

That last thought propelled me into action,
the fear. I ignored the burning in my chest. Dro
ing was not an option. Fear was not an option.
sister . . . my sister . . . goddamnit, she couldn't

I dogpaddled frantically, first this way, then
pushing water away with my hands, searching fo
for ground with my feet. There had to be somet
I could grab hold of, step up on . . . a log. How
was it? Had to find my way up . . . up to air. Bu
faster I paddled, the more water I found, and I fel
body began to sink. *No! Gelle . . . Gelle!*

Suddenly my toes tapped against something
beneath me, and I wanted to weep with reli
prayed it would be enough leverage. . . .

Despite my fear, despite every instinct that tol
to paddle, to move, I held still, sinking, sinking,
ing for both feet to find purchase. As soon as they
I coiled my body in tight, then sprang up as har
could.

Up! Within seconds, my head broke the surfa
the water, and I found air, glorious, sweet pre
air. I collected it in loud gasps.

I looked frantically about, my eyesight clou
"Gelle!"

No answer.

How much time had passed since she'd fallen
board? I knew fear and panic could warp time, be
at will . . . Had five seconds gone by? Five minu

slapped at the surface of the water with my hands, trying to stay afloat, gasping, coughing, gulping. "Angelle!"

The water soon claimed me again, sucking me under. The swamp wanted me, wanted us both, just as it had wanted the woman with the mole . . . I knew the ground was not that far beneath me. *Patient . . . patient . . .*

My feet soon found ground again, and I forced my body to the surface once more. At this rate, I figured the water to be only about six and a half to seven feet deep. Too deep for my height of five foot five, but shallow enough that I could keep bobbing up for air until I reached the side of the boat. Squat—jump—breathe. "Gelle!"

Squat . . .

Jump . . .

Breathe . . .

"Gelle!"

That time as I broke the surface, panic overtook me. Where the hell was the boat? I went down again . . . up . . . and that time the boat came into view, mere feet away, straight ahead. I'd simply bounced in the wrong direction.

Concentrate! You don't have time to make stupid fucking mistakes.

One more hard jump, and I got close enough to grab on to the side of the boat.

"Angelle!"

Hanging on for dear life, for my sister's dear life, I quickly swiped a hand over my eyes to clear my vision. I'd managed to grab on to the left side of the boat, the side nearer the cypress tree. The side nearer the dead woman. Her head bobbed closer, touching my right elbow

I screamed in revulsion and frustration, pushed her away. "Get the fuck away from me!" The water reclaimed her, swallowing her whole.

"Gelle!"

Still no answer. Nothing. How long now? Ten minutes? Twenty?

"Angelle . . . please . . . God, please answer me!"

I worked my way along the side of the boat, hand over hand, feet kicking, crying out to the moon, to the only light in this eternal black pit, "Help me find her! Please!"

As I pulled into a back kick, my knees suddenly bumped into something solid; then Angelle's face abruptly bobbed to the surface of the water.

"Jesus, Gelle!" I reached for her, managed to grab her ponytail, pulled her close. Crying, I hugged her to me with one arm. She was as pale as the seven that had brought us here. Her eyes were closed, her mouth partially open, and blood immediately began to ooze from a large gash in her forehead.

"Don't you die on me, you hear? Don't you be dead, goddamnit! Don't you fucking be dead!" I let out a sob, clutching my sister tight. I felt her chest move . . . barely. "I've got you now. I've got you. The water can't get you anymore. Neither can the dead woman. You hear? I've got you."

Breathing hard, I tried clearing my head. I had to get her to a flat surface . . . get her into the boat. CPR, that's what she needed, and I knew how to do it. I'd learned while doing research for a piece on rescue workers for the Dallas newspaper.

"Hold on, Gelle."

I couldn't see any land beneath the clump of trees where the seven had been, just slick tree trunks pressed close together. I *had* to get her into the boat . . . but how? Jesus, how? Maybe if I used my shirt—tied one sleeve to a tree, the other to her, used it as a pulley? It might keep her head above water until I could get into the boat and hoist her in. No . . . the branches of the cypress trees were too high, their trunks too wide.

How much time had passed now? Twenty minutes? An hour?

"Help!" I hoped against hope that a fisherman might be out working late and hear my screams. Or that there was a God, and that He did in fact send guardian angels. "Somebody help, please!"

No one came. No fisherman. No angels. Just the dead woman's leg as it resurfaced right beside Angelle's left hip.

"Get away from her, you bitch!" I screamed, as if she could hear me, as if it mattered. In some rational part of my brain, I knew I should pity the old woman. She was dead after all. Had probably died horribly considering the shocked expression death had locked onto her face. But I didn't pity her. As far as the woman was concerned, the only thing I gave a fuck about was that she stayed away from Angelle.

I pulled my sister closer; her face was now covered in blood. I had to do something and fast. Driven by instinct and desperation, I lowered my head, stuck a large part of her ponytail into my mouth, then bit down into her hair. I clamped onto the side of the boat with both hands and slid inch by inch toward the back and the boat motor.

Tugging Angelle along slowly, way too slowly, I finally made it to the motor. I ran a hand along its backside, searching, feeling for a chink, a notch, a knob, anything I could attach her hair to that would keep her face above the water.

How much time? A day? A year?

My forefinger tripped over something that felt like an upside-down U with a protruding lip, and my heart galloped. I pulled Angelle's ponytail out of my mouth, pulled her head closer to the motor, then wrapped her hair tight around the protrusion. When I was sure it would hold her mouth and nose above the surface of the black ink, I let go of her body.

In the gauzy moonlight, I saw more blood on her face, so much of it. Another sob gathered in my chest, knotted up into a hard ball that pressed and pushed against my heart, threatening to break it. But there was no time for crying. I kissed her cheek, blood and all, then went back to the business of getting my ass into the boat.

I pulled and tugged on the side of the skiff, tried throwing a leg over, anything to hoist myself up, but the weight of my jeans, the water, the slick aluminum made it impossible to find the right leverage. I wasn't a workout queen. My arms were those of a writer, conditioned at the wrist and fingers for typing out words on a keyboard, not hefting a hundred and twenty-five pounds of frantic, wet female over the side of a boat. Refusing to give up, I fought and kicked, pulled and grunted, the boat tipping one way, then the other. I kept Angelle's bloody face in my mind's eye, knowing if I didn't make it into the skiff and she died, I'd never make it through the rest of my life. Not being this close, only inches away from pulling her to safety.

Time passed now? A decade?

A thought pricked at my mind. What if I was already too late? What if Angelle was already gone and there was no chance to revive her? No! NO! I shook the image out of my head. I gripped the side of the boat as though I meant to rip it apart with my bare hands, then let out a growl of frustration so raw and primal it sent birds shrieking from the trees above us. I pushed, lurched, launching my body until I was folded in half at the waist over the side of the boat. It was all the leverage I needed to tumble my way inside.

I was scrambling to get to my feet when I remembered the snake. I froze for a moment, water dripping over my face, my hair, my clothes clinging to me like heavy scabs. Everything in the boat looked the same in the shadows. There was no discerning the towline from the flashlight from the snake from the rubber hose that ran from the gas tank. If I reached for the wrong thing, I could wind up with that moccasin's fangs embedded in my hand, poison pumping into my bloodstream. I'd be useless to anyone. But crouching on my haunches and dripping water into the boat wasn't doing my sister any good, either.

I got to my feet, spread my legs apart to maintain balance, then watched the floor for movement. More than likely the snake had fallen into the skiff from one of the tree branches that canopied overhead. I might not have known swamps, but I knew snakes. The desert had its fair share of the slithering bastards. After falling, it would have remained paralyzed for only a few seconds before coiling itself up for protection. Then, after assessing its surrounding and any potential threats, it would have quickly slid under something to hide. I had to find it and get rid of it. Couldn't take the chance of pulling Angelle into the boat, only to have it attack her.

Time? A millennium?

I stomped a foot, clapped my hands. "Where are you, you son of a bitch? Come out here!" I stomped again and again, harder and louder each time.

Finally, I saw something move from under the bench seat near the bow of the boat. Without thinking twice, I giant-stepped toward it, not caring if it was the rope or the flashlight jostled by the rock of the boat—it was going overboard.

In one swoop, I stooped, grabbed, felt the scratch of scales as it quickly wrapped around my wrist. "Motherfucker!" I squeezed the thick, slimy bastard back hard, then flung my right arm out toward the right side of the boat with all my might, releasing my grip at the same time. The snake sailed, writhing, twisting in mid-air, then dropped into the water with a loud *plooop!*

Now that it was out of the boat, I didn't even allow myself a breath of victory. I got on my hands and knees, feeling about until I found the long, hard handle of the flashlight. I grabbed it, beat it against my left palm, flicked the on-off switch back and forth, back and forth until it finally gave up and shed light. The beam was weaker now, yellow, but it was enough for me to locate the towline. I snatched up the free end of the rope, hurried over to the boat motor, then leaned over the side of the hull to attach the rope to Angelle.

"Hold on, girl, hold on. . . ." But I couldn't lean out far enough to secure the rope under her arms. The best I'd be able to do was wrap it around her neck, and that simply wouldn't work.

How much time now? Forever.

Not giving myself time to think it through, I threw a leg over the side of the boat and slipped back into the water. "It's going to be all right, you hear me?" With a series of tugs, pushes, tucks, and pulls, I managed to wrap the rope beneath Angelle's arms and secure it with a slipknot over her chest. "All you have to do is breathe now, you hear? Just breathe."

I clambered back into the boat, making it in on the first try this time. After grabbing the now taut rope, I braced myself, ready to give it a good hoist in order to pull her up, then remembered her hair was tied to the motor. With a growl of frustration, I leaned over and frantically plucked at the knot in her ponytail. Most of her hair pulled free, but a good handful had settled into a rat's nest that refused to untangle.

"Sorry. . . ." I grabbed the base of her ponytail and yanked, ripping the rest of her hair free. Her beautiful hair. She'd kill me. Even so, I'd welcome her anger. As long as she was breathing, she could stay pissed at me forever. Angelle's head bobbed underwater, and suddenly I was the one who couldn't breathe. "Gelle!"

I grabbed the rope and pulled as hard as I could, leaning back for leverage, hoisting, crying, begging silently for the strength to pull this off. Angelle weighed about as much as I did, but deadweight couldn't be measured in pounds. I felt like an ant trying to pull an elephant over a mountain. I heaved, cursed, screamed . . . then finally . . . finally her head and shoulders peeked over the side of the boat.

Grunting, straining, I pulled hard, harder, wrapping the rope around my fingers, around my wrists—tugging, tugging until my sister plopped onto the floor of the boat, her head bouncing against the supply bag.

I immediately threw myself over her, stuck a hand beneath her neck, lifted her head—pinched her nose closed, opened her mouth—blew my breath into it. Sister breath was the best . . . sister breath was the best. Then, after folding my right hand over my left, I placed both over her heart and pressed—pressed—pushed. One—two—three—one, two, three. Back to her mouth, lifting her head, pinching her nose—breathing, breathing. Only she wasn't. . . .

CHAPTER THIRTY-ONE

I became a machine meant for only one function—make Angelle breathe—breathe.

"Breathe, goddamnit!" I pounded on her chest—one, two, three . . . "Please!" The next round of chest thumping brought action. Angelle coughed, and water spewed out of her mouth and nose. I thumped the heel of my hand on her chest once more for good measure. More water flew out of her mouth.

I quickly rolled her onto her left side. "Can you hear me? Talk to me. Please, please open your eyes."

Her eyelids fluttered. She coughed again, spitting more water, then curled into a semifetal position.

I reached for the flashlight beside her, stuck the beam directly in her face, and pulled up her right eyelid. All I saw was the white of her eye. Blood dribbled from the gash in her forehead. I shook her gently. "Gelle, wake up! Wake up. Look at me, look at me, please."

Her body suddenly went limp against my hand, and my heart stopped beating. God, was she dead? After all that struggling to get her into the boat, I couldn't lose her now, couldn't!

"Gelle!" I wailed and shook her hard. In that moment, Angelle drew in a deep, shuttering breath; then her chest began the slow rise and fall of someone in a deep sleep. I sobbed with relief and pulled her to me, rocking—rocking. "Don't fucking scare me like that again. Just don't . . ."

The extent of my medical training had been my research on CPR, by far not enough knowledge to make a true assessment of Angelle's condition. All I knew for sure was that she needed a doctor. I had to find help.

After laying her head gently on the floor of the boat, I got to my feet and looked about. Water—shadows—trees, no matter which way I turned, it all looked the same. I glanced down and saw the face of the dead woman bobble up again next to the cypress tree. Only then, in that moment of stillness, did I feel sorry for her and wished I could help her. But there was really nothing I could do for her now. There was nothing anyone could do. Right now getting Angelle to a hospital was top priority. Later, once she was in good medical hands, I'd let someone know about the woman, tell them where to find her.

Then it suddenly dawned on me—how would I let anyone know where she was? Not only did I have the challenge of getting out here first, but I had to *know* where I was in order to direct someone else here. It wasn't as though I could say, "Just take a left across from the grocery store, then a right beside the dry cleaner's." I'd probably have to dowse to find her again. Just the thought of having to come back to these swamps made me shiver with nausea.

Staring at the woman's pale, wet face, I whispered, "If you know, tell me how to get out of here. Which way do I go? Tell me, and I'll send someone back for you. I promise."

The woman, of course, didn't answer—thank heaven.

Biting my bottom lip, I stuck my left hand out in front of me, the sixth digit flaccid and numb. I closed my eyes and concentrated on the landing, on seeing that long concrete strip where we'd backed up the car and launched the boat, the grove of trees where Angelle had hidden the car. That's where I needed to go. That's where I needed it to lead me.

Show me. . . .

I pictured Angelle's house, pictured Poochie inside, watching *GI Jane*, focused on the prayer tree and the shoes hanging from it. I thought of the shrimp stew, the *thump, thump,* thumping of Poochie's walker when she made her way down the hall.

Soon all those images filled my mind with the clarity of reality, and I felt the slightest twitch from my finger. A nugget of hope sent my pulse racing. I focused harder—on the bayou that ran next to Angelle's house—the night I saw Cherokee out there. I thought of Sook and Vern and the Bloody Bucket. My finger twitched again, then sprang to full alert, overlapping my regular little finger and my ring finger.

Pointing . . . pointing, northeast. Just as it did before. Then the firecracker sensation went off in my finger, and the pain was so intense I thought for sure it had literally blown off the tip this time. The same fire—burning that occurred each time it zeroed in on the children.

"No, no, not the kids. I have to get to the landing, get help for Angelle. . . ."

The pleading did nothing to change its direction. If anything, it intensified the pain. Experience had taught me that the heightening of any sensation usually meant I was close to finding whatever I sought. If that still held true now, we were closer to the kids than ever. What the fuck was I supposed to do? Angelle needed help in the worst way, but I didn't know how to get her to that help. If I tried going back to the landing without the aid of dowsing, there'd be no saving anyone.

"All right, come on, you've gotta get your shit together," I said, shaking my hands out like a boxer before a fight. I sorted through my thoughts, trying to find a logical solution.

My finger decided it wanted to be the only one with answers and spiked the pain to an all-time high. I doubled over, clutching my left hand to my chest. "Shhiiiit!"

Moments later, when the worst of the pain had passed, I leaned over and checked Angelle's breathing.

In—out—in—out. Good, nice and steady.

I stood up, sweat dribbling down the sides of my face, and gave thanks to the universe that she was still alive. "Gotta start the boat," I muttered, stepping over to the motor. "Can't do anything without starting the boat." I grasped the red bulb, squeezed it—squeezed it, the way Angelle had done. Then I pressed the start button and twisted the throttle.

Nothing. Of course nothing happened. Nothing but dead air and the smell of gasoline. Thinking I hadn't primed it enough, I grabbed hold of the bulb again and squeezed it a few times. How many times had Angelle done this? Five? Ten? Fifty? I added three more squeezes, then pressed the start button and twisted the throttle for all it was worth. The engine sputtered, coughed, then died, and a white plume of smoke filled the back of the boat. Shit, I was flooding the damn thing. I tried the start button once more, the throttle . . . This time the engine roared to life— which was all well and good, but now I didn't have a fucking clue about what to do next.

Eventually, by trial and error, I got us away from the bank and into the open stream. I soon puttered up to a cutoff and pushed the throttle back, intending to take a left. The waterway looked much wider there. A lake maybe? The Atchafalaya River? Logically, if it was the river, the waterway would eventually lead us to civilization. It had to. The bigger the water, the bigger the boat needed to navigate it. The bigger the boat, the bigger the chance there'd be channels leading to large loading docks, not small boat ramps like the one Angelle and I had used. There'd be buildings and people. Doctors. Lights.

The logic seemed plausible, so I steered left. Immediately, it felt as if someone had yanked the extra finger out as far as it would go, then began sawing on it with a rusted, serrated knife. I screamed in pain and held my left hand up to the night sky. "What the *fuck* do you want from me? What?"

The only answer was more pain, more sawing from the rusted knife . . . burning, stabbing pain. I had to turn around. It was telling me in no uncertain terms that I had to comply or else. Or else the pain would get so severe it might actually stop my heart.

It had taken over. *It,* that which I'd seen as a curse all my life. That which Angelle called on for help. That which had brought me years of embarrassment, seclusion, isolation, and fear. After all that pain over so many years, how dare *it* try to control me this way, *making* me go in a direction I didn't want to go! I slumped from the weariness of it all. From the pain. It took all I had to turn the boat around. As soon as I did, the pain dropped to a level just below excruciating.

Although forced into submission, the direction clear, I didn't know what I was supposed to do with the kids if . . . no, when, I found them. Two kids who'd been missing for . . . what? Three days now? Maybe without food and water? How was I supposed to deal with them *and* an unconscious sister? It was all so overwhelming and answerless that all I knew to do was pray that Poochie was standing at her prayer tree right now, calling upon her God, or anyone else's god, to help that dumb-ass desert rat who knew nothing about swamps or swimming, boat motors or kids. The dumb-ass who got herself stuck in the middle of it all, anyway.

With my right hand still on the throttle, I dropped down to my knees, then leaned over and grabbed the flashlight. Its beam had faded to little more than a fog lamp, but at least it was something. I aimed it ahead of me, saw nothing different than what I'd seen before, then moved the beam down to Angelle and watched the steady rise and fall of her chest. Good.

Left to the call of my finger, I got back to my feet,

twisted the throttle, and got the skiff moving again. The wind shifted to the south, and with it came an odd scent—a mixture of burning wood, cooked meat, and something rancid. The tail end of that aroma was so sour it seemed to stick to the hairs in my nostrils. In that moment, the electrical fire in my finger abruptly turned to ice, and instead of overlapping my other fingers, it aimed straight ahead, toward an inlet that appeared darker and narrower than any we'd traveled so far.

Knowing better than to resist, I slowed the boat down a little more and inched the skiff toward the mouth of the inlet. I aimed the flashlight ahead, but its beam was so weak I could barely see the nose of the boat.

Creeping along, I soon spotted an odd shape near the bank about fifty feet on my right. Thinking about the dead woman back by the cypress, I hesitated getting any closer, but the boat seemed to insist, nudging me nearer.

Closer . . . the odd scent growing stronger . . . closer, until I could make out a boat. It looked as though it was tied to a clump of skinny trees. Instinctively, I released the throttle, let the engine die, and the skiff drifted on its own toward the object.

It *was* a boat. My skiff's nose touched its bow, which was close enough for the meager beam from the flashlight to illuminate the biggest nightmare I'd ever seen in my life. Beyond the boat, in an opening no more than ten feet away from where I stood, two bodies— or what remained of their bodies—had been tied to metal rods that protruded from the ground, then burned beyond recognition. Brown, melted wax mummies with empty eye sockets. Both mouths were frozen in perpetual screams. I opened my own mouth . . . and puked over the side of the boat. *Jesus!*

When my stomach was empty, I chanced another look at the bodies. I couldn't tell if they were male or female. What was this place? Where the waters belched up bodies, stole children, housed gators and snakes bigger than Buicks? What the hell was going on here?

The boats tapped noses again, and the hollow *kathunk* of aluminum hitting aluminum drew my attention to the moored boat. It looked similar to the one we were in, same color, same length. Same descriptive registration numbers. The only difference was the name painted in large black letters along its left side.

BULLET.

Bullet . . . Bullet. The name rolled over and over in my head, trying to find a home. I'd heard it before, somewhere. . . . Oh, fuck! That was the name of Trevor's boat! *No, no, no . . . it can't be. . . .*

But I remembered Poochie saying that he'd gone out with some guy to check traps, only he was supposed to come home with the boat before going to work. He never did get home. Not before we'd left anyway. This had to be some sick coincidence. Certainly there had to be someone else in this damn area who had a boat with the same name. One of those bodies couldn't be Angelle's Trevor. It just couldn't!

I looked back at my sister to make sure she was still sleeping. Sleeping, not dead. If there was ever a time to be grateful for her being unconscious, it was now.

Jesus . . . Trevor . . . it can't be. . . .

I started the engine again, backed the skiff away, watched BULLET and the two charred bodies fade into the darkness. *Please, don't let it be Trevor. For Angelle's sake, for everybody's sake, don't let it be Trevor.*

With that silent prayer holding constant, I turned the boat in the opposite direction, and my finger changed sensations immediately. It went back to the firecracker. Back to the burning. Right . . . go to the right, Dunny . . . *It can't be Trevor!*

The weight pressing against my heart and intuition begged to differ. I forced myself to look away from that boat, away from BULLET . . . BULLET . . . BULLET. By the time my eyes focused on the direction I was supposed to be heading, where my finger led, I spotted a round yellow light off in the distance. It flickered and swirled, then stretched into the shape of a pyramid, growing higher and taller by the second. How could I have missed that light earlier? It was too big to be coming from a flashlight, and no way it was the moon. I thought about what Poochie had said about the feux fo lais, balls of light that led people deep into the swamp so they'd be lost forever. Although I didn't put any stock in the whole purgatory end of the tale, I couldn't help but wonder if what I was seeing now was in fact a feux fo lais. Too many weird things had crossed my path over the last couple of days for me to discount anything.

If this was a feux fo lais, was it a good one or an angry one? Was there a way to tell the difference? Poochie had said a good feux fo lais sometimes led lost fisherman back to shore. If I followed it, though, how would I know whether it was leading me home or deeper into the swamp, where I'd be lost forever? Fuck that. I was already lost. What more could it do to me?

Now the light flickered in multiple directions, like flames licking up from a large, swelling campfire. A silhouette suddenly danced across the backdrop of flames, and I felt my mouth drop open.

Wait—that *was a* bonfire! There was someone out there!

I was about to rev up the motor and shoot over there at full speed when I thought about the charred bodies—the dead woman by the cypress tree. There might indeed be somebody out there, but was it someone who'd offer help—or trap me in an even bigger hell than I was in right now?

Unfortunately, there was only one way for me to find out. . . .

CHAPTER THIRTY-TWO

Olm opted for a monument of fire instead of a wooden altar on which to place the heart offerings. And, oh, what a monument it was! It was in the same spot his father's burial shelf had been located, only it encompassed an area ten times the original size.

He'd spent hours chopping buttonwood trees with a short-handled machete to start the fire, then dragged in cypress logs, some almost as big around as his thigh, to build it higher. Once he had it roaring to the right height, he fed the flames anything dry he could find to keep them going. Anything to reach Tirawa. Anything that kept the fire roaring as loudly as his own spirit.

He'd never known any other time in his life when he'd felt this much excitement. This much hope. This much power. The time had finally come. All of the preparation, all of his hard work would soon be worth it. Moments from now, only bare moments, all he'd longed for would be his.

With a hop of joy, Olm made clicking sounds with his tongue and tossed an oak branch onto the fire. The wind whipped about and sent a shower of embers flying his way. He shielded his eyes, caught the scent of singed hair, then lifted his arms above his head and laughed uproariously.

Olm didn't know why it had taken him so many years to get to this place, for the revelation of Tirawa to come to him so he'd understand all that was possible. All things had their time, he supposed. Certainly he would not have appreciated the fullness of what was about to happen had it been given to him as a young man, a pup in his teens. Someone unfamiliar with the workings of his own body and mind, much less the intricacies of metaphysics.

He had years behind him now, had faced many struggles in life. Rejection, failure, never measuring up to others' standards, the butt of their jokes, of having that brass ring within reach so many times only to have it snatched away by someone quicker, faster, smarter. All of those experiences had definitely laid a strong foundation for true appreciation, something he believed Tirawa thrived on. Naked subjects, dependent, appreciative of his power. Addicted to the vast promises he gave to all who worshipped and sacrificed to him.

Olm glanced at his watch, noting how brash the simple piece of jewelry appeared on his naked arm against his naked chest. No warrior wore a Timex. But it was the only way for him to keep track of time, and he needed to have the timing exact for the sacrifice.

Five minutes left. Five minutes until the apex of the moon, and his life would start anew. The anticipation that had been building inside him for so long had reached an all-time high. It pushed from inside his body like a living thing, an eager animal wanting out of its cage. The feeling brought tears to his eyes, and he started to dance, pounded the ground with his feet in the rhythmic beat of the ceremonial Ghost Dance.

He felt fully alive, already renewed. He was like an olm tree, forcing its branches up from the center of a dead and hollow cypress stump.

"Hey-nah-hey-nah-hey-nah-hey. Hey-nah-hey-nah-oonah-hey. Hey-nah-hey-nah-oonah-hey." Olm raised his arms over his head as he chanted, beat the ground with his feet, spinning in a circle. So much had been given to him already. Bits and pieces of wisdom that had prepared his spirit to handle much more. First he'd been shown the old woman, told how to collect her blood to enhance tonight's sacrificial offering. Then Tirawa had given him the eyes of an eagle, allowing him to spot the two boaters who were getting too close to the knoll. He'd seen them on his way out here. His human self—his old self would have quickly hushed the motor on his boat, then run and hidden until the boaters had passed by. But that didn't happen. He no longer carried the weighty baggage from his old being.

Olm had spotted the crawfish traps in the men's skiff even from a distance. Seeing that, his old self would have assumed they were probably changing locations, looking for more productive waters. But the moment he saw them, Tirawa released to him an astonishing revelation. Serving Tirawa wasn't about an annual sacrifice used to please the mighty deity. It was a state of mind. It mean grabbing opportunities when he saw them, offering blood and life to the Great Warrior at every opportunity. The commander of the Morning and Evening stars deserved no less, and for those who understood that monumental concept, Tirawa's rewards were endless.

Attracting the boaters' attention had almost been too easy. Olm had faked an injury, then called to them for help. They'd come to him without hesitation. Once they were in his boat, checking the leg he'd sworn he'd broken, Tirawa gave Olm the power of a lion and the speed of a gazelle. Before either man knew it, he'd ruptured their hearts with his knife. Instead of dumping their bodies overboard, though, as he'd done with the old woman, Tirawa had demanded an offering of incense. He'd shown Olm the metal survey stakes hidden in a nearby thicket. Directed him to the rolls of wire and flagging in a compartment under one of the benches in the men's boat. Told him how to tie them to the stakes; then Olm had been allowed to complete the offering, using whatever method he thought would be most pleasing to Tirawa. So he'd taken the gasoline tank out of their boat, soaked both men until the tank was empty, then set their bodies ablaze.

No doubt the offering had pleased Tirawa, for he kept Olm's eyes sharp and his senses keen. Shortly after that fire offering, he'd spotted yet another boater. This one, however, had been outright brazen, having snuck in from the north, then tying his boat to a tree right on the very knoll where Olm kept the kids. His old self would have panicked and run off like a frightened rabbit, petrified at the possibility of being caught.

But once again, he didn't run. Instead, Olm snuck through the brush, hardly making a sound, creeping along on the balls of his feet the way his ancestors used to do during a hunt, bow and arrow or spear at the ready. Olm didn't have a spear or bow—but he had a knife. He'd stayed in the shadow of a tree trunk, held his breath, not making a sound, waited for his prey, who crunched and clonked through the brush like an oversized oaf, begging to be heard. Begging to be found. Begging to be sacrificed. And Olm had been more than happy to oblige. He rammed the knife into the man's chest up to the hilt, then dragged his body back to the clearing and tied him to a tree not far from the children. He, too, would be set ablaze, but only af-ter the hearts of the children were offered.

Lagniappe for Tirawa, who'd been so generous to him.

Olm glanced over at the tree where he'd tied the man and smiled. The man's eyes and mouth were open, paralyzed in perpetual surprise and fear, which he'd now carry throughout eternity. Olm wondered if the children's faces would freeze with that same expression when he killed them.

He checked his watch again. Another two minutes had passed. Only three minutes left.

Only three minutes to get the job done.

Olm hurried over to the willow, where he'd hid-den the metal bucket, grabbed it, and took off for the edge of the knoll closest to the children. Once there, he filled the bucket to the brim with sludge, then carried it over to the boy.

The boy began to cry immediately. "Please, don't,

mister! Please! I promise I'll be good and won't tell anybody. I promise I won't say a word. Just let us go. Please! Don't hurt us. Please don't hurt us!"

Grinning, Olm dumped the bucket of mud into the hole, which raised the level of silt to just under the boy's bottom lip. Olm frowned, pursed his lips. The mud should have gone higher, to the boy's upper lip. He must have miscalculated. He'd have to hurry. More mud. He needed more mud than he thought.

He ran back to the edge of the knoll, scooped up another bucket of mud, and brought it back to the boy.

"No! Please, I don't wanna die! I don't wanna die! Mama! Mama, please come stop him! Mama!"

Olm dumped the bucket of mud into the boy's hole. This brought the level of sludge above his upper lip, to the bottom of his nostrils. The boy's eyes went wide. Snot ran out of his nose and formed little rivers in the silt below it. Olm allowed himself a second of pleasure, as he watched the boy's eyes widen even more, the snot run, remembered his uncontrollable cries.

Now it was time for the girl.

Olm repeated the process of going to the edge of the knoll, collected another bucket of swamp slop, then carrying it over to her. He dropped the silt into the center of her hole. This time the silt level moved spot-on, settling just below her nose, just as the boy's was now. The only problem was there was no reaction from her. No fear. No tears. No begging for help. She simply sat there, head lolled back and to one side, eyes closed as if she were in a peaceful sleep.

Olm's pulse quickened as he considered the possibility that the girl might already be dead. What was he supposed to do with her if she was dead? The whole point of the sacrifice was the fear, the offering of the fear.

He calmed himself, recalling that the two kids had been his idea in the first place. Tirawa only required one. Two had been a matter of convenience, since they'd been together on the levee, and he'd thought surely two would grant him graces and benefits far beyond what one might bring.

Resigning himself to the fact that he might just have one life to offer, Olm scrambled back to the edge of the knoll and collected more mud. This would be the last for the boy. This bucket would take the silt level to the bridge of his nose, high enough so even if he leaned his head back, he still wouldn't find air. Only the boy's eyes would be visible. His terror-filled, horrified eyes.

Olm's plan had been to have the girl watch while he smothered him, or have the boy watch while he killed the girl, but the point was moot now. If the girl was already dead, the boy could easily assume as much, and wasting this bucket of mud on her would bring no extra benefit of fear in the boy. Killing the boy first, with the girl unconscious or possibly dead, provided no benefits either. But all that mattered, really, was Tirawa. And to that end, all he had to be concerned about was making sure the sacrifice was timed perfectly.

Standing at the foot of the boy's hole, Olm held up the last bucket of mud he intended to pour, and shouted, "Oh, Great Tirawa, I offer you the fruits of my labor, the sacrifice of fear and youth. Send to me, Great One, the collective knowledge of my ancestors. Hear me, Great Tirawa. Send to me all that runs through my lineage so I may stand powerful and prosperous on this earth. For this, I will become your prophet, forever singing the praises of your name, I will offer sacrifice upon sacrifice to appease your great and insatiable hunger."

With that, Olm tilted the bucket so only some of the mud slopped into the hole. The boy's head wiggled, his eyes growing so wide they looked like two stained moons.

Another tilt of the bucket. The plop of more mud. *"Ahna-hah-na-hey-nah-hey. Hey-nah-hey-nah-oonah-hey."* Though no one had ever told him a chant was required, Olm felt its necessity. When one lay with a lover, one felt compelled to say, I love you. To Olm, there was no difference. He was offering all, as he would to a lover. This sacrifice—his hard work—his heart—his soul—his voice—the fire. The raging fire, it crackled and popped, its flames soaring ever higher. Surely it had to be sweet music to Tirawa's ear. How could it not?

He glanced at his watch.

Thirty seconds remaining.

Olm lifted the bucket once more, held it steady, and counted backward from thirty. As the numbers decreased, something was pricking at the back of his mind. Something didn't quite feel right . . . sound right . . .

Still holding the bucket steady, Olm counted silently now. He listened carefully . . . past the crackle of the fire . . . past the nocturnal noises of the swamp . . . then he heard it. The sound of a boat motor.

And it was coming up on him fast.

CHAPTER THIRTY-THREE

The closer I got to land, the farther my mouth dropped. The fire I'd noticed earlier was no ordinary bonfire. It was a mountainous inferno that appeared to consume everything within reach, as if the entire island had been torched. The orange-red flames didn't just light up the night; they shocked the darkness from it.

I found myself so mesmerized by the height of it, the roar and thunderous rumble from it, that I didn't realize until it was too late that I was barreling toward the island's bank, which was now only mere feet away. Instinctively, my right foot sought a brake, my brain rolled its inner eye at the stupidity of the gesture, and the boat slammed into the bank. In an instant, the propellers ground to an abrupt halt in sludge and dirt, and I went flying headfirst over Angelle, who was still lying on the skiff's floor, toward the bow. My right side caught the edge of the bench seat, my head the aluminum abutment of the bow. White and silver lights burst into a sparkling fireworks display before my eyes.

Groaning, I waited until the fireworks dissipated, then grabbed the side of the boat and struggled to my feet. I held on to the skiff for a moment, catching my breath, waited for my legs to stop shaking. I glanced over at Angelle, clearly visible in the flood-light created by the fire. Although the jolt from the boat's impact had caused her body to slide sideways a foot or two, she looked no worse for the wear. A quiet peacefulness rested on her face, and I saw the gentle rise and fall of her chest, her eyes moving left to right beneath her eyelids as if she was in the middle of a pleasant dream. Satisfied that she was okay and feeling stability return to my legs, I stood up and took stock of my surroundings.

As far as I could tell, the island was shaped like a horseshoe, and I'd plowed into its south end. The fiery monolith stood over a hundred feet ahead, and even from here, I felt the intensity of its heat. The belly of the inferno consisted of a pyramid of logs, which told me that this blaze was no accident. Someone had purposely set it. But who would set up a bonfire out in the middle of nowhere? A camper might build one to cook, but certainly not one that big.

Dread began to grow and squirm in the pit of my stomach, seep into my bones. The images of the two charred bodies came to mind, but instead of seeing them as I had a short time ago, both unidentifiable save for the name on the boat that caused me to suspect one to be Trevor, the bodies belonged to Angelle and me.

Shivering, I peered over at the fire, watched it send giant gray clouds of smoke billowing, swirling, belching toward the sky. I felt hypnotized by the size and power of it all, the flames, the whirling, curling smoke. I had to force myself to turn away from it.

With the motor dead and the skiff all but cemented in mud, I didn't have the option to turn tail and run. I could either hunker down in the boat with Angelle or get out and see if there were any answers to getting us out of here. With Angelle needing medical attention, the decision was a no-brainer.

I got out of the boat and walked tentatively toward the fire, circling to the right. "Is anybody here? I need help. My sister's been hurt, and I need to get her to a hospital."

The only response was the crackle and pop of wood roasting in the flames.

"Hello? Anybody?"

Still no answer. I wasn't sure if that was a good or bad thing. I circled the circumference of the fire, which was so big it seemed to take forever to get to the other side. There was definitely no need for a flashlight here. No need for the moon. The flames did all the work, illuminating, defining every branch, every blade of grass. As I drew closer, smoke whipped across my face, curled up my nose.

"Is anybody here? Hello? Is any—Oh, *Jesus!*" A dead man tied to a tree, fifty feet away, if that, damn near sent me into cardiac arrest, paralyzed my feet. The world suddenly turned into a silent movie. I no longer heard the roar of the fire. Even in my shock, I realized I felt nothing from my extra finger, nothing cold to acknowledge the dead, which he most certainly was.

His arms had been pulled backward around the trunk of the tree, his hands obviously tied behind it.

His head was slumped forward, his shirt and pants stained with volumes of blood, which, judging from the knife protruding from the left side of his chest, had come from his heart.

That knife . . .

Of all the things my eyes decided to settle on in that moment, it chose the handle of the knife. Something about it . . .

Without thinking, I stepped forward, drawn closer to the dead man, to the knife. A red-handled knife . . . shaped like an exclamation point. My mouth went dry. I wanted to call out to Angelle, remind her where we'd seen it, then remembered she was back in the boat, unconscious. Remembered she hadn't been there to see it in the first place. She'd been sitting in the car, eyes snapping with anger.

I was the one who'd seen that knife earlier today. It had been stuck in a wooden cross at Woodard's church. It *had* to be the same one because it was too oddly shaped for it not to be. Even the policeman who'd pulled it out of the cross, that Beeno guy, had mentioned how rare it was. The memory of that incident jittered in my mind like faulty reel-to-reel film.

The knife . . . the church . . . the cop . . . how he'd shaken the knife at Woodard . . . and something . . . something else . . .

I was close enough now to the dead man to reach out and touch him. Although his head hung chin to chest, a sense of familiarity washed over me. I tilted my head slightly to get the advantage of an angle and inched up a step . . . then another. Who was this man?

Suddenly familiarity became horrid, absolute recollection. I gasped, threw a hand over my mouth. The dead man was Vern Nezat, Sook's husband. "Oh God," I muttered through my fingers. "God . . . Vern, no . . . not . . . Oh God . . ."

Someone must have fixed that faulty reel-to-reel because sights and sounds abruptly flowed into one smooth motion. The blood—the knife—the crackle, roar, pop, snap of fire—flames rising, falling, undulating, giant steeples in a perpetual state of rebuilding—dancing, whirling, billowing smoke—all of it now an IMAX of terror with surround sound.

Amidst the horror, my ears latched on to a new, odd sound, the *hrsshh, hrsshh, hrsshh* of someone running through dry brush. And the sound was getting louder, heading toward me. I peered tentatively over my shoulder, saw nothing, then turned slowly, fearfully to my left, where it sounded as if the noise was coming from.

I saw no one running toward me, only a large clearing a short distance away. It looked like a dirty moon with two dark eyes set in the center. I squinted, took a step toward it.

Dark eyes? Dark . . . Fuck! Those weren't eyes at all. They looked like freshly dug graves with two small heads poking up near the front of each. The sight took my breath away. The kids? Sweet Jesus, the kids! But their heads weren't moving. . . . Trembling, I inched closer. *Don't let them be dead . . . don't—*

The *hrsshh, hrsshh, hrsshh* sound was suddenly louder than ever, and it was followed by a primal growl of fury so loud it stopped me dead in my tracks, sent every hair on my arms, the back of my neck standing at attention. I whirled about and saw a man racing toward me. Bare-chested, eyes wild and filled with fury, teeth bared, arms raised with one hand wielding a short-handled machete. He screamed something, but I couldn't understand him. Adrenaline sent my heart flying to my throat and my pulse tripling in rate, but my brain wouldn't command my legs to move. It was too busy trying to figure out what was headed toward me.

The man looked and sounded like a charging animal, one unrestrained in its fury and focused on its prey. But he *was* a man . . . someone I knew . . . my brain rapidly sought and sorted . . . *The knife . . . the cop . . . the cop shaking the knife at Woodard . . . the cop taking the knife with him . . . taking the knife with him!* Son of a bitch, this wild man was the cop from Bayou Crow, the one they called Beeno! *What the fuck . . .*

"You *bitch!*" Beeno screamed, his legs gathering speed.

Instinct sent me spinning on my heels, ready to run. But I had nowhere to run to, no place to escape. *The kids . . . Sarah . . . Nicky . . . the boat grounded, Angelle in it, helpless . . . Vern . . .* I couldn't just leave them here.

I whirled back around to face Beeno—just as he launched and dropped me in a flying tackle.

Breathless, I waited for a cutting blow from the machete, but he must have dropped it because the next thing I knew he was on top of me, pummeling my face, my chest, my arms, my shoulders with his fists.

DEBORAH LeBLANC

I threw an arm up in defense, turned my head from side to side to deflect the blows.

"You goddamn bitch!" he screamed, spittle flying from his lips. His face was a red mask of hatred and rage, his lips curled up like a feral beast's. "You ruined it all!" He grabbed me by hair, forced my head up, pointed skyward. "Do you see that? Do you see that moon? *You fucking wasted it.* All my hard work, gone!" He swung down hard with a fist, plowing it into my right cheek. "Tirawa will get revenge, you'll see. He'll get revenge on my behalf." Then he screamed something incoherent and punched the top of my head. "You ruined it! Everything I've done . . ."

Suddenly his voice was lost to the roar of the fire, which sounded as if it had been amplified by a thousand. A rush of wind whirled about us—hot, so hot it made it hard to breathe. Gray smoke gathered, pushed against me, got into my eyes, my nose, my mouth. Hot—fire—smoke—dancing smoke and flames.

Beeno slapped me again, again, and the sound of his voice abruptly returned. "Manipulative, conniving, fucking bitch! How dare you interfere!"

"Get the fuck off me!" I screamed, and swung at him with both hands. He pinned them immediately, dropped his right knee on my chest, nailing me to the ground. He threw my arms out on either side of me, then immediately jabbed a fist into my face, my nose. I heard something crunch, felt a blast of pain, tasted blood in my mouth. I bucked beneath him, spat a bloody wad of mucus on his chest. "Get off me!"

Beeno howled with laughter; then his lips settled

278

into a snarl, and he swung his right fist, catching me on the ear. I felt his weight shift, as if he was ready to stand, and felt myself coil up inside, preparing to twist, roll out of his reach. But he lifted up for only a second, only to drop down again with a scream of fury, his knee slamming into my chest. Then his knee slid off, and he grabbed the front of my shirt in a fist, started shouting something in a language I didn't understand, had never heard before.

I tried pulling into a ball . . . couldn't breathe . . . my vision blurred . . . *Gelle . . . Sarah . . . Nicky . . . Gelle . . . Sarah . . .* Their names became my mantra for strength. I had to stay alive, had to remain conscious or God only knew what this maniac might do to them. Air . . . needed air. It felt as if my lungs had been split open, as if I were back in the water, drowning, everything turning inky black. *Gelle . . . Sarah . . . Beeno . . .*

In that moment, Beeno threw a left hook, catching me under the jaw. The world exploded into a million stars.

From a distant place, I heard him howl, like a wolf baying at the moon. Then he began to chant, his voice hoarse, his tone furious and determined. *"Oonah-hahna-hahna-hey-nah-hey. Oonah-hanah-hanah-hey."*

Through eyes nearly swollen shut, I saw him towering above me, one foot on my chest . . . gray smoke, curling, whirling, dancing . . . flames . . . chanting, chanting that sounded as if it came from the bowels of the swamp . . .

"Oonah-hahna-hahna-hey-nah-hey. Oonah-hanah-hanah-hey."

I felt the weight of him leave my chest, tried to roll . . . couldn't move. Saw him lift his arms above his head, the machete now glistening in his right hand. And as he continued to scream unintelligible gibberish, the smoke surrounded him, like ghostly shapes curling themselves about his body, flowing into his ears, his nose, his mouth. Through his very pores, flowing in and out.

Eyes . . . eyes everywhere now. No . . . not eyes . . . embers from the fire. I watched them settle over him, saw him swing the machete up, watched it swoop down and across. It missed my face by an inch. No doubt the backhand was coming. I felt it deep in my gut. Knew the next time he'd connect for sure. The next time it would all be over.

I saw the momentum of his body shift, heard the call of the blade in motion. With what little strength I had left, I lifted my left hand, putting up the only barrier I could between the blade and my face, stretched my fingers to block as much of the blow as possible.

Whoosh! The machete swung by . . . white-hot pain seared through my hand, raced down my arm and into my chest. My heart shuttered in its fury. I screamed, eyes opening as wide as the swelling allowed. So much blood pouring from my hand . . . from . . . from . . . my extra finger was gone! Gone! God, he'd cut it off! My screams turned into horrified shrieks that raked my throat raw. *Oh God . . . God . . .* I dropped my wounded hand at my side.

Over my own screaming, I heard Beeno roar in fury again, heard him start up the chant, saw that the smoke had almost obliterated him from view, curling around him.

I caught sight of the blade as he lifted it high. He wasn't going to come down at an angle this time. He was aiming straight down, right for my head. He was done with me. Through. Ready for me to die. I saw it in his eyes. In the snarl on his face. My mantra would be useless against such madness. Not even Poochie's God could stop him now.

I tried lifting my arms to cross them over my face, but they felt weighted with hundred-pound blocks of concrete. Tears stung my eyes. *Gelle, I'm so sorry . . . Sarah, Nicky . . . so sorry.* I felt something relax inside me, a giving way of sorts. I fought against it, didn't want to give up, wasn't supposed to give up. But the night was filled with a billion stars and a giant moon. I turned my head ever so slightly toward that moon and kept it in my line of sight, focusing on it, willing away the sound of Beeno's rage, the hefting grunt in his voice that told me he was lifting the machete higher. I didn't have to look to see what was coming. I didn't *want* to see.

Any second now . . . *Keep your eyes on the moon, Dunny. You hear, Gelle? Sarah? Nicky? Keep your eyes on the moon. . . .*

As I watched, the moon's soft white face began to darken . . . like the water I'd nearly drowned in . . . like the dark found deep in the swamp . . . just when I felt it ready to envelope me, bright light flashed in my periphery. The darkness paused then, waiting for me. . . .

Although I no longer saw him, I heard Beeno

screech in fury . . . heard the *blam!* of a shotgun blast, the loud thud of something hitting the ground hard.

Then, after a long, silent pause, I heard a familiar voice suddenly yell in triumph, "Now, take dat, you sumabitch, and *suck my dick!*"

Poochie?

Couldn't be . . . not out here . . . not way out here . . .

I tried turning my head to see, to make sure, but nothing on my body would move. The only external body part that seemed capable of functioning was my ears. I closed my eyes . . .

Heard . . . an odd sucking sound, like a cork being pulled from a wine bottle . . .

. . . a child asking, "Are you Superman?"

. . . a man's deep, gentle voice . . . "It's okay, I've got you. . . ."

A woman . . . "Dat's right! Dat's right, sumabitch, I got you!"

Then the stars, the moon, the world went black. . . .

EPILOGUE

At this very moment, the entire town of Cyler, Texas, was vibrating with activity. A parade down Main Street, children laughing, clapping, parents propping the smaller ones up on their shoulders—Roman candles spitting out brilliant red, green, yellow balls, the snap, whistle, and pop of Black Cat firecrackers and bottle rockets, sparklers that sizzled out far too quickly—folks chattering on front lawns around barbecue pits that roasted hot dogs, hamburgers, steaks, or chicken.

The Fourth of July had always been one of my favorite holidays. Not just because it commemorated the adoption of the Declaration of Independence, but because it celebrated the word *independence* itself. Freedom from control or influence of another.

Freedom. How precious a word. How relevant and powerful its meaning. Even more so to me now than ever before.

Nearly three months had passed since the nightmare in Bayou Crow, and so much had changed in my life in those few short months. I still carried a few stubborn bruises on my chest from Beeno's beating, but little more. The surgery I'd had on my hand to remove the rest of the bone Beeno had missed on my extra finger had gone well. I sometimes still felt naked and lost without it, though. Even after three months, I still reached for gloves before going out to the grocery store, or I'd unconsciously want to tuck that finger into my palm when I met someone on the street, then remember it was no longer there. It was a freedom that took a bit getting used to. The rest of the changes that came my way, however, I took to immediately. Especially the one before me now.

Sitting in a recliner, I folded my legs and tucked them up under me, rested my head on a hand, and studied my new family. Angelle was sitting on the floor in the middle of the living room on one end of a Monopoly board, grinning. She'd moved in with me about a month ago, once we'd finished burying Trevor and selling her house. She still had night terrors over her husband's horrid death, but they were becoming fewer.

"No, no, you can't have Park Place!" Angelle said, laughing.

The giggles that followed came from the little girl sitting on the opposite side of the board. She wore new jeans and a bright pink T-shirt with flip-flops to match. Her toes were wiggling in delight. The first time I'd taken Sarah Woodard shopping, the only thing she'd requested was that we not get dresses or shiny shoes. I was more than happy to oblige. Not only did we not buy either, but we shipped off to the Salvation Army the box of clothes her uncle had given us before we left Bayou Crow. No more patent leather—no more dresses.

"Ya gotta hand it over," Sarah said. "And the hotels on it, too!" She giggled again, and the sound made my smile broaden. She, too, still had nightmares, often screaming, "No more mud! No!" in her sleep. The doctors and counselors said she'd get better over time, but that the trauma had been so severe there was a chance her nightmares might never fully go away. Fortunately, the only physical scars that remained on Sarah's body were from the snakebite, which luckily hadn't been poisonous. It had healed beautifully and looked like two small freckles on her cheek.

Rusty Woodard had been more than happy to release Sarah into my custody, claiming that the *dee-mons* had invaded his niece and there was no hope of her returning to normal. The courts agreed . . . that the man was a hazard to the child, and when no mother or father stepped forward to claim Sarah, the state agreed she'd be better off in my care. I felt a little guilty because, secretly, I'd been glad when the girl's parents didn't show. Sarah was home now. *We* were her home.

Sarah laughed at the pretend-dismay look on Angelle's face and said, clapping, "I'm rich! I'm rich!"

Angelle laughed along with her. "You're a hard customer, I'll tell ya."

Beside Sarah lay Fritter, still lop-eared and wiry-haired, a permanent fixture in our home now, and Sarah's constant companion. His eyes roamed from Sarah to Angelle, then to me, and he gave me one of his looks, only this one seemed to say, *Thank you for letting me be here.*

I heard the soft hum of a motor from the hallway and glanced over to see Poochie riding into the living room on her scooter. She was humming "Jambalaya," an old Hank Williams tune about crawfish pie and filé gumbo, and tapping her fingers to the beat on the arms of the scooter. She winked at me as she circled around the coffee table to join Angelle and Sarah, and I winked back.

Poochie hadn't shouted out a bingo number in quite some time. Probably because she now frequented the bingo hall in Cyler. Every Wednesday night, I'd drive her out there, and more times than not she returned home with prizes, money, and a big toothy grin—toothy because Poochie had gotten herself a new set of teeth. Although she never said, I think the sudden interest in a set of choppers had something to do with Clayton, some old guy she'd met at the bingo hall her first time there.

Poochie's scooter was new, too, an updated version with compartments and a front basket for whatever bric-a-brac she decided to carry around. It hadn't taken her long to learn its operation. She zipped and zoomed around the house and every so often she'd give Sarah and Fritter a ride on it down the driveway.

So much smiling and laughing now . . .

I turned my attention to the large picture window that overlooked my front yard, and to the mesquite tree that Pop Pollack had tended to with such love and care. The lavender blossoms on the tree were gone, having given way to fruit that resembled dried green beans—and to multiple pairs of shoes of various sizes, shapes, and colors. As soon as Poochie moved in, she'd wasted no time laying claim to her new prayer tree. As far as I was concerned, Poochie Blackledge could fill every tree branch with shoes, socks, and gloves if she wanted to. I owed her my life.

Over the gentle laughter from the Monopoly game and Poochie's humming, I heard the crunch of gravel. I sat up to get a better view of whoever was headed down the driveway.

A black pickup was making its way to the house, and even from here I could make out the man behind the wheel. He wore a black Stetson.

"Dere he is," Poochie said, grinning. She winked at me again.

The smile on my face broadened.

My sister was smiling, too, although I wondered if seeing this man made her miss Trevor even more.

I got out of my chair and turned my attention back to the window . . . to him . . . to Cherokee.

Without a doubt, Cherokee had brought about the biggest change in me of all. According to Poochie, he'd been her accomplice at the knoll. That night, he'd shown up at Angelle's house, and Poochie told him what we were up to. She said his face got all dark, not with anger, but concern. She claimed she didn't have to convince him that Angelle and I were headed for trouble, because he already knew it. Somehow Poochie had talked him into taking her along in his boat to look for us. Cherokee's response to that had been "Poochie can be persuasive when she wants to." To which Poochie had responded, "Dat's right."

Obviously Cherokee was used to the swamps and had skills for tracking. He said it had been easy to follow the subtle, and not so subtle, trails that Angelle and I had left behind. Poochie swore that her prayers had been the biggest help in finding them. No one disputed that. Either way, the miracle had been that they'd been found at all.

Cherokee also added that finding us had been the easy part. What followed, though, had been the weirdest. How he'd heard Poochie scream in rage, then her grabbing the shotgun he'd brought along and blasting Beeno with it before he could stop her . . . not that he would have.

Every time the story was told, Poochie loved giving the details about how she'd raised that gun, given Beeno what for, and had never had a bad thought or bad dream about it since then. According to Poochie, God had given her peace about the incident, and she thanked Him every day for giving her a good aim.

Cherokee had stayed by their sides throughout the police investigations that followed that night. He helped retrieve that poor dead woman from the swamp and the bodies of those charred men. He also stood quietly by, attentive, ever watchful during Trevor's closed-casket service. He'd been with them for the reunion between Nicky and his mother, whom they'd found in a Baton Rouge rehab hospital. Cherokee had told Nicky's mother that if she ever felt herself sliding into trouble again to call him. To which I made sure to add, "And we'll take good care of Nicky for you."

Judging from the frequent phone calls between here

and Louisiana, Nicky and his mother were faring well. Nicky still referred to Cherokee as Superman.

When it was time to pack Poochie's and Angelle's belongings for the move here, Cherokee had been more than happy to lend a hand. Even helped with the sale of Angelle's house. He'd been there every step of the way—quiet, strong. He'd even made sure Pork Chop got on the straight and narrow so he'd be of decent help at the Bloody Bucket now that Vern was gone. In the beginning, Sook had talked about selling the grocery store and bar. She mourned Vern terribly and didn't think she'd be able to go on at the Bucket without him. Last I'd heard, though, the Bucket was still open, and Sook was still giving Pork Chop hell.

I guessed just like everything else in life, you can only take one thing at a time. People did the best they could. Lived and loved and died. But I didn't want to think about death now. I had life on my mind. And the man parking his truck in my driveway.

Before I left Louisiana, Cherokee promised he'd come to Cyler to see me. From the looks of things, he'd kept his promise. The sight of his strong face made my chest tingle, and as I watched him get out of the truck and walk toward the house—tall, straight, confident—the tingling turned to warm butter, flowing throughout my body. I felt my face flush, and my palms began to sweat.

I'd never felt anything like it before, and it brought a sudden rush of unexpected anticipation. I didn't have the extra finger as an indicator for anything anymore, but I couldn't help but wonder if my heart had taken over the job. If so, judging by the warmth spreading through me, it was signaling that there were bigger, better promises to come.

And for the first time ever, I believed in promises and looked forward to every one.

WIN WITH THE LEBLANC CHALLENGE:

- A *free*, four-year college education!

- $5,000 *cash* (USD)!

- $1,000 (USD) for the public school of *your* choice!

- A desktop computer!

- Bookstore gift certificates!

Contest ends March 1, 2009.

Visit www.theleblancchallenge.com for details, contest rules and regulations.

DEBORAH LEBLANC IS COMING TO TOWN!

See when she'll be in *your* neighborhood at www.deborahleblanc.com.

Master of terror

RICHARD LAYMON

has one word of advice for you:

BEWARE

Elsie knew something weird was happening in her small supermarket when she saw the meat cleaver fly through the air all by itself. Everyone else realized it when they found Elsie on the butcher's slab the next morning—neatly jointed and wrapped. An unseen horror has come to town, and its victims are about to learn a terrifying lesson: what you can't see can very definitely hurt you.

ISBN 13: 978-0-8439-6137-9

Bram Stoker Award finalist

MARY SANGIOVANNI

FOUND YOU

Those two simple words were like a death sentence to Sally. She recognized the voice, straight from her nightmares. The grotesque thing without a face, the creature that thrived on fear and guilt, had nearly killed her, like it had so many others. But it was dead...wasn't it? Sally is about to find out that your deepest secrets can prey on you, and that there's nowhere to hide...for long.

In the small town of Lakehaven something has arrived that can't see you, hear you or touch you, but it can find you just the same. And when it does, your fears will have a name.

ISBN 13: 978-0-8439-6110-2

DEBORAH LEBLANC

A HOUSE DIVIDED

Keith Lafleur, Louisiana's largest and greediest building contractor, thinks he's cut the deal of a lifetime. The huge old two-story clapboard house is his for the taking as long as he can move it to a new location. It's too big to move as it is, but Lafleur's solution is simple: divide it in half. He has no idea, though, that by splitting the house he'll be dividing a family—a family long dead, a family that still exists in the house, including a mother who will destroy anyone who keeps her apart from her children.

ISBN 13: 978-0-8439-5730-3

✂ # ☐ **YES!**

Sign me up for the Leisure Horror Book Club and send my
FREE BOOKS! If I choose to stay in the club, I will pay only
$8.50* each month, a savings of $7.48!

NAME: _____

ADDRESS: _____

TELEPHONE: _____

EMAIL: _____

☐ I want to pay by credit card.

☐ **VISA** ☐ **MasterCard** ☐ **DISCOVER**

ACCOUNT #: _____

EXPIRATION DATE: _____

SIGNATURE: _____

Mail this page along with $2.00 shipping and handling to:
Leisure Horror Book Club
PO Box 6640
Wayne, PA 19087
Or fax (must include credit card information) to:
610-995-9274

You can also sign up online at **www.dorchesterpub.com**.
*Plus $2.00 for shipping. Offer open to residents of the U.S. and Canada only. Canadian
residents please call 1-800-481-9191 for pricing information.
If under 18, a parent or guardian must sign. Terms, prices and conditions subject to
change. Subscription subject to acceptance. Dorchester Publishing reserves the right to
reject any order or cancel any subscription.